D1180527

DRAGON'S KIN

www.**books**at**transworld**.co.uk

Anne McCaffrey's books can be read individually or as a series. However, for greatest enjoyment the following sequences are recommended:

www.annemccaffrey.org

DRAGON'S KIN

ANNE
McCAFFREY

TODD
McCAFFREY

BANTAM PRESS

LONDON • NEW YORK • TORONTO • SYDNEY • AUCKLAND

TRANSWORLD PUBLISHERS
61–63 Uxbridge Road, London W5 5SA
a division of The Random House Group Ltd

RANDOM HOUSE AUSTRALIA (PTY) LTD
20 Alfred Street, Milsons Point,
New South Wales 2061, Australia

RANDOM HOUSE NEW ZEALAND LTD
18 Poland Road, Glenfield, Auckland 10, New Zealand

RANDOM HOUSE SOUTH AFRICA (PTY) LTD
Endulini, 5a Jubilee Road, Parktown 2193, South Africa

Published 2003 by Bantam Press
a division of Transworld Publishers

A catalogue record for this book is available from the British Library.
ISBN 0593 052870

Printed in Great Britain by
Clays Ltd, Bungay, Suffolk

1 3 5 7 9 10 8 6 4 2

Papers used by Transworld Publishers are natural, recyclable products made from
wood grown in sustainable forests. The manufacturing processes conform to the
environmental regulations of the country of origin.

To my brother, Kevin McCaffrey,
aka "The Smallest Dragonboy"

Anne McCaffrey

✦

To Ceara Rose McCaffrey—of course!

Todd McCaffrey

DRAGON'S KIN

PROLOGUE

When men first came to Rukbat, a G-type star in the Sagittarian Sector, they settled upon its third planet and named it Pern. They had set out to create an idyllic, low-tech farmers' paradise, escaping the ravages of the late Nathi Wars. They paid little attention to Pern's neighbors, as the entire solar system had been previously surveyed and declared safe for colonization.

Less than eight years—or "Turns" as the Pernese began calling them—after their arrival, Pern's erratic sister planet, the Red Star, came wheeling in from the outer edges of the solar system.

And then Thread fell from the sky. The thin, silvery wisps looked like no threat at all—until they touched flesh, or foliage, or anything living, including the bare earth. Then the Thread would grow, sucking the nutrients out of anything it could, turning soil into lifeless dirt, searing through flesh to leave nothing more than charred bone. Only metal, bare rock, and water—where Thread drowned—were safe.

The first Threadfall, catching the colonists by complete surprise, was devastating. Thousands died, many more were maimed, and countless herds of imported animals were lost.

Worse, the near approach of the Red Star not only brought Thread but also increased the stress on Pern's tectonic plates, producing earthquakes, tsunamis, and volcanoes.

The surviving colonists reorganized. They abandoned the richer but seismically active Southern Continent in favor of the more stable Northern Continent. There they built a "fort" out of an east-facing cliffside in which they could "hold" all the remaining colonists.

It was not enough. With their technology failing, they could not hope to get the ground clear of Thread long enough to harvest the food they needed for their survival. They needed another solution, a Pern-based system to rid the skies of Thread.

The colonists' biologists, led by the Eridani-trained Kitti Ping, turned to the indigenous fire lizards, small flying creatures that looked like miniature dragons. Using genetic engineering, the Pernese bred the fire-lizards into huge "dragons" that, by chewing a phosphene-bearing rock, could breathe fire on Thread, charring it right out of the sky before it could touch the ground.

These dragons, linked telepathically with their human riders, would form the mainstay of the colonists' defense against Thread.

In what was regarded as a mistake, Kitti Ping's daughter, Wind Blossom, created smaller, overmuscled, ugly creatures with great photosensitive eyes. Called watch-whers, they were useless fighting Thread in the daylight. But the resourceful Pernese discovered that the watch-whers were ideal for seeing in dark places, like the caves that became the Holds for the Holders and mines for miners.

As the colonists quickly outgrew their Fort Hold, the dragonriders found a new living space in an old volcanic basin. This, they called Fort Weyr.

The population continued to grow, and the colonists spread out across the Northern Continent. The dragonriders formed new Weyrs in the high mountains; the farmers and herders settled in new Holds on the plains below.

Under the leadership of the Lord Holders and the Weyrleaders, a new society developed, based on specialties and skills. Some specialties, particularly those requiring many years of training, became recognized as separate Crafts: Smith, Miner, Farmer, Fisher, Healer, and Harper. Levels of skill in a craft were recognized with the old guild appellations: Apprentice, Journeyman, and Master. Each Craft had one Master elected to preside over all Craft affairs: MasterSmith, MasterMiner, MasterFarmer, MasterFisher, MasterHealer, and MasterHarper.

Given the nature of celestial mechanics, after fifty Turns the Red Star moved too far from Pern for Thread to fall, and the threat faded away—until two hundred Turns later when the Red Star repeated its orbit, beginning a second Pass.

Again the dragons and their dragonriders rose into the sky to flame the Thread into harmless char. And again, as the Red Star receded fifty Turns later, the colonists returned to easier times and spread out to explore the abundance of Pern.

After another "Interval" of two hundred Turns, the pattern repeated and Thread fell again.

Toward the end of the Second Interval, with only sixteen Turns before the return of the Red Star, Thread, and the beginning of the Third Pass, a problem arose for the miners. The people relied on coal. Without coal, particularly the hot-burning anthracite, the Mastersmith would not be able to forge the steel that made the plows the farmers used, rimmed the wheels the traders used, and joined the leather riding gear the dragonriders used to fly against Thread. But by now, the easily acquired coal—the coal that came to the surface in huge, open seams—was nearly all mined out.

MasterMiner Britell in his CraftHall at Crom Hold realized that in order to dig deep into the mountains to get new coal, his miners would have to learn anew the old ways of tunneling and shaft mining. Working from ancient survey maps, the Master-Miner identified several promising subterranean coal seams, selected his most promising journeymen, and set them to the task of "proving" new mines. Those that succeeded would be made Masters and their Camps would become permanent Mines—with all the rank and prosperity associated with a minor Holder.

Although he admitted it to no one, MasterMiner Britell held his highest hopes for Journeyman Natalon and the group of hardworking miners he had inspired to join him.

Natalon had shown a willingness to experiment, which would be required to successfully master the new art of deep shaft mining.

He had enlisted watch-whers, hoping to use their abilities to detect tunnel-snakes and bad air—both the explosive gases and the odorless, deadly carbon monoxide which could suffocate the unwary.

From what Britell had heard, the watch-whers were something of a mystery—their abilities ignored as commonplace.

Britell planned on watching that Camp carefully, particularly keeping an eye on the work of the watch-whers and their bonded wherhandlers.

CHAPTER I

In early morning light I see,
A distant dragon come to me.

K indan was so excited that he practically bounced as he
ran up to the heights where Camp Natalon kept its
drum, fire beacon, and watch.

"They're here! They're here!" Zenor shouted down at him.
Needing no further urging, Kindan put on an extra burst of
speed.

Breathless, he joined his friend on the peak where they kept
the watch. Looking down at the valley, he could plainly see the
large drays rolling ponderously up toward the main Camp. Leading them were the smaller, but bright and cheerfully painted
domicile wagons owned by the caravanners.

From the watch-heights, not only could he see all the way

across the lake to the bend where the trail turned out of sight, but he could also see the fields on the far side of the lake, which had just been cleared, ready for their first planting of crops. Closer in, he could see where the trail forked, the more heavily traveled way heading up to the depot where the mined and bagged coal was stored, the lighter way leading toward the miners' houses on the near side of the lake.

Most of the houses were in three rows arranged in a U shape around a central square. The open, northern end of the U faced the road. It was there that smaller spice gardens had been planted. And it was in front of those, closer to the main square, that wedding preparations were in progress—for Kindan's own sister's wedding.

None of those houses were "proper" houses, built to withstand Threadfall. But Threadfall was a long way off—another sixteen Turns—and the miners were glad to have the temporary comfort of their own housing, convenient to the new mine.

Midway from the square to the hill was a separate house and a large shed. The house was Kindan's home and the shed housed Dask, the camp's sole remaining watch-wher. Dask was bonded to Kindan's father, Danil.

Hidden from the watch point by the bend of the hill was a much larger and sturdier dwelling—the full stone hold of Natalon, the head Miner in the Camp. North of it, separated by a walled-in herb garden, was a smaller but almost as well-built dwelling, the home of the Camp's Harper.

Just beyond the Harper's dwelling—the edge of which was visible from the lookout—the hillside, a spur from the western mountain, turned abruptly and the plain in front of it rose toward the peak of the mountain, with another spur about two kilometers distant forming a valley. Two hundred meters from the bend and a hundred meters west of the lookout was the entrance to the mine.

The boys knew the valley like the backs of their hands, even though it was changing daily and Kindan had been there only six months himself. They paid no attention to the view. Today, not even the novelty of the wedding preparations interested them: The two boys had eyes only for the trader caravan winding its way around the lake below them.

"Where's Terregar?" Zenor asked. "Can you see him?"

Kindan squinted and shaded his eyes against the sun with his hand, but mostly for show. The distance was far too great to make out one person in the whole caravan.

"I don't know," he answered irritably. "I'm sure he's down there somewhere."

Zenor laughed. "Well, he'd better be, or your Sis will kill him."

Kindan favored this comment with a glare. "Hadn't you better get back on down and tell Natalon?" he asked.

"Me?" Zenor replied. "I'm on watch, not a runner."

"Shards!" Kindan groaned. "I'm all out of breath, Zenor." He added in a lower tone, "And besides, you know how much Natalon wants to hear this news."

Zenor's eyes widened. "Oh, yeah, I do! Everyone knows that he was hoping your Sis would stay at the Camp."

"Right," Kindan agreed. "So just imagine how mad he'll be at hearing about it from me."

"Ah, come on, Kindan," Zenor replied. "There's good news with the bad—that's a whole caravan approaching, not just a wedding."

"Which he has to host," Kindan snapped back. He sighed.

"Well, if you insist, I'll go back down." He paused dramatically, eyeing his smaller friend. "But Sis said that I've got to wash Dask tonight."

Zenor's eyes narrowed as he considered this. "You mean, if I do the running, you'll let me help wash the watch-wher?"

Kindan grinned. "Exactly!"

"You would?" Zenor repeated hopefully. "Your dad won't mind?"

Kindan shook his head. "Not if he doesn't find out, he won't."

The added enticement of doing something unsanctioned brought a gleam to Zenor's eyes. "All right, I'll do it."

"Great."

"Of course, washing a watch-wher's not the same as oiling a dragon," Zenor went on. The thought of Impressing a dragon, of becoming telepathically linked with one of Pern's great fire-breathing defenders, was the secret wish of every child on Pern. But dragons seemed to prefer the children of the Weyr: Only a few riders were chosen from the Holds and Crafts. And no dragon had ever visited Camp Natalon.

"You know," Zenor continued, "I saw them."

Everyone in Camp Natalon knew that Zenor had seen dragons; it was his favorite tale. Kindan suppressed a groan. Instead, he made encouraging noises while hoping that Zenor wouldn't dawdle too much longer or Natalon would be wondering at the speed of his runner—and might remember who it was.

"They were so beautiful! A perfect V formation. Way up high. You could see them: bronze, brown, blue, green . . ." Zenor's voice faded as he recalled the memory. "And they looked so soft—"

"Soft?" Kindan interrupted, his tone full of disbelief. "How could they look soft?"

"Well, they did! Not like your father's watch-wher."

Kindan, feeling anger on Dask's behalf, stomped firmly on his emotion, remembering that he still wanted Zenor to run for him.

"Is the caravan getting closer?" he asked, hinting broadly.

Zenor looked, nodded, and sprinted away from the watch point. "You won't forget, will you?" he called back over his shoulder.

"Never!" Kindan replied. He was delighted at the thought of help with what he was certain was going to be a particularly thorough bathing of the coal mine's only watch-wher, the night before a major wedding.

◆

At the bottom of the hillside, after his long, warm scramble down, Zenor paused and looked back up to where Kindan was now standing watch. It was warmer in the valley and the air was thicker, partly from the moisture in the fields, and partly from the smoke already beginning to rise from the Camp's fires. Catching his breath, he turned to search for Miner Natalon. He steered for the largest knot of people he could find, figuring that the Camp's leader would be there. He was right.

Natalon was a rangy sort of a man who stood taller than the average man. Zenor's father, Talmaric, had called Natalon a "youngster" once, but only in a low voice. After hearing that, Zenor had tried to imagine Natalon as young but couldn't. Even though Talmaric was five Turns older than Natalon, Natalon's twenty-six Turns might have been a full hundred when compared to Zenor's meager ten.

Zenor considered calling out, but there was still a lot of confusion over the right title for Natalon. He'd be "Lord Natalon" if the Camp proved itself and became a proper Mine but that was still to happen and no one quite knew how to address him now.

Zenor opted for worming through the crowd and grabbing at Natalon's sleeve.

Miner Natalon was not pleased to have someone yank on his sleeve in the middle of an argument. He looked down and saw the sweat-stained face of Talmaric's son but couldn't remember the child's name. It had been so much easier six months earlier, when there'd only been himself and a few other miners seeking out a new seam of coal. But finding that seam, and still others after it, had been exactly what Natalon had hoped for—to start a Camp and prove it into a Mine.

Talmaric's son yanked again. "Yes?" Natalon said.

"The caravan's approaching, sir," Zenor said, hoping that "sir" would not affront the Camp's head miner.

"How soon, lad? Don't you know how to make a proper report?" a querulous voice barked above Zenor's ears. He turned and saw that the speaker was Tarik, Natalon's uncle. Zenor had had several encounters with Tarik's son, Cristov, and still bore bruises from the last meeting.

Rumor had it that Tarik was furious that Crom Hold's Master-Miner hadn't put him in charge of seeking out new coal. Another rumor, whispered quietly among only a few of the Camp's boys, was that Tarik was doing everything in his power to prove that Natalon was unsuited to run the Camp and that he, Tarik, should be placed in charge. The last set of bruises Zenor had gotten from Cristov were the result of an ill-placed comment about Cristov's father.

"How long until they arrive, Zenor?" a kinder voice asked. It was Danil, Kindan's father, and the partner of the Camp's only surviving watch-wher.

"I spotted them at the head of the valley," Zenor replied. "I imagine it'll be four, maybe six hours until they reach the Camp."

"They'd get here faster if the roadway were properly lined," Tarik growled, casting a reproving glare at Natalon.

"We must use our labor wisely, Uncle," Natalon answered soothingly. "I decided that it made more sense to fell more trees to use in the mines for shorings."

"We can't afford any more accidents," Danil agreed.

"Nor lose any more watch-whers," Natalon added. Zenor hid a grin as he saw Kindan's father nod in fierce agreement.

"Watch-whers aren't much use," Tarik growled. "We've made do without them before. And now we've lost two, and what've we got to show for it?"

"As I recall, watch-wher Wensk saved your life, Tarik," Danil answered, his voice edged with bitterness. "Even after you refused to heed his warnings. And I believe that your abusive behavior is what decided Wenser to leave with his watch-wher."

Tarik snorted. "If we had enough shoring, the tunnel wouldn't have collapsed."

"Ah!" Natalon interrupted. "I'm glad to hear that you agree with my reasoning, then, Uncle."

Tarik glowered. Then, to change the subject, he snapped at Zenor: "How many drays were there, boy?"

Zenor screwed his eyes shut in concentration. He opened them again when he had his answer. "There were six—and four wagons."

"Hmmph!" Tarik snarled. "Well, Natalon, if the boy's right, then those Traders have two drays less than we've got coal to trade." He fell to muttering darkly. "And all the time we've been spending working ourselves to the bone to get out that coal when we should have been building a proper Hold. What'll happen when Thread comes?"

"Miner Tarik," a new voice chimed in, "Thread's not due to

fall for another sixteen Turns. I imagine we'll have time to correct the problem before then."

Zenor looked behind him as a hand was laid lightly on his shoulder. It was Jofri, the Camp's Harper. Zenor smiled up at the young man who had taught him every morning for the last six months. Harpers were the teachers on Pern—as well as the archivists, news sources, and, sometimes, judges—and Jofri was as good a teacher as he was a musician.

Jofri was a journeyman Harper. He was due to return soon to the Harper Hall to complete his Mastery. When he did, he'd probably be too senior to return to a small Camp like this one. Instead, Zenor was sure that he'd be posted to a great Hold—perhaps even Crom—there to supervise not just the major Hold's children but all the journeyman Harpers dispatched to the small cots and Camps that spread out from the large Hold as its inhabitants expanded their territory.

Of course, maybe a new Harper would know more about Healing than Jofri, who had come to accept that in matters of Healing, Kindan's eldest sister, Silstra, was the Master and not he. Zenor swallowed when he remembered that the caravan approaching bore Silstra's future husband. And that, as a wife of a Smith, Silstra would leave Camp Natalon forever.

"Time or not," Tarik replied with a sneer, "you won't be here."

"Uncle," Natalon said, breaking up what he feared would be another nasty exchange of words, "whatever the result, it was my decision."

Natalon turned his attention back to Zenor. "Run down to the women at the cookfires and inform them that our guests are approaching."

Zenor nodded and took off gladly, not wanting to listen to more of Tarik's snippery. As he left, he heard Danil's voice above the others, "Do you suppose your replacement is also in the caravan, Jofri?"

Oh, no! Zenor wailed to himself. Not a replacement for Harper Jofri so soon!

———◆———

Back up in the watch-heights, Kindan followed Zenor's movements until he was lost in the crowd of elders. Nervously he waited until his friend exited the crowd and then he heaved a sigh of relief—Zenor wasn't in trouble and neither was he. He watched Zenor head down from the plateau toward the buildings and fields below and guessed that he had been ordered to let the rest of the Camp know that the caravan had been sighted. Tonight there would be a welcoming feast.

Kindan saw Zenor slow down as he approached the Harper's cottage. He was surprised to see Zenor stop and then dart around to the front of the cottage—out of Kindan's sight—and, presumably, inside. What was Zenor doing? Kindan guessed that he had stopped because someone inside the cottage had called to him. Kindan made a mental note to find out.

Then the first sounds of the arriving caravan distracted him and he turned his attention to it.

———◆———

The faint smell of pine sap came into the Harper's cottage on the breeze. Pine sap and something else, some subtle smells that made Nuella think instantly of—"Zenor, is that you?" she hissed.

The sounds of a runner stopping suddenly and skidding came through the window, followed by Zenor's voice in a whisper, "What are you doing here?"

Nuella frowned, irritated at his tone. "Come inside and I'll tell you," she answered testily.

"Oh, all right," Zenor grumbled. "But I can't be long, I'm Running." Nuella heard the capital "R" in his voice and knew that he was using kid-shorthand for "I've got the job of runner."

She held her next question until she heard his feet on the front steps. She made her way from the kitchen in the back down the hallway to the front door. A breeze, scented with the lake's moisture, wafted in as Zenor entered.

"I thought Kindan was the runner and you had watch," Nuella said.

Zenor sighed. "We switched," he said. Then, his tone brightening, he added in a rush, "He's going to let me help wash the watch-wher!"

"When?"

"Tonight," Zenor answered. "The caravan's arrived—"

"I heard," Nuella said with a frown. "Do you know if the new Harper's come? I wanted to meet him."

"Meet him? What will your father say?" Zenor demanded.

"I don't care," Nuella answered frankly. "If I've got to be cooped up all the time, at least I can learn something from the Harper. Work on my pipes some more—"

"But what if people find out?"

"The caravan's coming, right? There'll be a feast tonight, won't there? You're going down to tell them at the square, right?" Nuella asked, and then continued immediately, "So tonight, I'll dress up in bright and dark colors—trader clothes—and no one will know."

"The traders will," Zenor protested.

"No, they won't," Nuella said. "They'll think I'm just a miner dressing up to flatter them."

"What about your parents, or Dalor?"

Nuella shrugged. "You'll have to keep me away from them, that shouldn't be hard. Especially as they won't be expecting me."

"But—"

Nuella reached out, caught his arm, turned him around, and pushed him toward the door. "Go on now, or someone will be asking why you're so slow."

◆

By the time Kindan's relief arrived hours later, he had forgotten about Zenor's detour, his stomach rumbling with anticipation at the great smells of spice-roasted wherry rising up from the huge outdoor cooking fires below.

Usually, every family at Camp Natalon ate in their own quarters. Tonight, there were huge fires burning in the pits placed at the center of the square, and long wooden tables with benches had been drawn around them to provide seating for everyone, camper and caravanner alike.

Harper Jofri and several other musicians were playing lively music while the crowd ate happily.

Kindan managed to find food and a quiet seat far away from any further chores. Munching happily on the spiced wherry meat his favorite of his sister's excellent recipes—and drinking fresh berry juice, Kindan nevertheless kept his eyes and ears roaming, both to avoid any interruptions, like work, and to strain for any interesting gossip.

At the head table, in the center of all the tables, Kindan spied the head of the caravan and his lady but his eyes fixed most on his own sister and her fiancé, Terregar. The smith was of medium height but well-muscled. He wore a short, close-trimmed, dark beard that always seemed to be split by a smile made all the brighter by his twinkling blue eyes. Kindan had liked him from the first moment he'd met him.

Terregar and Silstra—their names had a good ring to them. But to him, and indeed all of Camp Natalon, his sister would always be Sis. Kindan wondered if there was a "Sis" in the Telgar Smithcrafthall already. Perhaps *she* was marrying someone from out of the Smithcraft and they were looking for a replacement. He wondered if Camp Natalon would ever find a replacement for his Sis.

Kindan found his eyes watering and decided that the wind must have changed and blown some of the ash from the fire toward him. He ignored the lump in his heart. He knew how happy Sis would be; he'd heard her say it so many times. And he couldn't deny that Terregar was a nice man. Still . . . it would be a lonelier place without his big sister, the sister who'd watched over all the family since their mother had died.

The wind changed, and the freshening breeze brought a new smell—bubbly pies! Kindan's stomach rumbled as he sought the source of the smell. He started to get up, but a hand pushed him down.

"Don't think about it," a voice growled in his ear. It belonged to the youngest of his older brothers, Kaylek. "Dad sent me to find you. You're to wash Dask now."

"Now?"

"Of course!"

"But all the pies'll be eaten!" Kindan protested.

Kaylek was unimpressed. "You'll get some tomorrow at the wedding," he said with a shrug. "Mind you clean him properly, or Dad'll have your hide."

"But it's not dark yet!" Kindan protested. Dask, like all

watch-whers, had been born with huge eyes that found the light of day hideously painful. Dask's eyes worked best at night. At night, there wasn't anything a watch-wher couldn't see. Many were the miners who owed their lives to the ability of a watch-wher to see a human body under the rocks and rubble of a cave-in.

A larger figure loomed over the both of them. Kindan could tell immediately who it was by the way that Kaylek shied away; Kaylek was always more frightened of their father than Kindan.

"You two are disturbing the meal," Danil said in a deep voice roughened by an age in the mines. He laid one large hand on Kaylek's shoulder.

"I told him to go wash Dask," Kaylek said.

Kindan looked up and met his father's eyes squarely. Danil returned the look with a slight nod.

"Well, it can wait until after the bubbly pies," he said. He shook a huge finger at Kindan. "I'm trusting that you'll do us all proud and make my watch-wher the envy of Crom Hold tomorrow."

"Yes, sir!" Kindan responded enthusiastically. The dreaded chore suddenly seemed a mark of great trust and respect. "I will."

Danil kept his hand on Kaylek, saying, "Come along, son, there's a craft girl you might like to meet."

Even in the failing light, Kindan could see Kaylek turn beet red. Kaylek, just Turned fourteen and still very wary of his new-found voice and manhood, was quite shy around girls his own age. Kindan managed not to laugh out loud, but Kaylek caught the look in his eyes and glared at his younger brother. Immediately Kindan sobered—for the look threatened retribution.

The smell of bubbly pies teased Kindan's nose, and he turned to hunt them out. Kaylek's retribution was sometime in the future—the bubbly pies were right now.

———◆———

The evening meal in the Camp's square was still going strong when Kindan started up toward the shed that was Dask's home. As he walked slowly and deliberately away from the bonfire and the crowd, a small shadow detached itself and followed him.

"Are you going to wash the watch-wher now?" Zenor whispered, panting as he struggled to catch up.

"Yes."

"Why didn't you get me, then?" Zenor asked, his voice full of perceived betrayal.

"You're here, aren't you?" Kindan replied. "If I went through the crowd looking for you, Kaylek would have noticed and done something to stop us."

"Oh." Zenor didn't have any older brothers and was completely unused to using guile to get his own way. But because he wanted an older brother just as much as Kindan wanted a younger brother they got along famously—even if there was no more than two months' difference in their ages.

They were about halfway there when Kindan noticed another shadow trailing beside them.

"What's that?" he asked, stopping and pointing.

"What?" Zenor answered promptly. "I don't see anything."

One of the things that Kindan really appreciated in Zenor was that his friend was a truly terrible liar.

"Maybe it was a trick of the moons," Zenor suggested, gesturing up to Pern's two moons, Timor and Belior.

Kindan shrugged and continued onward. Out of the corner of his eye, he noticed that the shadow was still following. He thought for a moment and came up with an interesting notion.

"Who did you talk to, today, at the Harper's?" he asked Zenor.

Zenor stopped dead in his tracks. So, Kindan noticed with satisfaction, did the shadow. "When?" Zenor asked, his eyes wide.

"When you went from Natalon down to the square," Kindan said. "I saw you stop and talk to someone—and I'd already seen Jofri in the group when you talked to Natalon, so it couldn't have been him."

"Me? When?" Zenor repeated.

Kindan waited silently for him to answer.

"Oh!" Zenor said suddenly as though actually remembering and not rapidly concocting a lie. "That was Dalor."

Dalor was Natalon's son, nearly the same age as Zenor and Kindan. Kindan didn't like the way Dalor took on airs about being the son of the Camp's founder, but he couldn't fault the boy otherwise. Dalor was often honest and had stood up for Kindan more than once when Kaylek had been picking on him. Kindan, for his part, had stuck up for Dalor when Cristov, Tarik's only son, picked fights.

Kindan gave Zenor a measuring look, but before he could ask his next question, Zenor said, "Won't your Dad be mad if he finds out that I helped wash Dask?"

"So we'd better make sure he doesn't find out," Kindan said.

Zenor gestured for Kindan to get moving again. "In that case, we'd better get done before my parents start wondering where I am."

Kindan considered teasing Zenor more about their shadow, but the look on his friend's face made him reconsider.

"Okay," was all Kindan said, starting up the slope toward the shed where Dask was quartered, next to the cothold his father had built.

Dask's shed was large enough for the watch-wher to lie on his side with plenty of distance from the walls. Straw was piled on the floor. Kindan opened the double doors carefully and chirped a quick note.

"Dask?" Kindan called softly. "It's me, Kindan. Dad asked me to get you washed for the wedding tomorrow."

The watch-wher uncoiled from his sleeping position, his head emerging from underneath his small wings and his bright eyes, like huge jeweled lanterns, reflecting the last of the twilight brightly back at the two boys.

"Mrmph?" the watch-wher muttered. Kindan crossed the distance between them quickly but cautiously, murmuring softly, reaching out slowly to scratch the ugly watch-wher on the ridge just above his eye.

"Mrmph," Dask murmured with growing pleasure. Kindan blew a breath toward the watch-wher's nose so that Dask would get a good smell of him and recognize him. Dask snorted and blew back. Kindan reached above the eyes for Dask's ears and stroked them.

"Good boy!" he said. Dask arched his neck and pulled his head out of Kindan's grasp to look down haughtily at the boy.

"We're here to wash you," Kindan repeated. Dask leaned down toward Kindan and blew another breath at him, then raised his head up and looked out past the curtain that had been hung inside the double doors. Kindan realized that Dask had seen Zenor. "That's right, me and Zenor," he said soothingly. "Come on in, Zenor."

"It's awfully dark in there," Zenor said, still standing outside the doors.

" 'Course it is," Kindan replied. "Dask likes the dark, don't you, big fellow?"

Dask blew an agreeing breath over Kindan's head and then swiveled his neck to peer curiously toward Zenor.

"The sun's down now," Kindan said to the watch-wher, pointing toward the lake. "Why don't you go for a quick dip and Zenor and I will freshen up your bed?"

Dask nodded and started out of the shed. Wide-eyed, Zenor backed out of the way as the watch-wher pushed by him. Then Dask gave a little happy chirp, flapped his wings once, and vanished. A cold breeze blew over Zenor from where Dask had been.

"Kindan, he vanished!"

"He went *between*," Kindan corrected. "Come on and help me tidy his bed. There should be some fresh straw near you."

"*Between?* You mean just like dragons?" Zenor looked from the spot where the watch-wher had been to the lake.

Kindan glanced consideringly at his friend and shrugged. "I suppose so. I've never seen a dragon go *between*. I heard their riders tell them where to go—but Dask does it on his own. He doesn't like all the bright fires in the square, so he's always going the faster way.

"Come on," he continued. "Give me a hand. He'll be back soon and then the work really starts."

Kindan was serious. They had just gotten fresh straw spread about in a satisfactory bed when another blast of chill air announced Dask's return. The watch-wher's brown skin was glistening with drops of water, and, with a happy noise, he shook himself.

"No!" Kindan bellowed. "Don't shake! We've got to get the dirt off you first."

Grabbing a long-handled brush and a bar of hard soap, Kindan directed Zenor to a bucket of scrubsand. Between them, they scrubbed the watch-wher from top to bottom, snout to tail. Both boys were wet and sweating by the time the watch-wher was clean and dry.

"There you are, Dask," Kindan said, pleased. "All clean and handsome. Just don't roll before the ceremony tomorrow."

Even in the low light, Kindan could see Dask's multifaceted eyes whirling with the green and blue of happiness.

"Whew!" Zenor breathed, sinking down to the floor by the doors. "Washing watch-whers is hard work! I wonder what it's like with dragons?"

"Harder," Kindan said. At Zenor's questioning look, he explained, "Well, dragons are bigger, aren't they? And their skin flakes and has to be oiled, too."

Kindan rose to his feet and gave Dask a hug and a pat on the neck. "Dask here doesn't need to worry about such things. He's tough!"

"I'm tired," Zenor said. "I can't imagine what it would be like to wash him all by yourself."

"We'd've been faster if your friend had helped," Kindan said.

Zenor jumped up. "I don't know what you're talking about! There's no one here but us."

"Who are you talking to?" a voice called loudly from outside the shed. It was Kaylek. "Kindan, if you've got someone helping you, Dad'll skin you alive!"

Zenor vanished into the shadows as Kaylek entered, looking suspicious.

"What are you talking about, Kaylek?" Kindan demanded coyly. "Can't you see I'm just finishing?"

"In about half the time I'd've expected of you," Kaylek muttered, peering into the corners of the shed. Behind him, Kindan could see Zenor carefully move the brush he had been using out of sight.

"I'm a fast worker," Kindan said.

"Since when?" Kaylek retorted. "I'm sure you had help. Dad'll lynch you—you know how he feels about people spooking his watch-wher." Kindan noticed that Kaylek never called Dask by his name.

"Whoever it is has to be nearby," Kaylek said, eyes darting this way and that in the dark shed. "I'll find him and then—"

A loud rattle of stones outside interrupted him.

"Aha!" Kaylek yelled and charged off in the direction of the sound.

Kindan waited until Kaylek's steps had faded into the distance before speaking again. "I think it's all right now," he said to Zenor at last. "But you'd better leave."

"Yeah, I guess I'd better," Zenor agreed.

"And thank your friend for making that diversion. I was sure that Kaylek was going to find you."

Zenor drew a breath as if to argue but let it out again in a sigh and left, shaking his head. Kindan listened to Zenor's footsteps as they faded in the distance, heading back toward the square. Then he bowed to Dask, said good-bye, and closed the shed.

Outside he paused. He turned his head in the direction he had heard the rattle come from. It was from a spot just a bit off the regular track between the mines and the square. For a long while he stood, trying to pierce the dark with his eyes. If he were bonded with a watch-wher, like his father was with Dask, he could have asked his watch-wher to see who was out there. Finally, Kindan gave up and made a guess.

"Thank you, Dalor," he said toward the darkness, as he headed back toward his bed.

Not long after he had left, a soft voice giggled.

CHAPTER II

Its skin is bronze, its eyes are green;
It's the loveliest dragon I've ever seen.

"Wake up, sleepyhead!" Sis shouted at Kindan. Kindan squirmed further into the warm blankets. Abruptly his pillow was pulled out from under his head. He groaned, startled by the sudden movement.

"You heard Sis, get up!" Kaylek said, roughly turning his youngest brother out of the bed.

"I'm up! I'm up!" Kindan snarled. He wished he had just a bit more time to remember his dream. Momma was in it, he was sure.

Kindan never told anyone about his dreams of his mother, not after the first time. He knew that his mother had died giving birth to him; he couldn't help knowing, because his brothers and sisters practically blamed him for it. But Sis—and his father, who spoke so rarely—both said that it wasn't his fault. Sis told Kindan how big a smile his mother had had when she held him in her arms. "He's beautiful!" his mother had said to his father. And then she had died.

"Your mother wanted you," Danil had told him once after Kindan had come home crying because his big brothers had told him that no one had wanted him. "She knew the risks, but she said you'd be worth it."

"Ma said you wouldn't need much looking after," Sis had said another time, "but you'd be worth it."

This morning Kindan didn't feel worth much of anything. He scrambled to get his clothes on, washed his face in cold water in the basin, and rushed to the breakfast table.

"Throw the water out and clean the basin," Jakris growled, grabbing him by the ear and spinning him back toward their room. "You're the last one who used it."

"I'll get it later!" Kindan yelped.

Jakris turned and blocked the exit. "You will not—you'll get it now or Sis'll give it to you later."

Kindan frowned and turned back to the washbasin. With his back to Jakris he stuck out his tongue. His bigger brother would have decked him if he had seen him.

Taking care of the washbasin ensured that Kindan was the last in to breakfast. He looked around for something to eat. There was *klah* to drink—cold. Some cereal, but not much, and no milk to go with it. The others hurried away, but Sis turned them back with either a growl or a frown, so they couldn't get away with leaving their dishes for him.

"You'll eat well tonight, Kindan," Sis said to him as he mournfully spooned his breakfast. Her eyes were particularly bright.

Kindan was confused for a moment, but then he remembered—there was a wedding tonight. Sis's wedding.

"Now, get out of here, you've chores to do," she said, shoving him affectionately out of the kitchen.

◆

First thing out the door, Kindan stopped. Sis hadn't assigned chores like she usually did. He turned back just as she came charging out.

"Go ask Jenella," Sis said scoldingly before Kindan could even open his mouth.

Jenella was Natalon's wife. As she was very pregnant, Sis had stood in for her ever since the families had moved up to the Camp, six months ago.

Kindan knew that there was no one worse than his own sister in a temper so he scuttled off immediately. He concentrated so hard on avoiding his sister's temper that his legs took him up to the mine entrance before he realized it. Rather than turning straight back, Kindan paused, eyeing the mine entrance thoughtfully.

Usually, one of the first tasks of the day for the Camp's youngsters was to change the glowbaskets in the mines. Today, because of the wedding, the mines were closed—except for those unlucky enough to have the job of working the pumps—so Kindan found himself in front of the mine shaft wondering whether the task had been canceled for the day. Even though no one would be mining that day and that night, Kindan decided that surely it made sense to change the glows so that the miners wouldn't have to go down into a dark mine the next day.

Kindan heard voices coming from inside the mine. He

couldn't make out what was being said, but he could tell that one was a man's deep voice and the other a young girl's voice.

"Hello!" he called into the mine, thinking that perhaps some of the caravanners had gone for a look at the mine.

The voices stopped. Kindan cupped an ear with his hand, straining to hear any sounds. Late at night, when the Camp's cook fire had burned down to mere embers and the chill winds from the mountains howled through the Camp's square, the older boys told all sorts of scary stories about ghosts in the mine. Kindan was *sure* that these weren't ghosts, but all the same, he wasn't too interested in going into a dark cave by himself.

"Hello?" he called again, hesitantly. He certainly wouldn't want to invite any ghosts to him.

There was no answer. Presently Kindan heard the steady sound of one pair of boots on the dirt floor of the cave. He stepped back from the entrance. A darker shadow appeared, then resolved itself into human form.

It was an old, silver-haired man whom Kindan had never seen before. The man looked haggard and his eyes were bleak, as though all the laughter had been leached from them and all the life had seeped away. Kindan took another step back and prepared to run. The child in the mine—the one with the girl's voice. Had this specter eaten it?

"You there!" the man called out.

As soon as he heard the deep, rich voice, Kindan knew that the man was no ghost. The accent was clearly from Fort Hold, and it held the cultured overtones of the Harper Hall.

"Yes, Master?" Kindan answered, not knowing what rank the man held and guessing that it was best to err on the side of caution. Was this Harper Crom's MasterHarper come to check on Journeyman Jofri? Or was he a Harper with the traders?

"What are you doing here?" the old man barked.

"I was here to see if the glows needed changing," Kindan said.

The old man frowned, brows furrowed tightly. His head swung around to look over his shoulder, but he stopped the movement almost immediately. "I was told," he said, "that no one was going to be up here today."

"Yes, there's a wedding," Kindan told him. "But I wasn't sure if Natalon wanted the glows changed."

"Well, they certainly could do with it," the old man said. The sound of a small rock falling behind him made him turn around and back again. "It can be quite dangerous down there. But I think—wait a minute!—are you Kindan?"

"Yes, sir," Kindan replied, wondering why the old man knew his name. He couldn't have known about . . . Kindan compiled a far too lengthy list of possible misdeeds before the old man made his next response.

"You are supposed to be at the Harper's quarters in about fifteen minutes, young man," the old man said. As Kindan turned to run back down to Jofri's cottage, the old man added, "Ready to sing and not breathless!"

"I will be!" Kindan shouted back over his shoulder, running as fast as his feet could carry him.

As soon as Kindan was out of earshot, the old man turned back to the mine entrance. "You can come out now, he's gone."

He heard the sound of light feet approaching the cave's entrance, but they stopped before their owner came into view.

"I know a shortcut, if you'd like."

"Through the mountain?" he asked.

"Of course." After a moment's silence, sensing the old man's reticence, the girl added, "I've used it loads of times. I'll show you."

The old man smiled and started back into the cave. "Well, with your guidance, I'll be happy to take your shortcut," he said, making a short bow to the figure in the dark. "Would I be right in guessing that it will get us there before the lad?"

The girl's answer was a mischievous giggle.

◆

Kindan arrived outside the Harper's cottage completely breathless. Zenor was already waiting.

"Kindan, you're just in time," Zenor said. "If you'd've been a few more minutes late—" He broke off, his eyes full of dark foreboding.

"What is it?"

"The Master wants to hear us sing," Zenor said. "He's already told Kaylek that he can't sing at the wedding."

Kindan's face lit up at the thought of Kaylek's reaction. Kindan wasn't surprised: Kaylek's singing voice sounded like a gravel slide, and he had no ability whatsoever to stay in tune. Whenever pressed about it by his friends, Kaylek would swear that he didn't like singing and that, anyway, he'd been a perfect singer until his voice had changed. But Kindan knew from tales he heard from his other brothers and Sis that neither of those statements were true; Kaylek loved to sing but had not one jot of musical ability.

Silstra had tried to figure ways to get all her siblings involved in her wedding, and her choice of Kaylek to sing was probably no more than a combination of nerves and running out of ideas.

Zenor nudged Kindan in the ribs. "Don't you get it? If Kaylek can't sing, who's going to do all his songs at the wedding?"

Kindan's eyes went round and his mouth opened in a big "O" of dreadful realization.

Just then, the door opened.

"Come in, come in, I can't stand dawdling," a voice growled from inside the cottage. It wasn't Journeyman Jofri's voice. It was the voice of the old man that Kindan had met up at the mine entrance.

Enraged, Kindan burst into the room.

"What are you doing here? It was bad enough that you went down the mines without Miner Natalon's permission, but to barge into a Harper's quarters—" Kindan cut himself short and a horrified look came over him. Kindan could feel his whole face burning in embarrassment. *Oh no!* Kindan thought to himself with a sinking feeling in the pit of his stomach, he's *the new Harper!* Our *new Harper!*

The old man did not take Kindan's outburst lightly.

"What do you think *you* are doing?" his voice boomed, filling the room not just with its volume but also with its intensity.

"Sorry," Kindan muttered, trying with the tip of his foot to dig his way into the floorboards of the cottage in a vain hope of escaping both his embarrassment and the Harper's anger. "I didn't realize that you were the new Harper."

"You didn't *think*, you mean," the old man roared back irritably.

Kindan hung his head. "Yes, sir." If there was one thing Kindan was good at, it was at being bawled out—he'd had *lots* of practice.

"You seem to have a knack for that, don't you?" the Harper noted tetchily.

"Yes, sir," Kindan agreed, his head on his chest and his answer going to the floor.

The new Harper eyed Kindan. "You're not related to that oaf I just sent out of here this morning, are you?"

Kindan glanced up at that, his fists clenched. It was enough to be in the wrong and caught out twice by the stranger, but only a family member had the right to call Kaylek an oaf!

"Hmm," the old man murmured. "You say nothing, but your body shows its support for your clan."

He stood up and strode over to Kindan. Putting a hand under Kindan's chin, he lifted the boy's head until Kindan was looking in the Harper's eyes. Kindan could not keep the anger off his face, and he refused to utter an apology. He matched looks with the Harper for as long as the Harper stared at him.

Finally, the Harper stood back. "Stubborn. But I've managed worse."

Kindan's nostrils flared.

The Harper ignored him, flicking his gaze to Zenor. "Well, come in, lad, I won't bite you!"

Zenor looked as though he were completely torn between the obvious fallacy of the Harper's statement and the blasphemy that a Harper could lie. He gave Kindan an inquiring look and, receiving no hints from his friend, stood dazed like a smallbeast stalked by a wherry until the Harper cleared his throat warningly. Zenor jumped into the room as though stung.

"Harper Jofri tells me that you sing well," the Harper said to them, dividing his gaze between the two boys. "But Harper Jofri is a journeyman who specializes in ballads and drums.

"I"—and here the Harper deepened his voice and increased his volume, so that his words echoed resoundingly through the room—"am a Master and specialize in the voice. So, naturally, I have been asked to oversee the evening's vocal arrangements."

Kindan looked up at that, amazed. Harper Jofri had often admonished the boys and girls of Camp Natalon that if they didn't behave he'd use the tricks that had been used on him by the

Harper Hall's vocal master. "Be good, or I'll treat you like Master Zist treated me," Jofri would warn them.

And here, standing in front of them, true to life and full of horrors, was that very same Master Zist.

Zenor's jaw dropped. Out of the corner of his eye, Kindan could see Zenor trying to get words out of his mouth, but it was obvious that all the air in him had gone into his eyes, for they looked ready to pop straight out of his face.

"You're—" Kindan realized that he was not immune from terror, either. "You're Master Zist?"

Beside him, Zenor had managed to close his mouth.

"Ah," Master Zist replied in satisfied tones, "you've heard of me. I am pleased to learn that Harper Jofri remembered my lessons.

"It remains to be seen how much he has taught you," he continued, raising a finger warningly. "I will not let my first day here—and this Camp's very first wedding—be marred by voices that are not in proper form."

Master Zist opened his hand and waved the two boys closer to him. "When you are ready, I shall hear a scale from middle C in harmony."

Kindan and Zenor glanced at each other; Harper Jofri had had them doing scales in harmony since they could first walk. Their eyes gleamed and they turned back to the Master, opened their mouths, and—

"No, no, no!" Master Zist roared. The boys caught their breath and rocked back on their heels in fright. "Stand up straight. Shoulders back. Take a deep breath and—"

Following his orders, the two boys started to sing the scales.

"Who told you to sing?" Master Zist yelled at them. After

they shut their mouths in horror, he continued, "I do not recall asking you to sing." He sighed. "It is obvious that you two must first learn how to breathe."

Zenor and Kindan exchanged looks. Didn't they already know how to breathe?

By lunchtime, Kindan was exhausted. He hadn't realized how much work it could be just to sing. Rather than letting them go, Master Zist sent Zenor to get their lunch and tell Jenella that the two boys would sing at the wedding. Zenor's eyes lit when Master Zist told them, but Kindan was too tired and still wary of the new Harper.

"You," Master Zist intoned after Zenor had left, "will practice the wedding chorale Harper Jofri had selected for your brother."

Kindan gulped. Kaylek would kill him for sure when he found out, and that song was a really hard one to learn.

By the time Zenor returned with lunch—it seemed to take forever—Kindan was sweating with effort and Master Zist was nearly shaking with rage.

"Leave the food here," Master Zist told him, "and take yourself away."

Instead of breaking for lunch, Master Zist insisted that Kindan continue his singing. No matter how hard he tried, Kindan could not master the song.

In the end, red-faced and bellowing, Master Zist threw up his hands. "You are not listening to me! You do not pay the slightest attention. You *can* master this song, you just choose not to. Oh, you are such a waste! To think your mother died giving birth to you! You're not worth it at all."

Kindan's fists clenched and his eyes flared with rage. He turned on his heel and ran out of the cottage. He got only a few feet before he was stopped by his sister.

"Kindan, how is it going?" she asked, too excited to notice his expression. "Isn't it great that Master Zist is here? Did you know that mother said he taught her our favorite song?"

Kindan took one look at her cheerful face as her words registered in his brain—and inspiration struck.

"Excuse me, Sis, I've got to get back to practicing," he said before he turned back to the cottage. Over his shoulder he added, "Everything's going great."

He barged back into the cottage where Master Zist still sat, waiting. Kindan pulled himself up to a proper singing posture, drew in a breath, and began to sing:

"In early morning light I see,
A distant dragon come to me.
Its skin is bronze, its eyes are green;
It's the loveliest dragon I've ever seen."

Encouraged by the Harper's silence, Kindan continued through the whole song. In the end, he looked truculently at the Master and said, "I can, too, sing. My sister says that I can sing as well as my mother. My sister says that I *am* worth it. And my father, too. And they should know—they were there when I was born." Tears streaked down his face, but he didn't care. "My sister said that my mother's last words were that I wouldn't need much caring but I'd be worth it."

Master Zist was in shock. "That voice," he muttered to himself. "You have her voice." He looked up at Kindan and there were tears in his eyes, too. "Lad, I'm sorry. I should never have said . . . I had no right . . . Could you sing it again, please? You have the same lyric quality she had."

Kindan wiped his tears and drew breath, but his throat was

still choked up with grief and anger. Master Zist raised a hand to stop him and went into the cottage's kitchen. He returned with a cup of warm tea.

"Drink this, it'll ease your throat," he said in a much kindlier and more subdued voice. While Kindan was drinking, Master Zist said, "I drove you too hard, lad. I have never driven a student so hard. I shouldn't have done it to you, either. It's just that— that I want this to be the best day for your sister and your father. I want to give them that."

"So do I," Kindan said.

Master Zist lowered his head toward him and nodded. "I see that you do, lad. I see that you do." He held out his hand. "So, let's start over and we'll do the best we can, together, eh?"

Kindan placed the cup beside him and shyly put his hand in the larger hand of the MasterHarper. "I'll do my best," he said.

"That's all I will ask of you," Master Zist promised. "And, with your voice, I think we'll both be proud of the result." He looked out the window. "We haven't much time, however, so we'd best concentrate on what you know, hadn't we?"

Kindan nodded in agreement, but his expression was be-mused. Master Zist grinned at him. "Why don't we work 'The Morning Dragon Song' into the ceremony instead of that solo?"

Kindan's eyes widened. "Could we do it just as Dask flies over?" he asked enthusiastically. "It'd be perfect!"

"The watch-wher can fly?" Zist was surprised.

Kindan nodded.

"Can all watch-whers fly?"

"I wouldn't know," Kindan answered honestly. "But weren't they supposed to be made from fire-lizards, the same as dragons?"

"Not much is known about watch-whers," Master Zist said. "For example, we know that they don't like light. But some people say that it's because of their big eyes while others say that they are nocturnal. Their wings look too small to support them."

"I've only seen Dask fly when it's late," Kindan said. "My father said something about how the atmosphere condenses at night, and air gets thicker."

Master Zist nodded. "That's so. I've heard the dragonriders say that it's dangerous to fly too high at night—the air has gotten thinner there. Perhaps the watch-whers are adapted to fly at night, and have smaller wings because the air is thicker then."

Kindan shrugged. The Harper made a note to himself to pursue the matter with the Harper Hall.

"Well," the Harper continued, "I think it would be marvelous for you to sing 'The Morning Dragon Song' when Dask flies over.

"Are you ready to begin now?"

"I'm ready, Master Zist."

———◆———

At the end of two hours, Kindan's back was drenched with sweat. Master Zist's instructions were more cordially delivered and Kindan obeyed them more readily than before, but they were still doing hard work—both of them, Kindan noted, as Master Zist wiped beads of sweat from his brow.

They were interrupted by a knock on the cottage door.

"Get the door, lad," Master Zist said in a kindly tone. "I'll make some tea. Unless I miss my guess, that's your father come to be sure that you're still alive and with your good clothes as his excuse."

Master Zist was not wrong.

"I've brought your clothes," Danil said. His face broke into a huge grin. "Ah, lad! This will be a grand day, won't it?"

Coming from his father, the words were practically a speech.

"Master Zist's gone to get some tea," Kindan said. "He says that it's good for the throat." He didn't add that Master Zist had said that it was good for the nerves, as well.

"I've been with Jofri all day," Danil told his son. "We've got the wedding platform properly raised and the whole square ready for the party."

"Where will the bride and groom spend the night?" Master Zist asked, entering the room with a tray. There were not just three cups of tea, but also some dainty pastries.

Danil blushed. "Oh, there's a trader custom that a bride and groom must spend the night in a caravan. Apparently Crom's MasterTrader instructed the journeyman in charge of this caravan to be sure that Terregar and Silstra followed *their* custom."

"Of course," Zist added with a wry look and a shake of his head, "anyone marrying cross Hold would be relying on a trader to move them, so no one would dream of upsetting them on that matter."

Danil picked up one of the dainties off the tray and bit into it. "This is good! And still warm! Did Jenella send them?"

Master Zist nodded. "Aye, they were just delivered." Kindan remembered that he'd heard the sound of a door opening shortly after his father had entered the front room.

Danil nodded. His face had gone serious. "Kindan, step outside for a moment," he said.

"Take your tea and a dainty with you," Zist said. Kindan scooped up one of his favorites, grabbed his tea, and headed outside.

Milla, who did all the baking and cooking up at Natalon's hold, loved making the tiny little snacks she called dainties. Milla's dainties were always different; sometimes they were confections, other times they were small, meat-filled pies, and yet other times they were deliciously spiced vegetables. The warm dainty Kindan had scarfed was made of spiced meat wrapped in a flaky pie crust.

Outside, the sun was well past noon, but its warmth did little against the fall chill that had settled into the valley. He shivered. It would be a cold evening, even with warm *klah* and hot mulled wine to keep him warm. He swallowed the rest of the dainty in one bite to give him both hands to wrap around the warm cup.

He could hear the rise and fall of voices from inside the cottage but couldn't make out the words. Bored, he walked over by the walled herb garden that separated the Harper's cottage from Natalon's hold. Natalon's place was too big to be called a cottage. Besides, it was built properly of stone. When the time for Thread got nearer, it would be turned into the entrance for a proper Hold dug into the cliffside—perhaps one day even as large as Crom Hold.

Kindan and the other youngsters had lived at Crom Hold for the better part of a year while Natalon, Danil, and the other original miners had sought out, found, and begun working the new mine.

Crom Hold was a vast set of tunnels and rooms dug into the side of a high, majestic cliff. Kindan had spent a lot of time running through—or cleaning—the vacant rooms that would again house most of those who looked to Crom's Lord Holder for protection when Thread started to fall from the sky.

Kindan shivered at the thought. Thread. Shimmering, long silvery strands that fell from the sky whenever the Red Star drew close to Pern. Thread. Burning, eating, destroying everything it touched—wood and limb alike. No green would be allowed to grow near the Holds when Thread returned. The mindless Thread could grow incredibly fast, or so Kindan had been taught, and wipe out whole valleys in a matter of hours.

Kindan squinted his eyes, trying to imagine how Natalon's hold would be converted into a proper Hold dug into the cliff-side. It certainly would have a great view of the lake below. But Kindan wasn't sure that he'd like being cooped up inside for the next fifty Turns.

Deep down, Kindan wasn't sure that he even wanted to be a miner. He squashed the thought firmly. His father was a miner and a wherhandler. Kindan should consider himself lucky to get a chance at either.

Miners were vital to Pern's survival. Without the firestone provided by other miners, dragons could not breathe fire; without those flames, dragons could not destroy Thread as it fell from the sky. The coal that Camp Natalon produced burned the hottest and produced the best steel. Still other mines mined the iron ore that went into the steel which made ploughs, shovels, picks, nails, screws, buckles, and countless other things which were vital to life on Pern. Yet others found the copper, the nickel, and the tin, which were blended together to make brass for ornaments and tableware. Indeed, the miners in the great salt mines of Southern Boll and Igen supplied all Pern with salt.

Watch-whers in mines were a recent addition, and Kindan knew that his father had done more with watch-whers and mining than any other. Dask, his father's watch-wher, not only could warn the miners of pockets of bad air, but was adept at digging and hauling ore. Kindan suspected, from snippets of conversations he'd overheard between his father and his older brothers, that Danil had even greater plans for the use of watch-whers in the mines.

While people were at their most alert during the day and

slept at night, watch-whers were the opposite, sleeping during the day and awaking at night. That was why they were used to keep watch in the great Holds during the dark hours of the night. In the mines, the night shift could do more excavating of new shafts than any of the day shifts because of the watch-whers.

But really, not much was known about watch-whers. Even his own father was largely self-educated—through his experience with Dask.

Kindan had heard that originally there had been two other watch-whers at Camp Natalon. One had died, and the other had left along with his handler. Kindan had heard his brothers complaining about it, and about Tarik's sour opinion of watch-whers.

Kindan knew that he would be extremely lucky if he were ever considered for a watch-wher egg.

Still, he really liked singing.

Kindan turned away from Natalon's hold to look down toward the lake and the cottages.

The cottages were built with rough-hewn stone to window height and timber the rest of the way. They were covered with long, high-peaked, overhanging roofs. It was possible that the roofs could be covered with slate and built to withstand Thread, but most people would feel safest in a "proper Hold."

"Kindan!" Danil's voice interrupted Kindan's reverie. He turned and followed Danil's beckon back to the Harper's cottage.

"I'll see you at the ceremony," Danil said to him. Then, to Kindan's surprise, his father leaned down and hugged him tight. "I love you, son."

Kindan fought back the tears in his eyes as he said, "I love you too, Dad."

Danil strode off briskly with a little trailing wave of his hand. Kindan returned to the cottage, his chest swelling.

Inside the cottage, Master Zist gave Kindan a long, penetrating stare.

"Your father's quite a man, lad," he said at last. "Quite a man."

Kindan nodded.

"One more time through 'The Morning Dragon Song' and then we'll go through the whole lot," Zist said to him. He held up a restraining hand as Kindan swallowed a lungful of air. "No! Not like that, lad. Remember what I told you." Zist placed his hands on his own sides and pressed them into his diaphragm. "From down here. Breathe up and down, not in and out."

◆

The wind tore through the Camp's main square as Kindan accompanied Master Zist down to the wedding platform. Both were dressed in their best clothes, Master Zist looking completely regal in his Harper blue. Kindan tried not to think too hard about how he looked, fearing that the rest of the Camp's kids would fill him in painfully on his appearance in many future encounters.

Master Zist must have guessed how Kindan felt for he chose that moment to say, "You look great, lad."

Traditionally, the marriage ceremony was performed in the morning, timed so that as the couple completed their marriage vows, the sun would rise, signifying the warmth of the new relationship and how it would lighten not only the bride and groom but also all those associated with them.

However, such a ceremony would mean that Dask could not attend. So Jofri had come up with the idea of performing the ceremony with the setting sun, instead, and lighting a bonfire as the final vows were made. Master Zist had seen no reason to contradict that.

Everyone in the Camp was gathered in the main square. The dining tables had been pushed to the edges of the square, while the benches had been arranged in rows in front of the wedding platform, which would be used after the ceremony by the musicians.

Kindan could smell fresh-cut branches of pine piled on the unlit bonfire. The wind died down as the sun continued its downward arc in the sky.

It was time.

Master Zist, holding Kindan's shoulder, guided him to his place on the platform. Kindan sketched a quick grin to Zenor, who was dressed in similar finery and stood on the opposite end of the platform. Seated next to Zenor was Journeyman Jofri, with his drums in front of him and his guitar placed beside him within easy reach. Master Zist moved slightly away from Kindan to stand next to his own pipes and guitar; Kindan guessed that Jofri must have set them up for the Master.

At a nod from Master Zist, Jofri began a long flourish on the drums. The people in their seats grew quiet. Out of the corner of his eye, Kindan could see his father and a radiant girl dressed in a marvelous gown standing at the back of the benches. Kindan realized with a start that the girl was Silstra!

Jofri changed his beat and the sound of Master Zist's pipes joined in. Everyone stood as Danil led Silstra down the aisle. At the same time someone lit the long row of torches that had been placed on either end of the benches.

A beam of light burst out from the sky above Silstra and followed her as she made her way down the aisle.

"Kindan, what is that?" Zist hissed in between his piping.

"That's Dask," Kindan said proudly. "He must be flying with a glow in his claws."

"Even as I see it, I can scarcely believe it," Zist whispered in awe. "Truly amazing."

Indeed, above the pipes, Kindan could hear the watch-wher's chirping voice in counterpoint to Master Zist's melody.

Zist's pipes stopped when Silstra reached her place on the platform, facing the audience.

Jofri began a different, more martial drum sequence and Terregar, resplendent in his craft's colors, started his walk up the aisle, accompanied by Journeyman Veran, the trader in charge of the caravan.

Again, Dask flew overhead, illuminating the groom from above as he had the bride.

Terregar's assumption of his position beside Silstra on the wedding platform was the signal for Kindan and Zenor to start their duet. Jofri introduced them with a flourish and Kindan started to sing only to realize that Zenor had not joined in.

Kindan looked frantically at his friend but saw that Zenor's eyes were skyward, watching Dask as he hovered over the wedding platform.

Kindan strengthened his volume to cover Zenor's lack until Jofri tapped Zenor on the shoulder. With a horrified look of apology at Silstra and Terregar, Zenor joined in singing the song with Kindan. A titter ran through the watching crowd.

After they had completed their song, Master Zist stepped to the center of the platform and started the ceremony. Kindan had seen three other weddings in his life, but he'd never participated in one before. He listened carefully to the words Master Zist used to ask Silstra if she would have Terregar as her husband

ANNE MCCAFFREY & TODD MCCAFFREY

and to ask Terregar if he would have her as his wife. Then Master Zist spoke of the changes that each had agreed to, and the joy that their union brought those gathered here and his hope that their union would bring joy to all of Pern.

"For now that these two are one, we are all more," Master Zist intoned. He placed Silstra's hand in Terregar's and kissed each lightly on the cheek. "To Terregar and Silstra!"

The crowd stood up and roared back: "Terregar and Silstra!"

"Long life and happiness!" Master Zist intoned.

"Long life and happiness!" the crowd roared back.

Master Zist stepped back from the married couple. He waited until the shouting had died down and then nodded to Kindan.

Kindan started his solo.

"In early morning light I see,
A distant dragon come to me."

But as he sang, he heard a strange echo. He tried not to look around and merely concentrate on his singing, but his expression must have been noticed by Master Zist, because the Harper surreptitiously pointed skyward—Dask was singing along! Kindan broke into a grin as he continued his song, working in Dask's counterpoint to the beat of the music and the spacing of the words. He finished with the opening refrain again:

"In early morning light I see,
A distant dragon come to me."

Kindan let his voice fade softly away. As his voice died out, Dask uttered one final, satisfied chirp.

A huge hand grasped Kindan's shoulder and Master Zist told him, "Well done, Kindan. Well done."

And then Silstra was hugging and kissing him, tears of joy streaming from her eyes. "You were wonderful, thank you!" Terregar shook his hand and clapped him on the back, and then the bride and groom marched back down the aisle. Veran gave Terregar a torch, and the two ceremonially lit the wedding bonfire, bringing the light of their union to the mining camp.

At that, the partying started. Master Zist and Journeyman Jofri started with a reel. Kindan had never heard a fiddle played before, but he found that its pleasant tones could be very lively.

As he leapt off the wedding platform, he was accosted by Kaylek. "Dad says that you're to change into everyday clothes now."

Kindan set off immediately for their cottage, where he changed quickly. On his way back, he spotted a girl about his own age standing beside a tree, listening to the music. Kindan had never seen her before, so he guessed that she was one of the trader girls.

"What are you doing here?" he asked, at peace with the world. "There'll be dancing as soon as the platform's cleared off."

"Dancing?" the girl repeated. "I don't dance."

"A trader that doesn't dance?" Kindan asked. "I could see a miner's daughter, maybe, but not a trader. Or are you afraid of the dance platform?"

"I've never been on one before," the girl admitted.

"I'm supposed to clear it off," Kindan told her, and started on his way with a wave of his hand.

"Wait!" the girl called. Kindan stopped. "Could you bring me down to the party?"

Kindan turned back and looked at her.

"I'm a bit shy," she offered hastily by way of explanation. She held out her hand to him. "If you could hold my hand—"

Kindan started to say no, but she raised the palm of her hand to stop him.

"Just until we get there," she said. She drew a deep breath and a hungry look crossed her face. "The food smells so good!"

"Well, okay," Kindan agreed. He took her hand and she stood up beside him. "I'm Kindan, by the way."

"I kn—I'm Nuella," she said.

"You know?" Kindan repeated. As they approached the torch-lit square he got a better look at the girl. "I've seen you before! You were with the Harper in the mine! You're lucky Natalon didn't catch you, or you would've been in a lot of trouble."

Nuella nodded and made a face. "I know," she said. "And I'm afraid he might have heard about it," she added hastily, "so if you could keep me away from him—I've never seen him, you know—I'd appreciate it."

Kindan thought for a moment as they continued their way down to the square. He realized that he probably didn't want to be seen by Miner Natalon, either, just to avoid being sent on an errand or given a chore. Come to think of it, if he could avoid anyone who might put him to work, that'd be just fine with him.

"All right," he agreed. "After we get our food, I know of a nice quiet spot where we shouldn't be seen."

Nuella giggled and said, "That sounds perfect."

The giggle sounded oddly familiar to Kindan.

Nuella asked Kindan to explain all the dishes set out on the buffet table. "You've never had tuber before?" Kindan asked. "Surely you must have."

"Oh," Nuella responded glibly, "I've had it before, but I don't think I've seen it prepared like this."

"Huh," Kindan muttered, surprised that someone had never had mashed tubers before. Shards, if it weren't for the fact that they were still warm, he would have avoided them in favor of something tastier himself.

They got their food and Kindan guided her to his special hiding spot. But it was occupied already.

"What are *you* doing here?" Zenor demanded when he saw them.

"Hiding," Kindan replied. "Just like you." He gestured toward Nuella. "Zenor, this is Nuella."

"I know," Zenor replied sourly, moving over to make room for them.

"We've already met," Nuella explained. She started to set her cup down beside her, but it spilled. "Oh, dear! Kindan, could you get me another cup, please?"

Kindan was reluctant to leave—his food was still warm—but Nuella had asked so nicely that, with a shrug, he found himself saying, "Sure." To Zenor he added, "Be right back."

❖

Zenor waited until Kindan was out of sight before he turned to Nuella. "Are you mad?"

Nuella turned quickly to Zenor. "He thinks I'm one of the traders."

"You weren't where you said you'd be when I came by," he said.

Nuella nodded. "I met Kindan while I was waiting for you. Anyway, what took you so long?"

Zenor shrugged. "I had to help set up the dance platform."

"Kindan was talking about dancing later," Nuella confided with a hint of wistfulness.

Zenor gave her a look of surprise and then said, "What are you going to do?"

"Well, I can't dance," she admitted. "Maybe I'll get tired or something."

"Anyway, if you tried, someone might see you and Dalor together and figure out that you were twins," Zenor said.

"They might not," Nuella argued. "We're not identical twins, we look different."

"Not that much," Zenor said. "You've both got blond hair and blue eyes. You look enough like him that you could take his place."

Nuella brightened. "Maybe that's it! I could switch with Dalor!"

"I don't think Kindan would want to dance with Dalor," Zenor said, laughing.

Nuella's expression deflated. "Oh," she said, "you're right."

"Still," she said after a moment, "he thought I was a trader girl. Maybe . . ."

Zenor was upset. "He's my friend. I don't want to lie to him," he said miserably.

"I wouldn't ask you to lie," Nuella said. "But he doesn't know—"

"And you don't want anyone to know," Zenor finished, having heard her views on this topic many times.

Nuella flushed. "It's not me, it's Father. He's afraid—"

"He's wrong, you know," Zenor said heatedly. "And what's worse, there's no way you can keep hidden all the time—"

"I've done well enough so far," Nuella retorted.

"*I* found you, didn't I?" Zenor shot back.

"Actually," she corrected, "I found you."

"Still, you've been here less than six months now—"

"As have we all—"

"And I've already found out," Zenor finished. "How long do

you think it'll be before someone else figures it out? A month? A sevenday?"

Nuella frowned. "It's just until Father proves the mine—"

"Shh! He's coming back," Zenor warned.

Nuella tentatively reached out to Zenor, grabbed his hand, and gave it a thankful squeeze.

"You know," he told her softly, "I could teach you to dance."

"Not tonight," she answered, her voice just as quiet. "But I'd like that, Zenor." She paused and added, "You're my best friend."

Zenor smiled in the darkness.

The food was mostly gone when Kindan went for his fourth helping. He must have been tired, because he didn't notice Kaylek until his older brother had grabbed his shoulder and squeezed.

"What are you still doing up?" Kaylek growled. "I thought I sent you younger lot to bed ages back."

"Just going now," Kindan lied, squirming away from his brother's grip. He could feel Kaylek's eyes boring into his back as he left, so he had no choice but to take the path that led from the camp's square uphill to their cottage.

His legs protested as he negotiated the gentle slope, and by the time he reached the cottage, he was all ready to climb into bed. He pulled some blankets over himself and was asleep before he could turn over.

He awoke early the next morning, shivering with cold. He quickly discovered why—his brother Jakris was in the bed next to him and had pulled all the blankets over himself. Kindan briefly tried to pull his share of the blankets back before he blearily remembered that Silstra would be leaving that morning.

He heaved himself out of bed and put on a set of workday clothes before he made his way into the kitchen. The fire was out and the room was cold. Silstra was normally the first up in the morning and laid the fire and got some oatmeal simmering in a pot and *klah* brewing beside it.

Now, it would be someone else's job. Rubbing his face to get the sleep out of it and some warmth into himself, Kindan decided that at least for this morning it would be him. He loaded the hearth with kindling and struck a fire. Soon he had the kitchen warm and breakfast cooking. The smell of *klah* filled the room.

"Morning," Dakin, Kindan's eldest brother, called as he strode into the kitchen. He poured himself a cup of *klah*. "Ah, I'm glad you were up first," he said, savoring the aroma of the *klah* while warming his hands around the cup.

"There'll be a hard day's work in the mines," he continued conversationally. "I'm sure that Natalon will want to make up for all the time lost frolicking last night."

"I wanted to say good-bye to Sis," Kindan said.

Dakin shrugged, glancing out the window to judge the time. "Well, you'd best hurry, then. The traders like to be on the road early."

Kindan started for the door, but Dakin called after him, "Wait up, Kindan. We'll fill some of the covered cups with *klah* and bring them down to them." His eyes lit as he added, "They might be a bit slow getting started this morning."

Kindan wanted to run down to the caravan, but Dakin slowed him to a more sedate walk. "If they're gone, Kindan, they're gone. But if they're not and we've spilt all the *klah*, we'll get no welcome."

The traders were just stirring as Kindan and Dakin entered their camp. Caravans were being packed up, and workbeasts rounded up and hitched into harnesses. Kindan looked around, wondering idly if he'd spot Nuella's wagon. His look grew quizzical as he noticed that there were no children at the trader's camp.

"Look, that must be theirs!" Dakin said, pointing to a wildly decorated caravan set off from the others.

Kindan trailed behind Dakin, his gaze everywhere as he took in the camp. Still he saw no signs of children.

"Hello the wagon!" Dakin shouted as they approached the wedding caravan. "We bring hot *klah*."

Dakin grinned as he heard sounds of movement inside the wagon. Terregar's head poked out from between the curtains.

"Hot *klah*?" he repeated wistfully.

"Well," Dakin responded consideringly as he handed the mugs up, "maybe just warm. It was a long walk from our cottage."

Terregar looked suspiciously at the first mug, but a slender hand reached out and snatched it from him before he could react.

"And a good morning to you, too, Sister," Dakin boomed jovially. His smile widened as he heard Silstra's answering groan.

Terregar shot him a reproving look, his free hand massaging his head. "Go easy, Dakin. You'll be married too someday, and you'll appreciate soft voices the morning after."

Dakin shook his head, still smiling. "I'll mine that seam when I find it. 'Til then, I'll go on as I always do."

Terregar shook his head ruefully but said nothing. Kindan tugged at Dakin's sleeve.

"Would you tell our sister that some of her brothers—the ones who know there'll be work today—have come to say our good-byes?" Dakin said to Terregar.

Terregar nodded and turned to listen to Silstra's voice from inside the wagon. He nodded at what she said, then turned back to Dakin. "She'll be out in a bit. First she's got to finish her *klah*."

"I don't blame her," Dakin replied judiciously. He spotted Trader Veran moving toward them with mugs in either hand. "Unless I miss my guess, your trader friends are starting out late this morning," he said to Terregar.

Veran arrived in time to hear this comment and nodded his head slowly. "Aye, with a night like last, we're not too quick to be on our way. I imagine that's the same in the mines, isn't it?"

Dakin pursed his lips consideringly and, finally, shook his head. "Hard to say. Miner Natalon has some fairly rigid ideas about a good day's work. On the other hand, I expect he knows—firsthand—that the miners are feeling their late night a bit more than usual and he's wary of anything that could cause an accident."

Veran nodded. "And there's nothing like a woolly head to cause accidents," he agreed.

Kindan ventured a comment of his own. "Are your children all asleep, too?"

Veran laughed. "Ah, no! I expect they're all up and about, back at Crom Hold." He leaned down toward Kindan and added conspiratorially, "After a night like the last, they'd be so wound up they'd never settle—and their parents would never forgive them!"

Dakin joined Veran in his laughter. "Well, we would have left our youngsters in bed if we could have."

Kindan glowered up at him, but Dakin merely tousled his hair in response. "We might have let one or two come to the party," he said to placate his youngest brother.

"And here's the lovely couple now," Veran said, spying Terregar and Silstra stepping down from the caravan. He raised his voice to a shout, "Did you have a pleasant evening?" He chuckled when he saw Terregar wince. "A bit too much wine, eh?"

Terregar grinned and, grabbing Silstra's hand, joined the rest of the group. Silstra broke free of his grip long enough to hug Dakin and Kindan.

"Old endings, new beginnings," Jofri's voice intoned cheerfully from behind them. Kindan turned to see that the Harper had all his gear wrapped in a bedroll, except his guitar, which was slung from his shoulder.

Dakin grinned and extended a hand to him and clasped him on the shoulder. "We'll miss you, Harper."

"I'm leaving you in good hands with Master Zist," Jofri replied. He looked down at Kindan and added, "As this one can attest."

Kindan was certain that he preferred Journeyman Jofri's easygoing ways to Master Zist's demanding discipline any day, regardless of the results.

His face must have shown it, for Jofri laughed. "Don't worry, you'll do fine with Master Zist. He was my vocal teacher, you know."

"But you never sing," Kindan protested.

Jofri laughed again. "And he's the reason." He shook his head, chuckling anew at Kindan's reaction. "I've no voice for singing—you must know that even at your tender years. Master Zist helped me to see it, even before my voice broke when I teened.

"He's got a gift to know how a voice will break," the harper continued. "I've never seen him wrong with it. If he says fine tenor, then it's a fine tenor you'll be. If he says lousy baritone—

well, then, he'll help you find a different way to beat your own drum."

He leaned forward to Kindan. "He's been through hard times." Kindan had the feeling that Jofri was entrusting him with a secret and his eyes grew large. "But he's one of the best. You listen and learn, okay?

"You won't get away with the tricks you played on me," Jofri added. He winked. "Okay?"

Kindan nodded his head dubiously. Jofri straightened up, grinned again, and tousled Kindan's hair. Kindan wondered to himself why everyone had chosen that day to tousle his hair. Perhaps it was because it was one of the rare days when it was obviously clean and they wanted to find out what it really felt like.

"Oh, and here's the rest of the sending-off party," Jofri said as he spied another group descending on them.

He was right. Kindan found himself sidling toward Sis as he saw not only his father and his six other brothers but also Natalon, his wife, his son, Dalor, and his uncle Tarik and nephew, Cristov, approaching.

Jakris and Tofir were still so sleepy that they couldn't hide their yawns, but Kaylek frowned at Kindan.

"We've come to say good-bye," Danil said, holding out his hand to Terregar.

Terregar wrapped an arm around Silstra's waist and drew her close to him. "I'll take good care of her, sir," he promised.

"I'm sure of it," Danil said feelingly. He started to say something more but closed his mouth and gestured to the rest of the family to make their good-byes.

Then it was the turn of Natalon and his family. Silstra hugged Jenella tight and wished her the best. Natalon gave Silstra a brief hug and muttered a few words to her that Kindan couldn't hear, and then it was time for Tarik and his son. Kindan wasn't surprised to see that neither Silstra nor Tarik were particularly sincere in their good-byes; Silstra had never had time for the surly miner.

And finally, the caravan was assembled. Veran waved farewell to the miners and a "move-out" to the traders, and the caravan began its slow way down the path curving down the hillside and around the lake on the way to Crom Hold.

Kindan watched until the caravans were lost to sight and only the dust marked their passage.

"Well," Danil said softly, "that's that."

Natalon clapped him on the shoulder. "It is."

Danil turned to him and said solemnly, "Miner Natalon, I want to thank you for the magnificent way you provided for the wedding of my daughter."

Natalon nodded, equally full of the formality of the moment. "Danil, it was my pleasure." He paused a moment, then added, "And now, we've got coal to mine."

CHAPTER III

Watch-wher, watch-wher in the night,
Guard our Hold, keep it right.
When the morning sun does come,
Watch-wher, then your job is done.

As the days turned into months, it seemed to Kindan that nothing much had changed. He still had chores to do. He still had to attend classes with the Harper. He still was bullied by Kaylek. His turns on watch or as runner for the camp were the same as always.

But in truth things *had* changed. He was now the first up in the morning and was always sure to have *klah* and breakfast ready for his family. His father asked him to check in on Dask in the mornings, and that was new, too.

In class with the Harper, Kindan started to notice that he saw less of Zenor in class and more of Dalor. In times past, it had always seemed that Dalor was either a very sickly child or that he was being overworked by his father. Either way, he used to miss at least two classes every sevenday, sometimes more.

Now it seemed like Dalor was in classes every day but one each sevenday.

Perhaps that change was explained by the other change: Master Zist. If Kindan had thought that Master Zist was a hard taskmaster when it came to singing, it was nothing compared to how hard he was when it came to teaching. No one could ever do anything well enough for the Master.

"Look at that! Do you call those letters?" Zist growled at little Sula one day. "How are you going to write a new recipe and share it with anyone, hmm?"

Sula had wilted under the interrogation. Everyone knew that she was hoping to join her mother, Milla, as a baker.

Another day, the Master reduced Kaylek to a red-faced gibbering wreck just by a series of probing questions on multiplication. "And how, young Kaylek, are you going to calculate the load a mine's supports must bear if you can't even figure out the area of the ceiling?"

Dalor got off no easier because he was the head miner's son. All the same, Kindan noticed that whenever the Master had been hard on Dalor before the lunch break, he would take special care to soothe Dalor's nervousness in the afternoon.

Kindan was the most obvious exception to Master Zist's hard teachings. When Cristov and Kaylek began to notice it, Kindan started to wish that the Harper would treat him as roughly as the rest of the camp's children.

"What is it with you?" Cristov sneered at him one day at break time. "Is it just because you can sing so well?"

"Can't be for much else," Kaylek decided.

But Kindan knew exactly why Master Zist never bore down too harshly on him. Early on, not long after Silstra's wedding, Master Zist and he had had another contest of wills similar to the heated exchange they'd had on the day they'd met. As before, neither had truly won the argument, but Kindan had recognized something in Master Zist's stubborn insistence that his students try their hardest and not be afraid to ask for help—and Kindan had decided to accept the challenge.

It had been difficult at first, but soon Kindan found himself relishing his time with the surly Master. He discovered that, by exercising a level of diplomacy that he had never attained before, he could survive the Harper's harshness and give back as good as he got without ever being branded as "disrespectful."

Kindan found, as he approached his eleventh birthday, that he could even work with Kaylek. His elder brother, plagued by Master Zist's remonstrations about his class work, had actually turned to Kindan for help.

Kaylek was smart enough to realize that work in the mines was dangerous and required more wits than temper. So he had swallowed his pride—as best he could—and had learned from his littler brother.

The morning of Kaylek's first day in the mines with his father and his brothers, Kindan was surprised to be awoken by a warm cup of *klah* thrust into his hands.

"I thought you might want to see us off," Kaylek said shyly.

Recognizing Kaylek's actions as a peace offering, Kindan quickly pulled himself out of bed. "Sure."

It was the dark of night. Kaylek and the rest would be going down in the shift that ran from just after nightfall to just before dawn, rightly called the "watch-wher" shift because that was when watch-whers were awake.

Careful not to disturb Jakris and Tofir, Kindan pulled on his clothes and followed Kaylek into the kitchen.

"Dad said nothing about you," Dakin said when he noticed Kindan.

"I'm just going to see you off," Kindan answered.

Dakin shrugged. "All right," he said. "You know Sis used to do that."

"Where's Dad?" Kaylek asked, looking around the room.

"In the shed with Dask, of course," Jaran, the second eldest, replied matter-of-factly.

"Let's go out and see if he needs any help," Kaylek suggested to Kindan.

"Only if you want Dask to snap at you, you will," Kenil said. Kaylek glanced at Jaran and Dakin for confirmation and saw that both older boys were nodding their heads.

"He's been a bit proddy recently," Dakin explained. He frowned. "I don't like it, nor does Dad."

"He's been like that before, though," Jaran said, apparently continuing a conversation that Kindan hadn't heard the start of.

"Come on, lads, time's a-wasting," Danil's voice called from outside.

They all put their mugs in the sink and started out the door, Kindan trailing.

He followed them all the way up to the mine entrance, where a group of miners waited. Kindan recognized one of the smaller ones.

"What are you doing here?" he demanded.

"I'm going down to help—my father said I could," Zenor answered, his voice full of pride. Talmaric, his father, nodded.

"It's only for today," Zenor added when he noticed Kindan's concerned look. Kindan brightened immediately.

"Wish me luck," Kaylek called to Kindan as he started into the mine.

"Good luck."

"What are you talking about luck for?" Kenil asked. "Miners don't need luck, they need caution."

"Sorry," Kaylek mumbled.

They swept from view, and Kindan went back to the cottage and his bed.

◆

It started with a silence. The children noticed it and gathered around the windows. Master Zist noticed only that the children were not paying attention to him.

"Get back here, now!" he shouted. He had just gotten them settled for the first lesson of the morning. One child turned his head toward him but quickly turned back.

Zist growled and strode over to the window, ready to bodily return his students to their seats. The tension in their small bodies unhinged his plan. He followed their gaze—they were all looking at the northern mine shaft.

"What is it?" he asked.

"Dunno," a girl replied, "something's wrong."

"How do you know?" Zist demanded.

One of the children shook his head and made a shushing motion. "Can't you hear? It's too quiet."

The sky outside darkened. Master Zist looked up and saw a thin raft of dark powder drifting down toward the lake from the direction of the mine shaft. Not smoke—coal dust.

"My father's down there!" one child wailed.

"And my brother!"

"Shh!" said an older child, cocking his head and listening very hard, his eyes never moving from the cloud exuding from the adit.

"There's been an accident?" Zist asked, catching Kindan's expression of open-mouthed horror, the look in his wide, shocked eyes.

Just then someone started cranking the mine alarm and abruptly, as if spilled out, people turned out of their houses and made for the entrance to the mine.

Kindan sat down hard on the edge of his desk.

"Are your father and brothers on this shift, Kindan?" Master Zist asked. Kindan shook his head, not as a negative but as a way to throw off the paralysis that had momentarily overtaken him.

"Yes, they are, Master. Dad is a shift leader and he has Dask with him today," Kindan managed to say. "We all have to go and help," he added after a moment. "There is a lot we can do, even if it's only carrying baskets to open a cave-in."

He stood up, and joined the older children as they began to file out, heading toward the shaft opening. Even as Master Zist tried to prioritize what he should do now, he saw Natalon, shoving his arms in his jacket, coming out of his house to take charge of the situation. Men and women were bringing equipment of all sorts—picks, shovels, baskets, stretchers—to the mine entrance. The thin soot that had first tinted the sky had grown to clouds of black coal dust.

Kindan's progress toward the mine was at first slow, but then the boy started to run. Master Zist looked around his classroom, now emptied of the older children, those who could be helpful in the emergency. Jofri had not informed him what his duties would be in the event of a problem, but keeping the younger children occupied seemed a good idea, so Zist hastily called his class to order. Through the window, he saw a group of miners, with torches as well as glowbaskets, entering the shaft.

"My dad's on this shift, Master Zist. May I go, too?"

The girl was barely eight and slight, as well, so Zist could not think what emergency task she'd be useful for.

"Do you have an assigned task?" he asked kindly.

"She's not old enough yet," one of the boys said authoritatively. "Nor am I. You have to be eight to be allowed to help. And bigger than Sula is."

"I could help. My mom has taught me ever so much," Sula replied with great dignity. "Sis taught her and I watched."

Zist knew that Sula's mother was one of the Camp's healers. He went to the child and pushed her gently back into her seat. "I'm sure you'll be a great help, once they discover what has happened. Until then, you must stay here." He gave her thin shoulders a little reassuring squeeze before he went to the head of the schoolroom and decided to teach this part of his class one of the new ballads he had brought with him. At a time like this, music could be a great comfort. Seeing him pick up his guitar caused the children to stop chatting and sit up attentively, though some of them continued to look over their shoulders toward the mine.

Master Zist could see Natalon and Tarik arguing, even as Natalon was urgently gesturing men to enter the shaft. The miners were carrying tools or pushing the wheeled carts that brought the ore out of the mine.

He wondered if that meant there had been a cave-in. But hadn't Kindan said that Dask was with his father? Watch-whers were supposed to have an excellent sense of smell which allowed them to detect bad air long before a person could.

When miners talked of "bad air" they were referring to either explosive gases or gases which could suffocate—either was deadly.

Strumming the opening chords to the new song, he began to sing, trying to look and sound as cheerful as he could, in order to distract the children.

He had barely succeeded in claiming the children's rapt attention when the mine's alarm let off three loud, sustained hoots, and everyone rushed to the window again.

The first thing that Kindan saw as he approached the mine entrance was Dask. His heart fell. Dask would never leave Danil unless ordered—or cut off by the cave-in.

"Where's Danil, Dask? Where is he?" Kindan asked as he approached. The watch-wher's flanks were gouged, deep wounds oozing the ichor that was a watch-wher's blood. He blinked his eyes painfully in the morning light and turned back to the mine entrance. Kindan followed.

"What happened?" Kindan asked, following the watch-wher.

Dask turned his head to look at Kindan and gave him the sound for "bad air."

"Why didn't you warn them?" Kindan asked.

Dask made an annoyed *bleek* and then the sound for *"fast."*

"It happened too fast?" Kindan repeated. The watch-wher nodded.

Inside the mine, Kindan could smell gas, sharp and bitter in his throat. It made him cough. The cave-in must have been caused by an explosion of trapped gas, he guessed. It must have been sudden, or Dask would have warned the miners in time.

The watch-wher trotted ahead in the tunnel, leading the rescue party to the jumbled mass of the cave-in. Before the rest of the party could reach him, he had already started clawing at the barrier, using his head to batter at the loose bits. Men stepped out of the way of the debris that his claws were throwing back. One of the men positioned a wheelbarrow so that it caught the flying rocks and dirt, clearing the ground as other men began to dig next to the watch-wher.

Now that the miners knew where to work, Kindan tried to get the wounded watch-wher to stop and save his energy. But Dask ignored him, burrowing on despite the ichor that was oozing from his various wounds.

Hours passed, all the while with Dask digging and the miners carting away the fallen rock. Painfully, they excavated their way through the cave-in.

"Natalon?" Kindan said, grabbing the miner's arm. "Let me take Dask back. He's bleeding."

Natalon looked over at the watch-wher. "We need him here now, especially as he seems to know where our men are."

"But . . . he could bleed to death," Kindan cried, tugging at Natalon's sleeve.

"Do what you can for him but don't stop him, lad," Natalon said. "Your father's on the other side."

Kindan ran all the way back out to where the injury station had been set up. He was surprised to see that the sun was past noon.

"Please, let me have some bandage rolls, Margit," he said to the woman who was setting out the supplies.

"Have they found anyone alive?" she asked, and he had to disappoint her with a negative shake of his head. He knew that her spouse was in his father's shift.

"Why would you want bandages then, Kindan?" she asked.

"Dask was hurt bringing out those he rescued," he said, gesturing toward the three men being cared for by the camp's healers.

"You want my good bandages for the watch-wher?" she demanded, affronted.

"If he bleeds to death before he finds your mate, it'll be your fault!"

"Why, you impertinent little scut!" Margit responded, swiping at him with the towel she had in one hand. He neatly sidestepped and, in doing so, scooped two rolls off the table and raced back to the mine entrance, avoiding the two men who were pushing laden barrels out to be emptied.

Kindan was panting with exertion when he reached the cave-in site. Splotches of greenish watch-wher ichor were visible in the light from the glows, but Dask continued to claw at the barrier. Kindan pushed in beside Dask, hearing the laboring gasp of the watch-wher's breath. When a sudden movement caused more dirt and stone to shower the creature, Kindan pushed up beside him and tried to bandage the deep neck wound that was pumping ichor out at much too fast a rate.

Muttering reassurances, he tried to get the watch-wher to slow down. Dask turned his head slightly, his eyes gleaming with irritation, and hissed at Kindan. Then he turned back to his task with renewed vigor. Ichor dripped faster.

"He has to stop, Natalon, or he'll bleed to death!"

Just then, they heard shouts from beyond the cave-in, urging them on. Frantically, Dask dug harder, with less control, showering the anxious Kindan with stones and mud. He shouldered deeper into the tunnel he was digging and renewed his efforts.

There was a loud cry as his heavy claws broke through the

last of the obstacle; the encouraging shouts from the freed miners were clearly audible.

"Run back to the entrance, Kindan," Natalon said, "and tell
them to bring in stretchers."

Kindan did not want to leave Dask's side, but Natalon pulled
him from the watch-wher and pushed him on his way. As he ran,
Kindan began shouting the good news, as well as Natalon's request for stretchers, to those waiting outside at the top of the
shaft. They came pushing past him in their eagerness to see who
had been saved, and Kindan followed more slowly, trying to get
his breath back.

Back in the shaft, Dask was lying in a lump, his big eyes fit-
fully gleaming. He didn't even pick up his head as Kindan knelt
beside him. The first of the rescued men was being hauled out
on a stretcher as Kindan tried to staunch the ichor that streamed
out of the neck gash.

"Oh, Dask, what have you done to yourself?" he keened as
he felt the unsteady neck pulse.

Dask curled his neck, placing his head on Kindan's lap and
sighing sadly. Kindan began to scratch behind Dask's ears,
soothing the beast as well as he could. And so, having led the
rescuers to the trapped men, Dask finished his life.

The boy had kept watching for the sight of his father's face or
one of his brothers among those led out and up to the surface. It
was when Natalon remarked that the last of the live miners had
been rescued, that Kindan gave up hope.

"We'll get the dead ones out now," Natalon said. He paused
beside Kindan, patting his head kindly. "Your father's neck was
broken, lad. And your brothers are half buried under the rubble.
We'll get their bodies before night falls."

Kindan sat there a long time, holding the heavy head of the watch-wher, absently scratching ears that were turning stiff, his lap covered in green ichor, until Natalon returned for a final inspection.

"Still here, boy? Come, it's nearly dark."

"But Dask is dead, Natalon."

Natalon crouched down beside the boy and saw his tear-streaked face. He mopped some of the tears from the coal-dust-smeared face and touched Kindan tenderly on the head.

"There's a big hole not far from here where I will see he is buried, Kindan, but you must come with me now. It's all over down here."

Natalon had to help the grieving boy to his feet, ignoring Kindan's repeated request to stay by the watch-wher.

"He made a good end, Kindan. He was a fine beast."

———◆———

Kindan found himself wandering among the wounded, looking for any of his brothers, his throat tight and tears streaming freely down his face. He went from stretcher to stretcher, fighting his way among the crowds, ignoring the calls of the women who were acting as nurses.

He heard a voice croak out his name and turned quickly.

"Zenor!" Abashed to realize that he had completely forgotten that Zenor had gone into the mine that shift, Kindan was at his friend's side in a second. Zenor was cut, bruised, and in shock. Kindan grabbed the hand Zenor had raised to him and held it with more force than he realized.

"Did—did they get out?" Zenor asked. A look at Kindan's face told him the answer. "My father?" Kindan shook his head.

"Your father?" Kindan's tears answered that question, too. "Dask did, though, didn't he? I heard him clawing through to us."

Zenor looked right into Kindan's eyes. "Kindan, he saved me. I would never have thought—"

"Dask was a good watch-wher," Kindan said over the lump in his throat.

Zenor shook his head. "Not Dask—I meant Kaylek. He and my Dad pushed me back as the mine caved in. He knew what he was doing, Kindan. They both did. But they pushed me back. They pushed me back . . ." Zenor's voice faded into sleep as the fellis juice he'd been given earlier took effect.

Kindan held his hand until Margit noticed him, hours later, sprawled beside his friend in sleep. Wiping away more tears from her own face, she fetched a blanket and draped it over him.

CHAPTER IV

I am too big to cry
And my voice is too shy
To sing my sad, sad song
Or say the words I long
To say to you   good-bye, good-bye.

The air was cold and the wind swept it through Kindan's clothes with a sharp bite. Winter was driving out fall, but Kindan was sure that it was always cold in the graveyard. The last words had been said, the rest of the Hold was drifting back down to the main Hall for a toast to the dead but Kindan held back, a small shape at the edge of the new graves.

His father had never said too much to him. As the youngest of nine children, Kindan had been one face among many. His elder brothers had always been remote, larger than life—nearly like Master Natalon.

All the same, Kindan felt that he should have said something more, should have left some remembrance. Jakris had made a carving, and Tofir had left a drawing, before they had both gone off with their new families.

Terra and her husband, Riterin, already had four children of their own and all of them young, so they had been willing to take Jakris, the eldest. Besides, Riterin was a woodworker, so Jakris's gift of carving would be well-appreciated in their household.

Tofir had been fostered to Crom Hold itself, where his gift with drawing would be encouraged and he might even take up mapping, a skill that was always needed in the mines.

"Kindan!"

Kindan turned his head toward the caller. It was Dalor. He ran up to Kindan.

"Father said you'd still be up here. He told me that you're to come down before you catch your death of cold."

Kindan nodded solemnly and set off behind the younger boy. Kindan had seen more of Dalor in the past sevenday than he had in many months, but he suspected it was Natalon's way of looking out for those beholden to him. Not that Kindan minded; Dalor was okay in a distracted sort of way.

Dalor cast a backward look at Kindan, partly to see if he was really following and partly out of sympathy for the youngest of Danil's sons.

"There's some mulled wine down at the hold"—only Dalor and his family called their large cottage "the hold"—"and father said we'd get some as soon as we got in."

———◆———

"Nine, can you believe it?" Milla was saying to Jenella, Dalor's mother, as they made their way into the hold kitchen. "Most of them Danil and his sons, more's the pity. And what's going to happen to poor Kindan now? They've placed the other two, and I don't see why they haven't placed him, too. It must be spooky sleeping in his place all by himself, poor lad."

Jenella, Dalor's mother, saw the boys and coughed pointedly at Milla. But Milla, who had her back to them rolling dough, didn't pick up on the hint. "Is that your cough come back? It's got chill enough now, but you don't want it what with you finally expecting another," she said.

She went on blithely: "Nine dead, three injured, and poor Zenor demanding his place in the mines for his father, not that I blame him, the way Norla, his mother, is dealing so poorly with it all." She placed the dough in rising tins. "And a shift leader short—what are they going to do?"

"Dalor, Kindan, you look chilled to the bone," Jenella said loudly, cutting across anything more that Milla might think to say. "Milla, could you be a dear and pour them some of the mulled wine that's on the stove? Getting up's so tiring for me right now."

Jenella was seven months pregnant. Kindan had heard that she'd been pregnant before but had lost the baby. Silstra had gone to help that night and had come back so distraught that her father had had to put her to bed.

"Oh!" Milla exclaimed, turning around. "I'm sorry, boys, I didn't see you. The mugs are there in the cupboard. Why don't you help yourselves so I can get these dainties into the oven?"

"Yes, ma'am," Dalor said politely. He was taller than Kindan and reached the mugs easily—Kindan realized that he would have had to get a stool or something to reach them and once again cursed his late growth. He was six months older than Dalor and still a whole hand shorter.

With mugs full of hot spiced wine in their hands—the spirit had left the wine when it was heated or Kindan would not have been allowed to drink it—the two boys found a clear spot at the bench and sat quietly, not trusting that their luck would last.

"Natalon will be sending for you shortly," Jenella told Kindan.

"Yes, ma'am—" At a sharp nudge and a glare from Dalor, Kindan corrected himself. "—my Lady."

Kindan had never been quite sure how to address Dalor's mother. Jenella had always seemed so less able than his own sister, but then again, if Natalon could prove Camp Natalon, it'd be Mine Natalon someday and Jenella would be the wife of a minor Holder.

But to prove Camp Natalon, they would have to mine the coal—and no one, aside from the investigating team, had been in the mines for the past sevenday.

It was normal, Kindan had heard the grown-ups say, not to go back to the mines until after all the bodies were recovered and the funerals had taken place.

"I heard Zenor's been put on father's shift," Dalor commented to Kindan. "With his father gone, there's no one else to provide for his family."

"How will he do his studies?" Kindan wondered aloud.

Dalor looked at him thoughtfully and then shrugged. "I guess he won't," he said. "Perhaps that's just as well, with Master Zist giving classes."

"Like you'd know," Kindan shot back, forgetting who else was in the room. He looked abashedly at Dalor's mother before muttering to Dalor, "Sorry."

Fortunately for him, Master Zist arrived at that moment. "Kindan, please come with me."

Master Zist led Kindan to the same great room that was

normally used by the resident Harper for classes in the mornings. There were three tables in the room, two long ones running the length of the hall and another smaller one set perpendicular to the other two. Master Zist usually sat at that table, with the hearth behind him.

Natalon and Tarik were seated at the nearer of the two long tables. At a gesture from Natalon, Master Zist and Kindan approached and took seats opposite them.

"Kindan," Natalon began, "I'm told that you wish to stay here in the camp."

Kindan nodded. He hadn't really thought much about what that meant until now. He'd have to be fostered. That, and he had heard enough whispered words by the adults to realize that he would never be allowed to stay in his cottage by himself. A quick look at Tarik made it clear who was hoping to move in. With Jenella expecting, Kindan could imagine that Tarik, his wife, and three older children would probably be grateful to escape the noise of a newborn.

Kindan felt a flush of anger come over him at the thought of Tarik moving into the cottage that his father had built for his family. Then another thought burned brighter in his mind.

"Sir," Kindan said, "what did the investigation find?"

Natalon cast a sidelong glance at Tarik, who stiffened and gave Kindan a sour look.

"As often happens when there are accidents like these," Natalon said, "the results are not conclusive."

Kindan sat up straighter in his seat, preparing to argue, but Natalon restrained him with an upraised hand.

"We *think*," Natalon said carefully, "that your father's shift had the bad luck to dig into some loose rock and that it caused a slide both over and behind them."

"But there was a smell," Kindan protested. "Dask told me there was a smell. I smelled it, too."

Natalon and Tarik exchanged looks. Tarik shook his head. "None of the men I spoke with talked of a smell," he said.

"Are you sure you understood Dask correctly?" Natalon asked.

"I thought it took years of training to understand a watch-wher," Tarik said sourly. "And the beast must have been in a lot of pain."

"It doesn't take years to learn the sounds for 'bad air,' " Kindan protested. "It and the other danger signals were the first I was taught." He did not bother to mention that his teaching in watch-wher lore had come from Silstra, and there had been a very little of it at that.

Tarik shook his head. "I saw no sign of fire."

"Could have been a small pocket," Natalon suggested, stroking his chin thoughtfully. "The blast would have started the cave-in."

"A pocket a watch-wher couldn't detect?" Tarik sneered. "The way Danil boasted, I thought they were supposed to have magic noses."

Kindan glowered at the older man, but Master Zist moved quickly to block Tarik's sight of him. He reached over and placed a hand on Kindan's arm and squeezed it warningly.

"If someone had driven a pick right into a pocket and made a spark, it'd all be over before the watch-wher could react," Natalon argued.

"See?" Tarik demanded, seeming satisfied. "What's the use of them, then? I say we're lucky to be rid of the last of them. We'll mine faster on our own."

Natalon prepared a hot retort, but Master Zist broke in. "What about Kindan?"

Natalon and Tarik looked startled, as though they had forgotten that Kindan was in the room with them.

"That house is too big for him," Tarik said. "There's plenty of others who could use the space better."

"And there's the memories," Master Zist said softly, as if to himself. "It's not good to linger where there are too many memories."

"Well . . ." Natalon said, consideringly.

"I could use the house," Tarik spoke into the silence. He looked at Natalon and said, "You've got a new one coming, and me and mine would just be too many underfoot."

"Well," Natalon said slowly, "if Kindan doesn't mind."

"It's not his house to give," Tarik said sourly. "The house will have to be emptied when Thread comes, anyway."

Kindan flushed at Tarik's brusque manner.

"That still doesn't answer where the boy will live," Master Zist noted, ignoring Tarik's response.

"He should foster with those who can handle an extra mouth," Tarik grumbled. "Maybe Norla could take him in."

Norla was Zenor's mother. Kindan liked her, even though she had always seemed a little overwhelmed by all her daughters. He'd be with Zenor, too, and that would be good. Or would it? Kindan wondered soberly. It would be awkward to have Zenor in the mines while Kindan was still in classes with Master Zist. No, maybe that wasn't a good idea. And Kindan wasn't sure he'd like to suddenly become big brother to four little girls, one of them still in diapers.

"He should go to the one with the least children," Natalon said, quoting the old, long-established rules regarding fostering. "Someone who's had some knowledge of raising children but won't be too heavily burdened by it."

He raised his head to gaze directly at Master Zist.

The Harper sat bolt upright, astonished. Clearly he hadn't anticipated this turn of events.

Tarik's eyes gleamed. "You know something of grief, too, Master Zist."

Master Zist glowered at him. Kindan had followed the exchange with growing alarm, but even so he could see how Tarik was trying to profit from others' loss and matched the Harper in his glower at the older miner. Tarik sat back and ignored their looks, a hint of a smirk on his lips.

"I don't—" Master Zist and Kindan said in unison and stopped in shock, looking at each other.

Natalon stood up, ending the discussion. "I think this will work out well, Master Zist. Kindan, you may ask anyone for a hand to haul up your things and an extra bed for you to the Master's cottage."

"I'll be glad to find someone for the job," Tarik added, a satisfied smile undisguised on his face. "If it's all right with you, Natalon, I would like to begin moving today."

———◆———

In the end Swanee, the camp supply man, and Ima, the camp's butcher, gave Kindan a hand moving his stuff.

"If you take the frame apart, you can carry it up in pieces," Swanee said to Kindan while he rolled the mattress up and heaved it over his shoulders. He tapped the empty frame. "There's good wood there," he said approvingly. "Get the slats first and then come back for the rest."

Under Master Zist's directions, they took two chests of drawers and a smaller clothes chest out of Danil's cottage.

"Your sisters will doubtless want these when they hear the

news," Master Zist said. "I'm sure you'll do well with just the chest, but set all of them up in your room."

"My room?" Kindan echoed. He'd never had a room of his own; he'd always shared with Tofir and Jakris.

"Well, you won't be sleeping with me," Master Zist said with a wry look.

"I'd best bring lots of blankets, then," Kindan said thoughtfully. For all their trouble, Tofir and Jakris had been enough to keep Kindan warm on the coldest nights—when they hadn't pulled the blankets off.

"If it's all the same with you, Kindan," Swanee said after taking a careful look around the cottage, "I'd like to take anything you don't need and give it to those that don't have. The rest I'd like to put up in storage. Tarik has enough stuff of his own."

Kindan heartily agreed to the request, and all three nodded in approval.

"Just a moment," Master Zist said, raising a hand. Everyone looked at him. "Kindan, is there anything special you'd like for yourself?"

Kindan thought about that for a moment. "Anything?"

"Anything," Master Zist agreed.

"Well, if I could have Mother's old table, the one with the hinged lid and the old music inside—"

"Music?" Master Zist raised an eyebrow.

Kindan nodded. "It was special to her, and to my father after . . ."

Master Zist raised a hand to stop him. "Ima, Swanee, can you see to it?" The two nodded in quick agreement. "Anything else?"

"Take a good look around, lad," Swanee advised. "If, after

we've distributed everything, there was something you'd forgotten we could always get it back, but . . ."

Kindan took a good look through the cottage. He stopped in the kitchen and looked at Master Zist. "Do you need any cookware or dishware?"

Master Zist shook his head. "The Harper's cottage is well supplied with both."

Kindan pursed his lips in a frown, thinking. Then he nodded. "I think that's everything, then."

Swanee gave Kindan a searching look and then nodded firmly. "Very well, we'll get your stuff up and distribute the rest. Thank you, lad, there's many will be grateful for what you don't need."

Kindan nodded mutely, not really understanding what the supplier meant.

◆

Nuella made Dalor tell her everything when he came upstairs.

"Kindan's moving in with the Harper?" she exclaimed when he finished his tale.

"And Uncle Tarik is moving into Danil's old house," Dalor said by way of confirmation. He was glad—that way he wouldn't have to listen to their uncle complaining all the time.

"Oh, but it's awful!" Nuella complained. "How will I get to see the Harper if Kindan's staying there?"

Dalor frowned, then said, "I don't know."

"And Master Zist was going to teach me the pipes," Nuella added sadly to herself.

"You're good already!" Dalor told his sister stoutly.

"Only you would know," Nuella said, feeling miserable.

"And Mother," Dalor corrected.

"This cave-in's set Father's plans back, hasn't it?" Nuella asked.

Dalor shrugged.

Nuella sighed. "I wish . . ." She sighed again, shaking her head, her wish unvoiced. After a moment she picked up her pipes and began playing a soft, sad song.

◆

Kindan was really surprised, hours later, to find himself sitting on his own bed, in his own room, with the sounds of the Camp's harper pottering about in another room.

Master Zist had popped his head in several times to ask, "Everything all right, lad?"

The first time, Kindan had nearly jumped with shock at the question and could only bring himself to nod mutely in response.

"Well, then, I've got some things to attend to," Master Zist had said. "If you need anything, you can get it from the kitchen. I'll be in my study and I'm not to be disturbed."

A quick glance at the Master's face told Kindan that disturbing him would *not* be a wise thing to do at all. He had nodded quickly but said nothing.

"All right, then," Master Zist had said, to fill in the silence. "Get yourself settled in and we'll have dinner when I'm finished with my work."

Now Kindan heard voices from Master Zist's study. A younger voice and the Master himself. Curious, Kindan listened more carefully. The young voice sounded a lot like Dalor, but he couldn't hear it clearly enough to be sure. Maybe Master Zist was trying to catch Dalor up on all his missed lessons. It occurred to Kindan to wonder if perhaps Dalor had received extra lessons from Journeyman Jofri, as well. Perhaps because he was Natalon's son it had been decided to keep him out of all the rough and tumble of the everyday classes. Kindan knew that all the kids in the camp thought that Dalor was a bit sickly. Although, come to think of it, Kindan couldn't recall ever seeing Dalor coming down with anything. Perhaps Jenella, who'd lost so many babies in childbirth, was being careful with Dalor and keeping him in whenever he got the slightest bit sick. It didn't seem likely to Kindan . . . and the voice didn't quite sound like Dalor's. He wondered if he was allowed to open his door to hear the voices more clearly.

As he pondered the notion, another voice joined in. Kindan immediately recognized the voice as Miner Natalon's. It seemed as though Natalon was not pleased about something. He heard the youngster's voice, as well, and Master Zist's. Judging by the rise and fall of the voices and their tones, Kindan was certain that whoever owned the younger voice was someone well known to Natalon. So it was probably Dalor, Kindan decided. Maybe Natalon was annoyed to find Dalor bothering the Master, Kindan guessed.

The voices rose in parting and Kindan heard two sets of feet walk to the front door and leave. A while later Master Zist walked into the hallway and knocked on Kindan's door.

Having never been afforded such a courtesy, Kindan didn't know how to respond.

"May I come in?" Master Zist asked after a short wait.

Kindan opened the door. "Of course, Master Zist."

Master Zist entered the room and looked around. "All settled, then?"

"Yes, thank you," Kindan replied.

"Good," Zist said, nodding emphatically. "Come along, we'll eat in the kitchen."

Kindan smelled the hearty beef stew before he saw it bubbling on the hearth in a pot he recognized from Jenella's kitchen. He looked around for the dishes and cutlery and set the table.

Master Zist served them and they ate in an awkward silence. Kindan finished his stew quickly and waited politely to see if he could have seconds. Master Zist noticed this but continued to eat in slow, deliberate bites. By the time the Master was finished, Kindan was squirming in his chair.

"Dessert?" Master Zist inquired.

"Well," Kindan began, then blurted, "I was wondering if I could have some more stew."

Master Zist gestured to the pot. "There's only you and me here, Kindan. You may have what you want."

As Kindan refilled his plate, Master Zist regarded him thoughtfully. When Kindan returned to the table, the Harper said, "When we are alone, Kindan, you may always help yourself. You just have to ask."

Kindan, mouth full of stew, smiled and nodded.

"You had a lot of older brothers and sisters, didn't you?"

Kindan nodded again.

Master Zist sighed. "I was the eldest in my family. I can't quite imagine how it must have been for you. But I can guess that you were probably the last to get seconds . . . or dessert."

"It wasn't all bad," Kindan said. "Sis made sure that I always got to eat something." He made a face. "But Kaylek always tried to steal my desserts, when we had them." His face took on a sadder, more introspective look.

"You didn't get along with Kaylek, did you?" Master Zist inquired gently.

Kindan shook his head. "No, not until just before—" He looked troubled. "Zenor, my friend, he told me that Kaylek saved his life." Tears formed in Kindan's eyes. "He was always mean to me, but he saved Zenor's life."

"It's a bit hard to grasp, isn't it?" Master Zist commented. "I have been surprised how often people who only seem to be bad have turned out to be selfless when it really matters."

Kindan nodded in wordless agreement.

"Kindan, do you know what harpers are supposed to do?"

"They're supposed to teach, and to sing songs at gathers, and play instruments," Kindan said, not quite sure he had the right answer.

Master Zist nodded. "That's part of their job. Harpers also gather information and pass it along. We preserve knowledge. We help with the healers."

"My sister did some healing," Kindan offered.

Zist nodded acknowledgment. "And we also try to smooth things over."

Kindan looked puzzled. Master Zist sighed. "We listen to everyone and try to help when we think it's appropriate."

Kindan tried hard to look as though he understood, especially because he'd finished his stew and his mouth was watering for dessert and he knew that Master Zist would keep on talking until Kindan showed that he understood what he was saying.

Master Zist smiled in wry amusement. "We are trained to be good observers, too. Sometimes we don't pay attention, but we're trained." He rose, taking Kindan's dish with him, and served them the dainties that the baker had sent over

"A harper's trained to watch and listen, as well as to play and sing," Master Zist said after he'd had a bite of the dainty.

Kindan nodded, his mouth full.

"And a harper's trained to keep secrets," Zist added.

"I can keep a secret," Kindan said.

Master Zist wagged a finger at him. "Ah, but there are some times when you have to let others keep secrets, too. Can you do that?"

Kindan looked doubtful.

"Well, we'll see," Master Zist said. "For now, I expect that you won't try to overhear any conversations I have in my study or kitchen. If you hear something and you want to talk about it, you come to me. I'll tell you whether it's a secret or not. Can you do that?"

Kindan nodded.

"Good lad." Master Zist finished his dainty, saw that Kindan had finished as well, and stood up. "You do the dishes and get some sleep. Tomorrow we'll start with your lessons."

"Lessons?" Kindan repeated.

Master Zist nodded. "Lessons," he repeated. He nodded toward his study. "Harpers also take notes. Jofri left me his. And he noted that a certain son of Danil's was not only good at singing but showed an interest in becoming a Harper."

Kindan's eyes lit with astonishment. "He did?"

Master Zist nodded solemnly, but his eyes were twinkling. "He did," he affirmed. He waggled a finger at the door. "Now finish up and off to bed with you."

◆

It seemed to Kindan that his new life was far more strenuous than his old life. And sadly, very different. He still had duty on the watch up the cliffside hundreds of meters above the mine entrance with its splendid view of what most folk simply called "the valley," but which he and the Harper had started to call "Natalon's Valley." Now, however, he was not just one among the many but the lad placed in charge of all the younglings on watch duty. That job might have been Tofir's or Jakris's had they remained, but Kindan was shocked to realize that he was the oldest boy in the camp who wasn't working in the mine itself.

The first day he'd looked down from his perch and had seen Zenor, dressed in overalls cut down from a pair of his father's, Kindan had felt a mixture of shame, awe, and sorrow. Shame that he wasn't going down into the mine, as well; awe that his best friend Zenor was doing such a grown-up job; and sorrow to see the bitter proof of the disaster that had claimed not only the lives of his own father and brothers but also Zenor's father and his childhood.

But Kindan found that his new duties left him with little time to reminisce—whether on purpose or just because the camp was so short of able bodies he could not guess. When he was sure the watch was set up properly for the day and runners had been arranged to be ready at all the usual spots, he found himself in charge of a group of sturdy boys and girls nine and ten Turns old helping to trim the branches from trees felled the day before by the Camp's adults.

Zenor's mother, Norla, found that her years of dealing with younglings were put to good effect as she found herself in charge of a daily crèche of all the Camp's infants while their mothers helped out planting the fields below or working the herb gardens or helping cut trees into timber for the mine. It was, Master Zist had suggested, a good way to immerse her in activity while keeping

her close to her youngest children. Before, the task had been ro-
tated amongst all the women with infants, but now Norla's cottage was filled with diapers in various stages of use, and mothers
stopped in whenever they could to check on their babies, giving
the widowed Norla more contact with the rest of the Camp than
she would have had otherwise.

The hill of coal on the other side of the valley from the mine
grew steadily in size, but not without cost.

Kindan heard but kept to himself many late night conversations spoken in low voices in the Harper's cottage. With the exception of Tarik, nearly all the miners had come to pay their
respects at one time or another to the new Harper. Many returned. All were worried.

"Sure, we're getting coal enough, but for how long?" was the
common complaint. "Without new diggings, we'll soon be reduced to either working the pillars or . . . just giving up."

Kindan hadn't been surprised the next morning when he had
been asked to explain to the MasterHarper what was meant by
"working the pillars."

"A coal field's a huge field underground," Kindan had said.
"There's rock on top of it that's pressing down. When we dig, we
leave large pillars of coal untouched to help support the rock
above—"

"But that's not the only way to do it, is it?"

Kindan nodded. "You could build in supports and then pull
out the pillars. In fact, if the field weren't so huge, or when it's finally mined out—probably not before the end of the coming
Pass or even longer—"

"More than fifty Turns?" Master Zist was impressed.

Kindan nodded again. "The seam's a good three meters wide,
and there's acres of it down there. The Camp would have to be

proved and then they'd drill some more shafts, one for air and the other just for coal, and they'd probably make roads on the level wide enough for workbeasts to haul the coal out, instead of just men with carts or wheelbarrows."

Master Zist sighed, shaking his head at his own ignorance. "Let's get back to the pillars."

Kindan nodded. "The pillars keep the rock above the coal from bearing down on the field and crushing the coal. They support the weight. If you work your pillars—"

"Then you run the risk of crushing the whole field?" Master Zist guessed.

Kindan smiled at the Harper. "Exactly!" he agreed.

"So when would it make sense to work your pillars?"

Kindan shrugged. "I don't know everything about mining, Master Zist," he admitted reluctantly.

"Just give me a guess, then," the Harper allowed.

"Well . . . I can think of two times: when you need to get coal out in a hurry and you're not going to keep mining; and when you've mined everything else and you're willing to build up new pillars to bear the load while you work the coal pillars," Kindan said.

"So either way, it's the end of the mine, is it?" Master Zist asked.

"Yes," Kindan agreed in a troubled tone. If the mine were to close, he thought, what would happen to him?

Master Zist must have guessed his thoughts, for he punched Kindan lightly on the shoulder. "Harpers can work anywhere, lad." He looked at the window. "And speaking of work, we've both chores to get started."

◆

Classes with the MasterHarper were different, too. They had been different before from those with Harper Jofri, but now, as a fostering in the Harper's cottage, Kindan was aware of his unique position. He found himself backing Master Zist's gruff ways out of his strong sense of loyalty, when before he would have done his stubborn best to undermine the Harper's discipline.

Dalor noticed it and said nothing; Cristov noticed it and taunted him about it. Tarik's son had always lorded his position over the other children in the Camp, but now he took special pains to rub Kindan the wrong way, taking every opportunity to remind Kindan that he was now sleeping in *his* room and how nice Kindan's old house was.

Kindan took the abuse as long as he could, until one day he caught Cristov leaving the hold on his way back to his house for lunch. One deft hook of his leg and Cristov was sprawled in the mud and snow that was the pathway between Miner Natalon's hold and the rest of the camp.

"You need to watch your feet," Kindan said to him roughly. "As well as your tongue."

Cristov jumped to his feet, but before he could do any more, a huge hand grabbed Kindan by the ear and dragged him back into the hold.

"I'll deal with this," Master Zist's deep voice said. Cristov's opened mouth closed into a sly grin as he watched Kindan being hauled away.

"Wipe your feet," the Harper told Kindan when they reached the entrance to the hold. Kindan complied, still smarting at the grip on his ear, and followed the Harper back into the classroom.

"Sit," Master Zist ordered, indicating a seat at one of the long tables. Kindan sat and raised a hand to rub his injured ear.

ANNE MCCAFFREY & TODD MCCAFFREY

"Leave it alone, you earned the pain," Zist told him. "Now I want you to tell me what you did wrong and what you should have done."

Kindan furrowed his brow and tried to ignore his sore ear. "He's been saying—"

"Remember that you're training to be a harper," Master Zist reminded him. "Words are supposed to be *your* trade."

"But—"

Master Zist held his hand up, and Kindan stopped. "Tell me three good things about Cristov," the Harper ordered.

Kindan closed his mouth and thought. "Well, he's strong."

Master Zist raised one finger and gave Kindan an encouraging look.

"His mother likes him."

"That's a good thing about his mother," Master Zist said wryly.

"Aren't harpers supposed to be trained at the Harper Hall?" Kindan asked, hoping to change the topic.

"A Master may take an apprentice wherever he is," Master Zist responded, "and send him on to the Harper Hall later." He raised his hand with the one finger extended. "But you have not finished."

"Um, well . . . he's not good at figures . . . or writing—"

"Those are *faults*, not virtues," Master Zist said with a sigh.

"I know," Kindan protested, "I'm just trying to think—"

"I see," the Harper said. "Well, this is taking too long and we've both work to attend. So, to help you think, in addition to your other chores, you will go down to Tarik's every evening after you've done your usual chores and wash all their clothes for them. You will continue doing this until you can report to me three virtues of Cristov. And you will apologize to Cristov for your behavior."

"But—but—" Kindan spluttered. "How will I get Cristov's mother to let me do their laundry? I can't imagine her being too eager to let me do it."

"How you get her to do it will be up to you," Master Zist told him. "But do it, you will."

Kindan rolled his eyes.

Master Zist wagged his finger at him. "I don't think that rolling your eyes will work with Dara," he said. He rose from his seat. "Get going; there might be a bite to eat left in the kitchen if you run."

"What about you, Master?"

"I," Master Zist stretched to his full height and assumed a lordly pose, "have a date with a young lady." Catching Kindan's surprised look, he added with shushing motions, "Go on! Off with you!"

◆

It took Kindan two grueling days to come up with three virtues Cristov possessed: honesty; loyalty; integrity. He managed to ingratiate himself with Dara by explaining that he had fond memories of doing laundry in his old house and could he please do a few loads for them to relive the memory? Cristov looked ready to die of laughter at the question and Tarik looked sour, as always, but Dara relented after giving Kindan a long, searching look.

All the same Kindan was delighted when he reported his findings to Master Zist and got out of his extra chore.

"Describe the house to me," Master Zist ordered then.

Kindan started to run down the layout of the house from memory, but the Harper stopped him with an upraised hand.

"No, not how you remember it, how it *is*."

Kindan struggled to find words, fumbled, and shook his head.

"A harper must learn to observe," Master Zist said. "Wherever you go, you must be observant." Under the Harper's questioning, Kindan slowly recalled all the details of Tarik's house and the items inside it. He was surprised to discover how much he knew of the state of the house, even though he had not consciously set out to learn it.

"Good," Master Zist said at last. "It is late—you'd best get to sleep."

Kindan looked rebellious.

"Tomorrow, we shall meet at the Hold for the evening," Master Zist said. "We'll celebrate winter's end, and I'll need you to have your wits about you and help on the drums."

Kindan was surprised. Master Zist had started him working on the drums almost as soon as Kindan had moved into his cottage, but he had never suspected that the Master, always short of praise, would let him perform with him.

"Don't be so surprised," Master Zist said. "I can't play all the instruments by myself, you know. Now, to bed with you. Tomorrow will be long enough without the evening's festivities at the end of it."

◆

The next day Dalor had morning watch on the cliff heights. Kindan, woken up well before dawn by the Harper, had as his duty the setting of the watchers. After a hasty cup of *klah*—breakfast would come later—he set off in the dark looking to meet Dalor at the bottom of the path up to the cliff heights.

The winter snow was still on the ground, but there had been no new snow for over a sevenday and much of it had turned to slush with the warming weather. Kindan walked carefully, enjoying the crunch as each of his steps broke through the thin layer of ice that had formed over the snow during the cold night.

There was no sign of Dalor. He waited a few moments and then, aware that he had other duties, he set off for the hold.

The instant he opened the door, he smelled trouble. There was something wrong with the air. He had learned enough about bad air in the mines to have some guess as to what had happened—the chimney had been blocked, or something had caused all the gases from the hearth to spread into the hold and not leave it.

All his training told him to duck to the ground where the air was cooler and might still be breathable, but Kindan knew that time was of the essence.

"Fire! Help, help! Fire!" Kindan shouted at the top of his lungs. He started fanning with the door to suck some of the air out, but he knew it wasn't enough. He had to get a draft going. He ran from the kitchen door around to the front, all the while shouting as loud as his lungs would allow.

At the front he opened the great doors of the hold and fanned them a few times.

Master Zist came running over. "Lad, what is it?"

"Bad air!" Kindan said. "I could smell it when I went into the kitchen for Dalor. I've got the door to the kitchen open and I'm trying to get more air in but—"

"Fire! Help, help! Fire!" Master Zist bellowed. Shapes were approaching from different directions. Kindan looked around. Help might be too late. He ducked into the hallway.

"Kindan!"

"It's okay," Kindan shouted back. "I'm little, I don't need as much air as others. If I can get upstairs, I can open the windows and maybe wake them up."

The air on the stairways was definitely bad, Kindan realized as he started up them. He took a few good lungfuls and then held his breath, suddenly grateful for the dares he'd had with Kaylek on who could hold their breath the longest. His eyes were stinging as he reached the landing. His fingers fumbled with the window latch, but he got it open finally and took a few deep breaths before he turned to the bedrooms.

He opened the first door, ran into the room, and heaved open the first window he could find. He heard the shouts of others entering the house and running up the stairs. He shook the person in the bed—it was Dalor. Dazed and confused, Dalor looked up.

"Come on, Dalor!" Kindan shouted at him. "Bad air, come with me!" Suiting actions to his words, he grabbed Dalor's arm. Shortly, he had the other boy leaning against him and started him out of the room, fighting his own light-headedness as he did so.

Some men met him at the door. One grabbed Dalor and threw him over his shoulders and the other grabbed Kindan and did the same, despite his protests.

Suddenly Kindan was outside, spread out on the snowy ground, taking deep, steady breaths. His head ached.

❖

Something was wrong. Someone was calling her name, but it seemed as from a great distance.

"Nuella! Nuella!" It was Zenor's voice. A smile played across

Nuella's lips. Zenor. She really liked him. Her friend. The first friend she'd made at the camp. Her only friend. She tried to move, but her limbs felt heavy, like stone.

"Nuella!" Zenor's voice drew nearer. Dimly Nuella heard a door open, and then she felt someone shake her, grab at her. She was picked up and dragged out of her room.

"The air's bad, Nuella—I've got to get you out," Zenor said.

Bad air? Nuella thought to herself. Outside? The first faint stirrings of alarm grew inside her, but she was too heavy and tired to move. Outside— She wasn't supposed to be outside.

"Not outside," she murmured. Zenor, panting and hauling her down the stairs, didn't hear her.

"Are you all right, lad?" Master Zist asked, kneeling down beside Kindan. Kindan nodded feebly, wished he hadn't for the way his head felt, and managed to gesture a question with an open hand. "The others? They seem all right, thanks to you."

Another person dropped beside Kindan. It was Natalon. "Thanks, lad. We would have died in our sleep, if it hadn't been for you."

Kindan sat up more, managed a sickly smile for Natalon, and looked around. Jenella was being wrapped in a blanket, her eyes streaming with tears; Swanee was beside her, coughing deeply. Kindan's eyes narrowed as he saw Zenor helping a young girl get her breath back. He looked up at Master Zist and raised an eyebrow inquiringly. The Harper cocked his head and shook it just slightly.

Kindan jumped up, ignoring the pain behind his eyes, and grabbed Dalor, with a conspiratorial look in his eyes. He jerked his head toward the girl and Dalor's eyes grew wide. Kindan shook his head again and walked nonchalantly with Dalor over to Zenor and the girl.

Zenor had placed a blanket over the girl's head. He looked up curiously as Kindan approached. Kindan raised a quick fingers to his lips as he moved to block the girl from the view of the others.

"Come on, Dalor, you can get warmed up at the Harper's fire," Kindan said loudly, motioning for the girl and Zenor to stand up.

After that, it took only a little bit of work to arrange it so that Dalor was covered by the same blanket as the girl, and the four of them marched carefully to the Harper's cottage, Kindan talking loudly the whole way.

It was possible, he hoped, that things had happened too quickly for anyone but him to notice that two children had been brought out of Natalon's house, instead of just one.

Safe in the kitchen, all four of them warmed themselves by the fire. Dalor and the girl, still in their nightclothes, were shivering more than Kindan and Zenor.

"How'd you find us?" Dalor asked, his lips still blue.

"You were late for watch," Kindan explained.

"Thanks," Dalor said.

The girl reached up a hand hesitatingly toward Kindan and brushed his cheek. "Thank you, Kindan," she said.

"You're welcome, Nuella," Kindan replied. At Dalor's hiss of surprise and Zenor's widened eyes, he added, "Master Zist has taken me as his apprentice. He says that a harper has to keep secrets and has to respect the secrets of others." He turned to the cupboard and pulled out some mugs.

"Zenor, will you help me bring some warm *klah* while *Dalor*," and Kindan emphasized the one name, "warms up here?"

Zenor grinned broadly at his friend. "Sure."

Kindan winked at Dalor's surprised look and said, "I'll see you later."

◆

By that evening, everyone in the camp knew that the chimney had been blocked, apparently by a freak crack of brick, and that Natalon's hold had been thoroughly aired and there was no danger to anyone attending Winter's End there.

All the same, the great double front doors and the windows of the long room were wide open to reassure any worriers. The two long tables that by day served students were pushed to either side of the room, and the teacher's table was pushed all the way to the far end of the room from the hearth so that there was a good warm area for dancing.

Kindan and Master Zist were situated on top of the long table pushed against the wall. The Harper instructed Kindan to keep a simple beat on the drums, to accompany the songs.

The drumming was so basic that Kindan could spare his attention to observe the partygoers. The whole of Camp Natalon was fewer than two hundred people, including the smallest baby, but such a crowd should have filled the room nearly to bulging. As it was, Kindan calculated that less than a quarter of the Camp's inhabitants were present.

And no wonder—regardless of what the miners knew about bad air, not even Milla the baker could be coaxed back into the kitchen that morning to make her dainties. Natalon's lady, Jenella, was still suffering from the combined effects of the bad air and her pregnancy and was confined to bed.

The absence of others was easier to understand—Zenor had

four little sisters and his mother to look after. And, because of the cave-in that fall, it was still necessary to work two solid shifts, so the second shift was still in the mine. A third "air" shift had been organized to keep the air pumps going through the night, but that consisted of only four people working in two pairs and they were mostly the youngest, the oldest, or the least skilled.

Kindan was so lost in his thoughts that he didn't realize that Master Zist had stopped playing until the Master was speaking in his ear, having gotten up from his chair and walked over to where Kindan was seated. "Keep up that beat, lad, while I go mix with the crowd."

Kindan nodded without breaking beat and watched as the MasterHarper climbed down from the table and made his way over to the refreshments. Kindan beat a bit harder as the Harper approached that table, and his hint must have been taken, for Master Zist tossed a backward wave at him—he would bring Kindan back some refreshments on his return.

Still playing instinctively, Kindan scanned the small crowd to pick up snippets of conversation.

"Caravan coming in to pick up our coal— " It was true: With the snow melting, there should be a trader caravan in any day now to take the last six months' worth of mined coal

"—hope they bring some apprentices—" Natalon had sent a drum message to the MasterMiner in Crom asking for more apprentices.

"—no use, they'll be the worst, or who'd let them go?"

Kindan sighed, as that last comment made too much sense. Any apprentices that could be freed to go to a new mine would never be the best apprentices—they'd be kept on by their Masters at the current mines. Some of them would just be young and eager, but others might even be more trouble than they were worth: lazy or shiftless.

"—without a watch-wher, how are we going to be safe?" Kindan's ears pricked up at that snippet of conversation, trying to identify the speaker.

"—there's been too many accidents, especially since—" Kindan guessed that the speaker was about to say "the cave-in," but the voice had slipped away from him in the general noise of the hall. Kindan agreed with whoever had said that; there'd been minor accidents once or twice a week since the cave-in that had killed his father and Dask. Partly, as Kindan had heard Natalon tell Zist one late evening when they both thought him asleep, because they were working hard with few people, and partly because it was just the nature of working underground where any carelessness could easily result in an injury.

Kindan searched the crowd and spotted Panit, one of Tarik's old cronies, stumping about with a cast on his foot. The old miner had not been paying attention and had let a trolley get away from him and run over his foot.

"At the end of the day, it's the head miner who's to blame, isn't it?" Panit asked a small knot of worried-looking miners gathered around him. Kindan stiffened. "Maybe the problem's not watch-whers, but leadership."

Kindan strained to see the reactions of the other miners but only succeeded in losing his beat. With a quick flourish, he jumped back into it, but not before several heads turned in his direction, Panit's being one of them.

"When you're listening in," Master Zist murmured in Kindan's ear, appearing suddenly at his side, "it's important not to be noticed."

Kindan managed a sickly smile in return. "Sorry," he muttered back.

Master Zist nodded. He thrust a mug and a plate of snacks at Kindan and said, "Take a break."

Not long after that, the Gather broke up. Kindan and the Harper were the last to leave, bowed under the weight of their instruments and the length of their day.

Kindan could never remember how he got into his bed that night.

◆

"Master Zist! Master Zist!" Dalor's cry woke Kindan far too soon. He stirred groggily, frightened by the tone of Dalor's voice.

"Eh? What is it?" Master Zist called out from his room as Kindan tumbled into the kitchen.

"It's my mother," Dalor said, face pale with fright. "The baby's coming early."

The Harper emerged from his room, still in his bedclothes. He took one look at Dalor and turned decisively to Kindan. "Go run to Margit's and get her up here." He turned back to Dalor, "I'll be along as soon as I get some clothes on. You get on back. Start the cook boiling water, if she hasn't already." His tone turned softer as he took in the look on Dalor's face. "It'll be all right, lad. Now off with you!"

The moment Dalor was out of earshot, Kindan told the Harper, "Margit's not much at midwifery. Silstra did most of that, and Harper Jofri."

"Journeyman Jofri learned his healing after I'd thrown him out of my singing class," Master Zist said. Then he sighed. "And I learned my singing after the MasterHealer threw me out of his healing class."

Kindan looked alarmed. The Harper made shooing motions with his hands. "Get off, now! We'll cope."

Kindan chivvied Margit along as fast as he could when he woke her but she was not to be hurried. They reached Jenella's room in time to hear Milla, who was standing in the doorway, wail, "It's too soon, it's too soon!"

"No, it's not," Margit said matter-of-factly. "It's a month before normal time, and that's close enough." She drew herself closer to the baker and said harshly, "And if you can't get yourself under control, you'll go back to the kitchen."

Milla, who wouldn't miss the excitement for gold, sniffed and drew herself up, but closed her mouth.

Kindan, carrying Margit's work things, followed her into the room. Natalon was holding Jenella's hand. Master Zist had arranged sheets and blankets discreetly and placed himself to receive the baby.

Margit shouldered the Harper aside to make her own inspection. Satisfied, she went to Jenella's side. "You're fine, dear, just fine," she assured her. "When the next contraction comes, just bear on down. You know the drill."

Dalor stirred uncomfortably from his spot in the room. Master Zist glanced at him, eyes narrowed, and then turned to Kindan. "Lad, get Swanee to cook some towels in boiling water. We'll need to clean the baby when it arrives. Take Dalor to help you."

Kindan gave the Harper a quizzical look, then enlightenment dawned and he grinned. Dragging a reluctant Dalor after him, he left the room.

Out of earshot, Kindan said to the other boy, "If we work it right, we can get your sister in to substitute for you some of the time."

"Oh, please," said a figure appearing out of the shadows. It was Nuella. "I'd like to be there; Mother will want me."

"But if Margit or Milla—" Dalor protested.

"They won't know if there's only one of you in the room at a time and you wear the same clothes," Kindan said. "Not in all the excitement."

"That will only work if you wear my cap," Dalor said, pulling the cap he usually wore off himself and stuffing it on Nuella's head.

"And put your hair under it," Kindan said. Nuella took the cap off, twirled her hair up into a bun and stuffed the cap back on.

"Perfect!" Dalor said. "You look just like me."

"But if you forget the cap or it falls off, you'll be caught out," Kindan warned. Dalor looked frightened.

Nuella settled the matter, telling Kindan, "When you go down, be sure to have the cook sterilize the sharpest knife she has—she'll moan, but don't listen—that'll be to cut the cord. Have her put it on one of the boiled rags so it stays sterile."

Kindan started down to the kitchen wondering just when Dalor's sister had taken charge.

All the same, his plan worked perfectly. Kindan deftly managed it so that Dalor and Nuella switched off every quarter hour. After Jenella's first wide-eyed recognition of her daughter and Nuella's subtle nod in Kindan's direction, Jenella calmed down with a grateful smile and clasped Nuella's hand tightly.

When the baby came, Margit deliberately stepped away to let Master Zist receive it. Kindan got the distinct impression that she wanted to place the burden—figuratively and literally— in the Harper's big hands. And that's how it turned out. One moment the Harper was leaning in, calling soothing words to Jenella, and the next moment there was a little snuffle and a slight mewing sound.

"Kindan, come here with that knife," Master Zist ordered. When Kindan came around, he saw the small newborn still attached by its umbilical cord.

"Make a loop with the cord," Master Zist instructed. As Kindan complied, the Harper said to Natalon, "Come cut the cord and welcome your new daughter into the world."

Natalon, with a proud look at his wife and a big smile on his face, cut the cord. Margit took the baby from Master Zist, quickly wiped it off with the sterile towels, and looked up for blankets to wrap the baby in.

"I'll get them," Nuella offered, hastily leaving the room.

Margit followed her departure with a penetrating look, saying to Jenella, "You've got a good lad there. Usually it's only the daughters that know where the baby things are kept."

"Dalor's been talking about this for a while," Kindan said, improvising quickly. "Although I think he was hoping for a brother."

"He'll be pleased with a sister, I'm sure," Natalon said. He gazed happily at Jenella. "I know I am."

Dalor returned, sweating visibly, with the baby things and passed them on to Margit, who wrapped up the newborn and passed her to Jenella.

"I don't know what the Harper thinks," Margit said with a nod to Master Zist, "but I think she's perfect."

Kindan was surprised to see that Master Zist's face was flowing with tears.

Margit's face fell when she noticed. "Oh, Master Zist, I'm sorry, I'd forgotten you'd had one of your own."

Master Zist nodded, wiping his eyes. "I did," he said after clearing his throat. He looked to Jenella. "I'm sorry, but your lass looks the same as mine did when she was born."

"What was her name?" Kindan asked softly.

"Carissa," the Harper murmured. He forced a smile on his face and looked toward the proud parents. "And what are you going to name this bouncy one?"

Natalon and Jenella exchanged glances. "We don't know yet."

"There'll be plenty of time for that," Margit agreed. "Now why don't you leave while I help Jenella and her babe get settled in." And she backed up her words with determined shooing motions with her hands. "Milla, you can stay and help."

By the time the others had collected downstairs, the early morning light was showing. Natalon bit back a curse. "I'm late for my own shift!"

"I think they'll understand," Master Zist told him.

"I had Swanee send word, Father," Dalor added.

Natalon gave him a grateful look and let out a big sigh of relief.

"It'll be a long day for all of us," Master Zist said to Kindan as they made their way back to the Harper's cothold. "But that's the way things go, sometimes."

Kindan nodded in agreement but was robbed of words by a huge yawn.

"Some *klah* will help you start the day," Master Zist said.

Kindan had a great tale to tell as he set the watch. It was still bitterly cold in the watch-heights so he stayed on to gather kindling and firewood as the first watcher got settled in. He was back down the hill in time for classes with Master Zist and back up again at lunchtime, when the morning mist was finally lifting, to spell Renna, Zenor's eldest sister, while she got her lunch.

So it was he who first saw the trader caravan approaching.

CHAPTER V

A baby's cry, a mother's sigh,
Sweet things make a day go by.

Being the first to spot the trader caravan, Kindan quickly sought out the Harper who was handling, between yawns, a class of busy younglings.

"Natalon's in the mines," Master Zist said when Kindan told him. "You'll need to send someone to let him know." He paused consideringly. "Do you know what else to do when a caravan arrives?" Kindan nodded. "Well, you'd best get it done, then."

"But I've only Turned eleven," Kindan complained, wondering how he would get such oldsters as Swanee and Ima to do his bidding.

Master Zist looked down his nose at him. "Then it will be an interesting challenge for you."

"Right," Kindan said, catching on at once. "I'll figure something."

By the time he met Ima, the camp's butcher, Kindan knew what to say. "There's a caravan coming in. Master Zist sends his compliments and asks if you could prepare enough extra meat to feed another twenty."

He used the same strategy with Milla and Swanee. It worked every time. Finally, having set everything in train, he decided that he was the right one to deliver the message to Natalon in the mines.

He had kept Kaylek's second set of coveralls, but as he hurriedly put them on, he discovered that he was still a bit too small and had to roll up both the sleeves and the legs. Kaylek's hard hat fit once he adjusted the headband—perhaps, he thought ruefully, Kaylek's teasing about his big head had had some measure of truth in it. Properly attired, though without good work gloves, Kindan made his way to the mine entrance.

Inside the mine, he was pleased to recognize Zenor. Zenor was tired and grumpy. "All I ever do is work topside," he groused. "Honestly, Kindan, I saw more of the mines when you and I had to change the glows."

"Natalon has you working the pumps?" Kindan asked rhetorically. When Zenor nodded miserably, Kindan clapped him on the shoulder. "Well, he must trust you a lot, putting his life in your hands like that."

Zenor brightened a bit at the thought. "Really?"

"Really," Kindan replied. "You're what keeps him breathing."

"And it's hard work, too," Zenor agreed. He was on a rotation, resting from the constant work of the pumps but on call for running the lifts. "I hadn't thought of it that way."

"I've got to deliver a message from Master Zist," Kindan said. "Can you lower me down?"

"A message?" Zenor repeated, leaning in toward Kindan, curiosity shining in his eyes.

"There's a trader caravan approaching," Kindan told him confidentially.

Zenor's eyes widened as he turned to look at the other five working the top of the mine on his shift, contemplating how this inside bit of gossip would go over with them. "I hope they brought apprentices," he said fervently. "I could trade places and get down the mines myself."

Kindan grinned. "There's an idea," he said. "But Natalon needs to hear this, too. Can you lower me down?"

"Sure," Zenor said, heading to the lift controls. "Hop in."

Before lowering the lift, Zenor made a careful check of Kindan's gear and changed the glow that was strapped to the front of his hard hat. He thrust a heavy sack at him, too. "Bring these glows on down with you; they'll be calling for them soon enough anyways."

At the bottom of the shaft, Kindan climbed off. He was met by Toldur, one of the miners.

"I was just about to go for those," Toldur told him, nodding approvingly at the sack of glows Kindan had brought.

"I've a message for Natalon from the Harper," Kindan said.

"I'm going back to him," Toldur replied, throwing the sack over his back with the ease of long practice. He double-checked Kindan's gear, muttered about the too-long coveralls, and motioned for Kindan to follow him.

The solid rock of the mine shaft immediately gave way to the soot black of coal. Kindan had been in the mines before, but he always took the chance to examine the changes and take in more detail. And this was the first time he'd been in the mine since the cave-in.

"We're taking a different road from the one your father was on," Toldur commented.

Kindan studied the shoring along the way. The trees nearest the campsite would have to be cleared long before Thread came again, so there was no shortage of timber to support the roof of the mine, but there *was* a shortage of labor to cut the trees. Kindan had been on many work parties that had trimmed the branches off felled trees, or had helped to cart the finished beams and planks to the supply shed up by the mine entrance.

He measured distance by counting glows along the way. Toldur paused a few times to replace dim glows with new ones from the sack Kindan had brought. Glows were placed every three meters, Kindan knew, so he knew that they'd gone sixty meters before they saw Natalon's work party.

Toldur had to shoulder his way into the group to carve a path for Kindan. The rest of the crew took the opportunity to take a quick break from their labors. There was a line of carts on the track that they'd filled with coal.

"What is it, Kindan?" Natalon asked cheerfully.

"There's a trader caravan approaching," Kindan told him. The other miners perked up at that and began talking happily among themselves, hoping that there were new apprentices in the caravan or wondering whether the traders brought some of the things they'd been missing, such as new fabrics—"for the wife"—or pickaxes—"never can have enough."

"When do you think it'll arrive at the camp?" Natalon asked.

Kindan pursed his lips thoughtfully. "Probably just as your shift ends." The other miners, who had gone quiet to hear their conversation, raised a cheer over the news. Kindan could see the weary acceptance in Natalon's face.

"Master Zist's got all the welcoming preparations under way,"

Kindan assured him. "He wanted to know if you would let him host another evening in the hold's great room."

Natalon nodded his assent. "And, if there're new apprentices, they'll need to be assigned shifts and lodging," he added, diving into the administrative side of his job with a deep sigh.

"Master Zist asked if he and Swanee couldn't consider that," Kindan said, happily stuffing words into the Harper's and the camp's supplier's mouths. He knew how tired *he* was from all the excitement of the past day, and he hadn't been working shifts, nor was it his wife who'd given birth that morning. He worked up a smile. "I believe Master Zist said that it would be an interesting challenge for him."

Natalon gave in with a wave of his hands. "I'll leave it to him then." He turned to his crew. "You lot get back to work. You've had enough of a break."

He put a fatherly hand on Kindan's shoulder. "I'll walk you back to the shaft," he said. As soon as they were out of earshot of the others, he asked, "Did you see how many coal drays they had with them?"

Kindan frowned, trying to remember. He had only just seen the head of the caravan in the rising fog. "It was still foggy," he admitted. "I think there were four."

Natalon looked puzzled. "We've enough bagged coal for five, I think, nearly six. If they've only brought four it'll be months before we sell all our bagged coal. If they've brought six . . ."

Kindan had learned a lot in his months with the Harper. The camp could supply many of its own needs—lumber, coal, meat, some herbs and greens—but they needed flour, fabric, finished metal goods like pickaxes, spices, and all the little incidentals that made living more than just drudgery. Those goods had to be paid for, and coal was the way the camp paid for them. Traders preferred bagged coal, dry and ready to sell. They charged a penalty for wet coal, and another penalty for loose coal.

If the caravan had only brought four coal drays, then the camp could only buy goods equal to that amount. But if the caravan brought six coal drays and Natalon had only enough for slightly more than five, there might be a bigger problem: No trader made a profit hauling half-filled wagons or, worse, empty ones. The trader could well decide to move on to another Camp in hopes of getting a full load. There'd be another caravan along soon that'd take what bagged coal Camp Natalon had, but it'd be at least another month.

Kindan knew how the miners would feel to see a caravan leave without trading, even if the Camp had enough goods to carry it through until another caravan arrived. He could only guess at the unease the new apprentices would feel to arrive at a Camp that couldn't buy the goods the traders had brought.

Except for the coal bagged and set aside in a dry cave, all the coal that had been mined in the fall and winter was in a huge pile covered with melting snow. The warmer weather would easily see it dried out, but that couldn't be expected for at least another three sevendays or more—far longer than any trader would be willing to wait.

"How long would it take to mine enough coal to fill a sixth dray?" Kindan asked.

Natalon raised his eyebrows in surprise, then nodded in comprehension. "Master Zist asked you to consider all possibilities, then?"

Kindan shrugged. "I'm certain of four drays . . . but if there were more out of sight, then there might be six altogether. It never hurts to be prepared, does it?"

"No, it doesn't," Natalon agreed heartily, looking at the sturdy supports he'd placed along this tunnel. "Although," he said with a stern look at Kindan, "it's better to be accurate than to guess."

"I know," Kindan agreed mournfully. "Next time I'll stay until I'm certain that I've seen the end of the caravan."

Natalon looked at Kindan and noted the set of his jaw and the slump in his shoulders. It was obvious to him that Kindan had really thought through all the implications of his mistake and would not repeat it.

"Good," Natalon said firmly. "So how much to fill a sixth dray, eh?" He pursed his lips thoughtfully. "If we worked three shifts, maybe two or three days." He sighed. "But we can't work three shifts. I've no one trained to be a shift leader for the third shift."

"So it'd take four days with two shifts?" Kindan guessed. Natalon agreed. "But how long will it take to fill the drays?"

"Usually we take the working shift and have them fill the drays," Natalon said. "With ten men in two shifts, we can fill the drays in a day or two."

"So, what if we could form a third shift to fill the drays while the other two kept on mining?" Kindan wondered. "They'd fill the drays in about three days, wouldn't they?"

Natalon considered the question and finally nodded. "Yes."

"So all we have to do is convince the trader to stay on an extra day," Kindan said.

"Maybe," Natalon allowed. Then he shook his head. "But traders don't make profits sitting around. They're just as likely to decide to go to another Camp for their coal."

"They'd lose time with that, too." Kindan shook his head. "Why don't I ask the Harper to help out? I'm sure he'll enjoy the challenge."

Natalon chuckled. "You've used that phrase twice now, lad," he noted. "Is it one dear to the Harper?"

"Yes," Kindan agreed, suppressing a grin. They had arrived at the mine shaft. "Let Master Zist take care of it, please. He managed the birthing—I'm sure this will be nothing for him."

Natalon laughed aloud at the comparison. "All right, Kindan, you may tell Master Zist that I leave it all in his capable hands."

"I will," Kindan said, tugging on the lift ropes to signal his ascent.

◆

Master Zist was amused at Kindan's creative solutions to his challenge but not at all amused that Kindan had managed to dump Natalon's problems squarely in *his* lap.

"Well," he said when he'd digested all the news, "if I'm to play the Holder while Natalon's resting and Tarik's working his shift, you'll have to play the Harper." He ignored Kindan's horrified expression and continued blithely, "I'm sure that Swanee has got his lists together and can talk all that's necessary about supplies and payments, but he strikes me as an *honest* man, and that's not the best sort of person to deal with traders."

Kindan stoutly declaimed Swanee's honesty. "Well then," the Harper said, "there you go. Traders are honest in their own way, too: They'll always give you what you pay for, but they don't go out of their way to be sure to give you their best price. That takes bargaining. Traders love to bargain."

From the glint in Master Zist's eyes, Kindan got the impression that the Harper enjoyed bargaining himself.

"Bargaining," the Harper continued, "takes lots of talk. And talk is what a Harper does best." He wagged a warning finger at

Kindan and added, "Although you'd never find a Trader willing to admit that a Harper could out-bargain him.

"So," he concluded, "it'll be up to you to provide the entertainment while I provide the bargaining."

"But I only really know how to drum!" Kindan protested.

Master Zist snorted. "And what were you doing at the wedding?"

"I thought you didn't want me to sing," Kindan said.

"Except when I tell you to, or there's no choice," Master Zist corrected. "And I'm telling you *and* there's no choice."

"Oh." Kindan's forehead puckered in thought.

"Something else is troubling you," Master Zist noted.

"Well . . ." Kindan began slowly, considering his words carefully. "I've always been taught not to lie, and yet it seems that I've told an awful lot of lies recently . . . I've always found that lies tend to come back to me."

Master Zist nodded. "When have you lied?"

"Well, I said that you'd asked for the things to be set up for the Gather tonight."

"And did I not send you on that task?" Master Zist asked. Kindan nodded slowly. "So you said what you said in order to do what I asked you to do, isn't that so?" Kindan nodded. "That's not a lie, Kindan. That's being a good subordinate."

"A subordinate?" Kindan repeated, unfamiliar with the word.

"Like Swanee is responsible for the supplies but works for Natalon," Master Zist said, giving an example. "Or a shift leader working for the head miner. A subordinate is someone who has been given a task by his leader and sometimes uses the authority of that leader to accomplish it.

"If you had said, 'Master Zist asks you to make me some

bubbly-pies' when I never did, that would be a misuse of a subordinate's powers," the Harper added. "A subordinate does walk a tender line between lie and truth. A subordinate is supposed to guess what his leader wants and guess correctly." He wagged a finger at Kindan, eyebrows crunched tightly together in warning. "You don't want to be wrong when you're my subordinate."

Kindan shrugged in wary acceptance. "But what about at the birthing? You didn't ask me to see to it that Nuella was present, and we fooled Margit and Milla. If that's not a lie, it's certainly stretching the truth."

"That was a difficult situation," the Harper agreed. "You did well, by the way. Lies and secrets are related, Kindan. Secrets breed lies. Because Natalon wants to keep Nuella a secret, for reasons that I'm not allowed to tell you, you had to create some deceptions."

"But if secrets are so bad, why do so many people have them?" Kindan asked.

"Because sometimes they are the only thing some people can truly call their own," Master Zist answered with a sigh.

"Well, I can't see how long Nuella will remain a secret," Kindan said. "Both Zenor and I know about her, and we've been in the Camp less than a year."

Master Zist nodded. "I have pointed out the same to Natalon," he said. "But he has his reasons."

"Because she's a girl, or because she's blind?" Kindan asked. Kindan had guessed she was blind the day he'd found Natalon's hold full of bad air—but he wasn't certain if that was Natalon's reason for keeping her concealed.

Master Zist smiled at the youngster. "That was a good try—offering me a choice in hopes of getting me to reveal the secret," he said, "but I've been a Harper longer than you've lived.

"And it was perceptive of you to notice Nuella's condition," the Master continued. "Perhaps from that, you can make some conjectures"—he held up a hand when Kindan opened his mouth—"which, as my apprentice, you'll keep to yourself."

"I would have figured it out sooner if I'd seen her any other time but when the traders were here," Kindan remarked. "I thought she was one of them."

Master Zist nodded in understanding.

"In such a tight community as this Camp, everyone knows everyone else and most everyone has the same things," he continued. "Oh, there are a few special trinkets or family heirlooms, but mostly no one has more than another. So some people have secrets all their own. Or they have secrets because they're afraid how others would react if the secret were ever known."

Master Zist gave Kindan a wry grin and added conspiratorially, "Most of the time, other people wouldn't care a bit for another person's secret. But, as I said, a secret makes a person who's got nothing else feel special. Which is why Harpers are instructed"—and Kindan heard the special emphasis on the word "instructed" as an instruction to him—"to respect the secrets of others."

"So when is a secret a bad thing?"

"A secret's a bad thing when it can be used to hurt others, or when it hides a hurt," Master Zist said quickly. "You've an obligation, again as a harper, to expose a secret like that when you find it."

"What sort of secret is that?" Kindan asked, mentally running through the small list of secrets he'd discovered about other people.

Master Zist made a sour face. "I once knew a man, a hard man, who when he'd taken too much wine would lose his sense and temper. When he did that, he'd beat his children." His lips tightened. "That's that sort of secret."

Kindan shivered at the thought. "So a bad secret is the sort of secret that when people know it, they can help?"

Master Zist considered his words before responding. "I suppose you could say that," he replied. He got up, finished the last of the *klah* he'd been sipping, and gestured for Kindan to follow. "We'll talk more of philosophy later. Right now we've got work to do."

There *were* six coal drays in the trader caravan. All the camp youngsters and women turned out to greet the traders who had walked up in front of the coal drays.

"You're the first fresh faces we've seen in six months!" Milla exclaimed, passing out dainties she'd made especially for their arrival.

"Tarri," a woman in her early twenties said, extending a hand to Milla and looking around at the rest of the crowd. "Journeyman Trader."

Master Zist stepped through the crowd with Kindan not far behind. "I'm Master Zist, pleased to meet you."

Tarri's eyebrows went up at the sight of a MasterHarper here at this small camp, but she quickly schooled her expression and gladly shook his hand.

"I've seven apprentices from the MasterMiner along with me," she said, nodding to a knot of miners clustered nearby.

Kindan smothered a puzzled look. He'd heard Natalon tell Master Zist that eight apprentices had been sent—not seven.

"We'll be glad to have them," Master Zist said cheerfully,

ANNE MCCAFFREY & TODD MCCAFFREY

waving to the group. Under his breath he said to Kindan, "Where are we going to put them?"

Kindan whispered back, "They'll have to go where there's the most room."

Master Zist's eyes widened in a combination of alarm and glee. "That'd be Tarik's place, wouldn't it?"

Kindan gave an imperceptible nod.

"Master Zist, would you know where the coal drays go?" Tarri asked. From her expression, Kindan guessed that she expected the Harper wouldn't.

"If you follow the fork in the road back there, you'll come right to the depot," Master Zist answered calmly.

Tarri nodded thanks and turned to the other traders, issuing orders. In a moment she turned back to the Harper.

"I imagine Miner Natalon will be wanting to talk about supplies and the price for his coal," she said.

"Miner Natalon's on shift at the moment and has asked me to show you the courtesy of his hold," the Harper replied, bowing and gesturing toward Natalon's hold with one hand. "If you'll follow me, I'm sure you're parched from the journey and wouldn't mind a bit of refreshment."

The young trader nodded agreeably and strode on to the hold, side by side with Zist.

"Do you know where we're supposed to go?" a boy scarcely older than Kindan asked of the remaining crowd before Kindan could follow the Harper.

"He'd be just the lad," Milla told him, pointing at Kindan. "Why don't you get the apprentices settled, Kindan, while I go serve the traders?"

Kindan suppressed his disappointment at not being able to

stay around to learn the latest gossip but admitted, with a nod, that he was outmaneuvered and outranked by the baker.

"I'm Kindan," he said to the gathering apprentices. "I'm sure we can get you settled in. If you'll follow me."

In the end, Kindan managed to foist four of the apprentices, two older and two younger, onto Tarik's Dara—mostly through fast-talking that alluded to how much esteem she'd gain in fostering the lion's share of the new apprentices. Dara's eyes, at first wary, grew quite appreciative as she imagined breaking the news to Tarik. Kindan, who thought Tarik would hold his privacy in higher regard, was not so sure of the miner's reaction.

Toldur's wife, Alarra, was glad to take in two—the older Menar and young Gulegar—while Norla happily took young Regellan when Kindan hinted broadly that he'd be on the opposite shift from Zenor, giving her a constant chance of someone who spoke "adult words" nearby.

With the apprentices all settled, Kindan went back to the Harper's cothold to spruce up, change, and get his drums. Inside he was surprised to hear the soft sounds of someone crying in Master Zist's study.

It was Nuella. The glows in the room were dim; Kindan realized that no one had had a chance to change them.

"What's the matter?" he asked as he caught sight of her sitting in one of the large chairs. Nuella looked up at the sound of his voice.

"I—I—Master Zist was supposed to teach me," Nuella said shakily. "I thought maybe I'd gotten it wrong so I went back to the hold only—only I heard him talking to someone else. So I came back here."

"Oh, things got all mixed up because the caravan's come in," Kindan said.

"I didn't hear the drums," Nuella protested.

"Well, that's because there's no one at the relay yet, I expect," Kindan said, referring to the drum relay midway between Crom Hold and Camp Natalon. "I spotted them and then got awfully busy between Master Zist and your father."

"But it was a girl's voice I heard talking to Master Zist," Nuella said.

"That's Tarri, the Trader," Kindan told her.

"A girl can be a trader?" Nuella sounded surprised.

Kindan shrugged. "Why not? Although I think Tarri is older than that. She's a journeyman, by her shoulder knots."

Nuella sniffed. "I heard Milla say that a girl could be a baker or a mother, but that was all a girl was good for. She was complaining to Mother about it."

"I can't understand why Milla would complain," Kindan said without thinking. "She's a pretty good baker."

"Mother wants to name the baby Larissa," Nuella said in an abrupt change of topic. "She's all worried whether the baby can see. She doesn't want—"

Kindan realized that Nuella was telling him her secret.

"I'm sure the baby is fine," Kindan said, sounding far more like Master Zist than himself. Nuella heard it too and frowned at him.

"Mother says that you can't tell when they're first born," Nuella went on. "Sometimes it's years before they lose their sight." She paused and bit her lip nervously before continuing in a rush: "I could see just fine all the way until I was three. And then . . . things just started to go blurry and dim. Now everything is just splotches . . ."

With a look of determination she stood up, steadying herself against the wall for a moment with an outstretched hand, and walked over to the door where Kindan stood. "Master Zist keeps the furniture in the same place," she said appreciatively.

"I know," Kindan replied. "He keeps yelling at me when I move it."

"Father's afraid of what the others will say if they find out," Nuella said. "That's why he was so glad to get Tarik to move out. Cristov almost found out once, you know."

"Why is your father so worried?" Kindan blurted.

Nuella scowled, and shook her head angrily. "He's afraid that we'll be shunned," she said bitterly.

"Shunned? But you've done nothing wrong," Kindan said, wondering why the ultimate punishment—expulsion from society—could even be considered.

"Not like that," Nuella corrected him. "His mother was blind, too. There aren't that many blind people, you know."

Kindan nodded, then said, "I know."

"Well," Nuella went on, "I heard him and Mother talking about it several times. Arguing, really. My father's afraid that people will wonder what's wrong with *him*, if his children are blind. And they won't trust him. And he's afraid that no one will marry Dalor." With a catch in her voice, she added, "He doesn't think I'll ever get married."

"So he wants to keep you a secret?" Kindan asked. Nuella nodded. "I don't see how. Master Zist knows, *I* know, and Zenor knows. It was a wonder others didn't figure it out the other day."

Nuella snorted. "Some people who have perfectly good eyes only see what they want," she said. "I usually wear clothes to match Dalor's. Once Milla brushed right by me without even noticing."

"And what a choice bit of gossip she'd make of you," Kindan replied.

"She would, indeed," Nuella agreed, adding bitterly, "And then Uncle Tarik would spread the gossip throughout the camp. 'If he can't make decent children, what sort of miner can he be?' "

Kindan considered her words carefully. He could see Tarik saying such spiteful things, and he could imagine there would be some who would listen. Certainly Tarik's cronies would. And they'd repeat the gossip. And, if anything went wrong, like the bad air in the hold, there'd always be some who would start believing the gossip.

"All the same, you're going to be found out sometime," Kindan said.

Nuella nodded. "I've been telling Father that ever since we came up here. And I *want* to get out. But he keeps telling me to wait until the right time. He had hopes—before the cave-in . . ."

Kindan felt his throat tighten as he remembered all that had been lost in that cave-in. Master Zist had kept him so busy that it was only in his sleep—his nightmares—that he remembered the past, and his family.

"There's a Gather tonight," Kindan said. "I've got to get over there."

"I won't hear it if I stay here," Nuella said, downcast. She held up her fingers, which were dotted with tiny pinpricks. "Mother says that everyone does this. I'm not sure—"

"Oh, they do!" Kindan said reassuringly. "I saw Zenor with the same pinpricks—diaper pins, right?—with his sisters."

Kindan could tell that his words had relieved Nuella's fears. One thing bothered him, though. "How long has Zenor known?"

"Oh, since the first sevenday we moved here," Nuella said with a grin. "He fell off the fence when he was trying to get away from Cristov and hurt himself pretty badly." She made a face. "I heard him crying. I couldn't just leave him there for Cristov to find and probably kick, so I bundled him up to my room and bandaged him up and we've been friends ever since."

Kindan made a rueful face. "Well, your secret's safe with him, that's for sure. I'm his best friend and he never told me."

"Good," Nuella said firmly, causing Kindan to glance up at her. "He wouldn't be much of a friend if he couldn't even keep a secret from you, would he?"

"Well . . ."

Nuella nodded. "I see, you think that because he's your friend he should tell you all his secrets, is that it?"

Kindan's frown grew more thoughtful. "Well . . ."

"But now you *know* that anything you've ever told him he's kept secret—even from me," Nuella pointed out.

That thought cheered Kindan up. "Wait a minute! It was you who threw those rocks when we were cleaning Dask! You warned us. But how did you know . . ."

"There's a difference between keeping a secret and keeping out of sight," Nuella said primly. She giggled. "Or out of hearing. I may not see, but I can hear better than anyone in the camp. And I can smell better, too."

Kindan didn't say anything so Nuella continued, "I heard you and Zenor talking. I heard what you were talking about. I wanted to help you, but I hadn't been invited and I wasn't supposed to let anyone know about me so—"

"You hid out and listened in," Kindan finished. He flashed a smile at Nuella that faded as he realized she couldn't see it, but her hand reached out toward his face, found his lips, and traced lightly over them.

"People think that you can't hear someone smiling," she said, her fingers still on Kindan's lips. "Maybe it's not really *hearing*, either, but I can feel it somehow." She drew her fingers back. "I always thought you'd have a nice smile," she said. "I was right."

"Thanks," Kindan said, feeling a bit awkward. He found himself touching his own lips, as though feeling them for the first time. "But I've got to get over to the Gather. Let's see what we can do for you."

In the end, they used the Harper's clothes basket. A brightly colored robe and a hat made Nuella look like she might as easily be a trader or a miner. At Nuella's urging, Kindan applied a bit of makeup to darken her skin color.

"Make sure you bring some pipes," she said as they headed out the door.

"I don't play pipes," Kindan protested.

"I do," Nuella replied with a grin.

◆

They arrived just as the great hall was being set up. Master Zist and Trader Tarri were parked in a corner with a plate of Milla's best dainties and a jug of good *klah* close at hand. Master Zist's eyes widened as he saw Kindan's companion. Kindan gave him a don't-worry look, to which the Harper replied with an I'd-better-not-have-to grimace.

Kindan helped Nuella up onto the table where he'd performed the evening before, settled her on a stool somewhat behind him, and set up his own drums.

"I'd like to hear your pipes, Nuella," Kindan said.

Nuella obligingly started into a lively little song. Master Zist looked up, caught sight of Nuella on the pipes, and gave Kindan another probing look. As the song came to the end, Kindan said to her, "That was great. How many more do you know?"

"I'm best at that one," Nuella admitted. "But Master Zist has had me practice on four others."

Kindan nodded to himself. "Well then, I'll make you earn your keep. I'll start with the drums and when I'm tired, I'll ask you to do a song. I won't ask you to do more than one song for my three, can you do that?"

"I can," Nuella said. "But I've never had to play for very long."

"You'll find that if you get enough rest in between sets you can play as long as they'll let you," Kindan assured her. Nuella smiled and Kindan was struck by how much she looked like her brother—only prettier. Her sharp blue eyes really lit up when her cheeks curved in a smile.

Kindan bent closer to her and said for her ears alone, "Sometimes I'll want to leave you for a bit so that I can hear what people are saying. There are things they'd say when they don't know anyone's listening that they'd never share with the Harper."

Nuella nodded. "It's a pity the place will be so crowded," she said. "I can hear much better than you."

"I'll bet you can," Kindan agreed. "And if you listen in when I'm playing and tell me what you hear later, I'd be grateful."

"Okay, I will."

The first hour went marvelously. Every time Kindan caught sight of Master Zist's eyes, it was only to get a cheerful wave or nod. Nuella's piping was a great relief for Kindan, who mingled with the crowd—mostly women and younger folk—and caught tidbits of gossip as he did.

He was pleased to discover that everyone thought Dara lucky to have four apprentices put up in her place. A sour note was Dara herself who, as Kindan had expected, had discovered that Tarik was not thrilled to see his privacy so eroded. Kindan suppressed a smile at the thought of Tarik's displeasure.

Having acquired a generous tray of dainties and a jug of cool water from an appreciative Milla—"And who's that lovely lass playing with you?"—"I think she's a trader."—Kindan returned to start another set. Just as he'd begun a new, gentle drum set, he felt Nuella stiffen behind him. He glanced back her way quickly in time to see her strain her nostrils meaningfully. A blast of cold air mingled with the warmer air of the room; Natalon had returned from his shift.

A hand on his shoulder warned Kindan that Nuella had crept beside him. "He's gone to change, first," she said. Then her tone brightened. "Zenor's here!"

Indeed, at that very moment, Zenor entered the room. His face was newly scrubbed and he arrived with his mother and young sisters all in tow. He gave Kindan a jaunty salute and turned toward the banquet laid out on the far wall, only to turn back again with a start.

"He's seen me, hasn't he?" Nuella whispered. Kindan could only nod, which he realized a moment later would do Nuella no good, but apparently she had felt his movement through her hand, because he felt it leave his shoulder and heard the faint sounds of her regaining her chair.

It was going to be a very interesting evening, indeed, he thought to himself.

◆

"Have you lost your mind?" Zenor hissed at Kindan as soon as he could break away from his mother. As Nuella was doing another of her pipe solos, Kindan had found himself back among the now much larger crowd filling the great hall. "Or has she?"

"Aside from you, Zenor, who will know?" Kindan asked. "We darkened her face, hid her hair, and she pretty much stays up there. The traders will think she's one of us, while the rest of the miners will think she's one of them."

"Well, her father and mother will know differently, won't they?" Zenor said, lips pursed tightly. "And if Tarik finds out—"

"Well, he'll never hear it from me," Kindan assured him. He had been surprised to hear, from his rounds of the Gather, how little regard the rest of the miners had for Tarik. In fact, Kindan got the distinct impression that they were all only putting up with him as a favor to Natalon. Oh, there were a few—two, to be exact—who thought highly of Tarik, but Kerdal and Panit were old cronies of Tarik's and even the talk from their wives led Kindan to believe that their loyalty was due to hopes of high rewards from Tarik rather than any actual camraderie they felt toward him.

"But what about her parents?" Zenor persisted. Before Kindan could make any reply, Zenor's jaw dropped. He grabbed Kindan's arm and turned him around. "Too late."

Kindan saw Natalon and Jenella enter the room. The new baby was in Jenella's arms. Behind them, Kindan saw a wide-eyed Dalor looking all around the crowded room. Kindan leapt forward to greet them.

"My Lord, my Lady," Kindan said to Natalon and Jenella, executing the sweeping bow that Master Zist had drilled into him over the past several sevendays. "Master Zist extends his welcome. He is there," Kindan pointed, "in conversation with Trader Tarri."

Kindan waved toward the table on which the musical instruments had been placed, from which Nuella was playing a lively pipe ditty. "I am lucky to have someone who chose to accompany me tonight," he said. "I'm sure you've never met her before. I was given to believe that she is one of the trader's group who wanted to sit in on the festivities. I hope you don't mind."

Natalon listened to all of Kindan's speech with an abstracted air until his wife grabbed his arm urgently and turned him toward Nuella. Jenella gave Kindan a piercing look.

"If I've done wrong, my Lady," Kindan said, "I am sure I could ask the lady to step down."

Natalon glared for a moment at Kindan, then at Nuella. Jenella tightened her grasp on his arm and shook her head. "I have always wanted to hear the pipes played," Natalon said after a moment's thought.

Dalor, who had been behind his mother and father and not quite concentrating on their conversation, suddenly stiffened as he noticed Nuella and then relaxed again as he digested the conversation in front of him.

"She plays very sweetly," he declared. He gave Kindan a look that was part thanks, part warning. Kindan nodded in acknowledgment.

"Well, I must get back to my duties." Kindan inclined his head toward Natalon and Jenella and strode quickly back to the musicians' table.

As Nuella's song came to an end, Kindan whispered to her, "That went well."

"Not from what I heard," Nuella whispered back. Kindan blushed at the thought of her hearing what he'd said—not so much for the words but for his ham-fisted way of saying them.

Chagrined, he turned back to the crowd. People were growing restless, waiting for a new song. Instead of reaching for the drum, Kindan opened his mouth and sang the first song to come to his mind. It was "The Morning Dragon Song."

Partway through the first verse, a haunting counterpoint joined in. It was Nuella on the pipes. Kindan nearly stopped singing, he was so surprised by the beauty of her melody. Instead, he raised his voice slightly and let her weave her pipes through the song.

As the last words faded away, Nuella's piping chirped a last response and faded, into a silence that Kindan hadn't heard all evening long. Then there was a thunderous applause. Kindan was thrilled to see Master Zist on his feet clapping as loudly as the others. Even more astonishing was Nuella's voice in his ear: "Can we do another?"

◆

In the end, they did six more duets before the night was over. Zenor even managed, with Kindan's connivance, to sneak a dance with Nuella.

"She'll follow your lead," Kindan told him. When Zenor looked balky about dancing, Kindan said, "It's either her or one of your sisters, you know that."

Nuella was radiant as Kindan handed her down from the table into Zenor's arms. Kindan suppressed a smile as he saw Nuella school her expression before Zenor could see it. With matched let's-humor-Kindan looks they took their places on the floor.

Master Zist joined Kindan on the musician's table with his fiddle for a rollicking song that challenged the dancers to keep up. Kindan smiled as he watched Nuella and Zenor navigate their way through the song—with the occasional squeak over a squashed toe.

"They're too young to match, and you're too young to be

matchmaker," Master Zist whispered in Kindan's ear when the song was over.

"They're friends," Kindan replied. "And at a Gather the only thing they can do together is dance."

When Nuella returned to the table, she was tired but exhilarated.

Master Zist waved Kindan off with a meaningful look. "You take a break, lad. This young one and I will see what a fiddle and a pipe can do."

Kindan nodded back and walked over to the banquet table. There were none of Milla's dainties left and scant else to eat, but there was good clear water, mulled wine, and *klah* for the taking. Kindan's stomach grumbled as he wolfed down a few vegetables, but he really wanted the water more and it was a while before his thirst was slaked enough to let him wander the room.

He was pleased at all the praise he got from trader and miner alike for his singing. However, he knew that Master Zist was expecting him to do more than bask in praise, so he made himself small and wandered toward the knots of people he'd noticed from the musician's table.

"So the watch-wher didn't come?" Kindan heard a voice say. "What of it? Can't recall much good ever coming from one." The voice belonged to Panit, one of Tarik's men.

The other men in the crowd weren't so sure, it seemed. Several wondered why the apprentice with the watch-wher had decided not to come. Kindan heard an undertone of worry in their voices.

"Been too many cave-ins," one voice grumbled.

"Lazy people, that's what it is," Panit replied. "They get lazy, thinking a watch-wher will save them. They get careless. We're better off without 'em." There was a pause. "But it bothers me that Natalon's so keen on having one."

Kindan snuck away, troubled. He *knew* that watch-whers were important. Shards! Wasn't it Panit himself whom Dask had pulled out of the mines? If people were bothered about working without a watch-wher, why *not* get more? And why would Panit want people to think Natalon was lazy? If they thought the head miner was lazy, would they want to stick at working the mine? Or would they leave like that unnamed apprentice and his watch-wher?

◆

After the Gather, when Kindan and Master Zist had trundled back to their cothold, the Harper called Kindan into the study to talk.

"You and Nuella did a remarkable job on 'The Morning Dragon Song,' " Master Zist said.

"Thank you."

"I'd like to work with you on some other vocal pieces," Master Zist continued. "I think we should try a duet."

"What about Nuella?" Kindan asked.

Master Zist shook his head sadly. "When the traders leave, she'll have to 'leave' with them."

"But you teach her, don't you?"

"Yes," Master Zist allowed, "and I am very careful in how I schedule her lessons."

"I don't understand why Natalon wants to keep her a secret," Kindan said, his face reflecting all the injustice he felt.

Master Zist shook his head. "I cannot tell you why—that is Natalon's secret."

"Nuella told me. It seems like a bad secret," Kindan replied.

"Your drumming was good tonight," Master Zist said, changing the subject. "I will start you on learning drum sequences, and you can start training some of the other youngsters—"

"I'm as old as Zenor!"

Master Zist raised a cautioning finger to his lips. "As I was saying, some of the other youngsters who are too impetuous and could use the exercise to burn off some of their excess energy."

Kindan accepted this new assignment with a shrug. "What happened with the trader?"

Master Zist smiled. "I thought I did rather well, there. I asked her about the state of the trail up here, and when she told me how muddy it was, I suggested that she could do with a delay of a few days to let the roads dry out more."

His eyes twinkled. "Naturally, she caught on immediately that we wanted the delay for some reason and we commenced to bargaining."

As Master Zist explained, Trader Tarri tried to negotiate a lower price for their coal, but Master Zist countered by pointing out the risks of losing a fully loaded coal-dray on the slippery trail back down to Crom Hold. That would not be good for the trader's profits at all. He pointed out that it also would not do for the trail to Camp Natalon to get a reputation as dangerously slippery. So Master Zist offered that the camp would pay half their food and board for an additional day. Tarri demanded that the miners send out parties to spread gravel on the worst parts of the trail, saying that it would benefit the miners more than the traders. Master Zist countered with an offer of enough gravel to spread over the difficult parts but the traders would have to do it themselves.

"She said, 'Done.' And that was that." Master Zist sat back in his chair looking quite pleased with himself. "And how did you get on with settling in the new apprentices?"

Kindan explained where he'd found lodgings for all the new apprentices.

"I suspect you're right about Tarik's reaction to housing four," Master Zist said when Kindan had finished.

Kindan snorted derisively. Master Zist raised an eyebrow inquiringly.

"Did you hear what Tarik's men are saying about Natalon?" Kindan asked.

"No," Master Zist began slowly. "My apprentice has not yet seen fit to tell me."

Kindan felt himself flushing.

"Sorry," he said and proceeded to repeat everything he could remember of the conversations he'd heard at the evening's Gather. At the end he looked up at the Harper and asked, "Why is it that Natalon puts up with Tarik? And why does Tarik seem to hate his own nephew so?"

Master Zist sighed. "I was hoping maybe you could tell me," he said ruefully.

"And watch-whers," Kindan said, adding them to the list as an afterthought. He wrinkled his brow.

"And why didn't that apprentice come to the Camp?"

"That maybe I can answer," Master Zist said. "I happened to work my way around to that very question with Trader Tarri."

Kindan was all ears.

"From what I gather," Zist continued, "and she was very circumspect about it all, it seems that the apprentice in question decided that his Master's wrath was less troubling than life in this Camp."

"The only thing *I* fear more than my Master's wrath is death," Kindan said with an apologetic look at the Harper.

Master Zist laughed. "Yes, and that was exactly Trader Tarri's observation."

"So you think the apprentice was afraid of dying in the mine?"

"Or losing his watch-wher," Master Zist remarked. "I doubt the bonds between watch-wher and wherhandler are as strong as that between dragon and rider, but the loss must be pretty hard regardless."

"It is," Kindan said with feeling. "I was not bound to Dask and it still hurts."

Master Zist reached out and squeezed Kindan's shoulder gently. "I know, lad. You've been through a lot. Better days are ahead."

"The other miners were complaining that we need watch-whers in the mines," Kindan said. "But Panit said that only lazy miners need watch-whers." He shook his head, sadly. "Panit's one of Tarik's men, but Dask still saved him."

"Well, we've the new apprentices now," Master Zist reflected. "Let's see how things work when they're in the mines, eh?"

Kindan nodded blearily.

"And now to bed with you, lad," Master Zist said. "It's way too late and you've been up late two nights running. You sleep in tomorrow."

◆

The first trader caravan marked more than the end of the winter thaw. Sevenday after sevenday caravans rolled in at all hours of the day, loading up with coal and heading back out again to Crom Hold, or farther to Telgar, where the Smithcraft made the steel that rimmed the wheels of the drays, formed the bodies of the pot-bellied stoves and ovens that Milla so loved, was turned into plowshares, dragon's tack, and countless other things that could only be made from steel.

Natalon had decided that with the new apprentices he could start a third shift. He set them to building a second mine entrance, farther down the mountainside, closer to his hold. While Tarik and his cronies grumbled about work with no reward, the rest of the miners were relieved to know that there would now be more than just the one entrance to the mine.

Natalon promoted his old friend, Toldur, to lead the new shift. Zenor tried desperately to get himself assigned to the new shift, in the hope of "finally getting *into* the mines" and was bitterly disappointed when Regellan was chosen instead.

"Look at it this way," Kindan said, trying to cheer up his friend. "With Natalon you get on just at dawn and off just at dusk—the babies are all asleep by then. Regellan gets off his shift tired, only to be woken by your littlest one every morning."

Zenor glowered but said nothing more. Kindan couldn't think of anything to say that might cheer up his old friend. Later, he realized sadly that he didn't have all that much to say to Zenor anymore. Zenor was rarely in class with the Harper, never on the watch-heights, and always tired from his long days in the mine.

Kindan was always dealing with the younger ones, setting the watch for the watch-heights, learning drum lore and messaging, and rarely found himself with a night to himself. Not sharing the same experiences, they found they had little in common these days.

On the other hand, Kindan found himself talking a lot with Nuella. Master Zist had allowed her to join in their music-making occasionally, and the three of them had spent many happy hours making music or listening while one of them played a solo. Privately, Master Zist told Kindan that Nuella's voice was "passable," but that didn't stop any of them from enjoying her efforts.

Kindan also found himself enjoying the evenings when it was just he and Master Zist. Early on, they had found that their voices complemented each other's marvelously. The Harper delighted in finding and composing new duets for them.

As spring gave way to summer and summer faded into fall, Kindan felt happier than he could ever remember.

CHAPTER VI

Cromcoal, Cromcoal, burning bright
Warm the cold of winter's night.
Cromcoal, Cromcoal, underground
Where the best of all coal's found.

For all the dangers of the mines, it was true that Natalon had found a rich vein of coal. Rumor had it that the Master-Miner himself had spoken favorably of it. Still, it would take more than favorable words for Camp Natalon to become Mine Natalon, a mine permanently listed on the Crom Hold master list—with Natalon as its leader.

Accidents in the mines continued to plague their efforts. "Without a watch-wher, we haven't a chance of knowing where the ground's good or not," miners grumbled in Natalon's hearing.

Natalon did not need to hear the grumbling—he knew it himself. Regardless of his uncle Tarik's sour opinion, Camp Natalon needed another watch-wher. He'd said as much to the MasterMiner, who had listened appreciatively and had told him that he'd ask the Lord Holder to put their name on the list. But Natalon knew how long that list was, and their Camp was the last on it.

Strangely, it was Master Zist who brought him the news. Or rather, it was the harper drums and Kindan.

The boy had been practicing with the message drums and all the drum rolls for many days. Zist had put him in charge of training the group of lads that Natalon had elected to be the Camp's drummers, so it was natural that Kindan was up on the heights when the message came in. It was an odd message, and while he could transcribe it, he didn't understand it.

He brought it down to Master Zist, who had just finished with the first years. *Aleesa will trade,* the message read.

Zist read the message, gave Kindan an undecipherable look, and then said to himself, "Well, I suppose I'll have to show this to Natalon."

Kindan found himself tagging along behind the old Harper. Zist turned back once, waggled his white eyebrows at the youngster, and continued on his way.

Natalon was at the mine entrance, talking in a low voice with the shaft foreman. He looked up at their approach, frowning slightly as he recognized Kindan.

"It concerns him," Zist said, answering Natalon's look and handing him the note.

"Hmmph," Natalon grunted, taking the note and glancing at it. "So, she'll trade, will she? Doesn't like the cold, I'll bet." He eyed the cloudy sky. "And it'll be a very cold winter, that's no doubt."

"You realize that she can only trade you the chance," Zist

said, his eyes traveling from Natalon to Kindan. "The rest is up to the lad."

"Yes, I understand," Natalon replied. He looked sharply at Kindan. "They say blood tells. You'll have a chance to prove it now."

Master Zist nodded agreeably and laid a hand on Kindan, guiding him away from the miner.

"Blood tells?" Kindan repeated.

Master Zist nodded. "You'd better hope so, youngster. Natalon's betting a winter's supply of coal on you."

"Master Zist!" Natalon shouted down the hill to them.

The Harper looked back and waved to show that he had heard.

"Light the beacon and show the flag for a dragonrider," Natalon yelled.

The Harper waved his arms in acknowledgment.

Kindan's eyes bulged wide. "We're going to send for a dragon?"

"That'd be a first for you, wouldn't it?" Zist asked, his face breaking into a wide grin. "We'll have to ask for a ride—Aleesa's hold is too far away and we'll need swift transport."

"A dragon! Do you think it'll be a bronze or a blue or—" Kindan was overwhelmed with anticipation.

"We'll be glad of whichever we get. And you'll be doubly so." Master Zist glanced back up the hill as they reached the clearing. "I only hope that Natalon's as good a bargainer as he is a miner."

◆

That night, when he and the Master were seated for their dinner, Kindan raised the issue that he had kept in the back of his mind the whole day. "What is up to me, Master Zist? And who is Master Aleesa?"

Master Zist's eyes glinted under his white eyebrows as his mouth curved up in a smile. "You have learned to keep things to yourself, I see."

"You've taught me that there are times to listen and times to talk," Kindan agreed.

The Harper's smile faded. "This is a time to listen, then.

"You've heard how badly the Camp needs another watch-wher," he continued. "After that wherhandler apprentice declined his assignment here, Natalon figured—rightly, I believe—that we would not get another anytime soon."

"Is Master Aleesa the Master of wherhandlers?" Kindan asked, wondering why he hadn't heard anything about this from his fathers or brothers.

"No more than there is a Master of fire-lizards or a Master of dragons," the Harper responded. Kindan raised an eyebrow, mimicking Master Zist's own questioning expression. "Master Aleesa is the wherhandler of a queen watch-wher. Her 'Master' is an honorary title. Natalon's trading for an egg."

"Blood tells . . ." Kindan eyes grew wide as he comprehended Natalon's meaning.

"You want me to raise a watch-wher?" he asked in a shocked whisper. He struggled not to blurt out, "But I want to be a Harper!"

Master Zist faced him gravely across the table. "Natalon thinks—and I have to agree—that unless we can get a watch-wher soon, the mine will fail."

Kindan took a deep breath, clenched his mouth tightly shut, and lowered his eyes from the MasterHarper's. Slowly, he found himself nodding in agreement.

◆

The beacon was lit and the flag flew for two whole days before there was any sign of an answer. At last a dragon appeared in the sky, swooped around the flagpole, dipped over the beacon, and then blinked out of existence—going *between*, to somewhere else.

Kindan, whose duties had been stretched to include manning the beacon fire, saw the dragon and waved excitedly at it as it performed its antics and disappeared. His tale was the talk of the camp with the youngsters. Zist listened appreciatively and gently guided him to crafting a better tale, so that by the end of a sevenday, Kindan's story took a full fifteen minutes to tell and left all eyes peering up to the sky, hoping for a glimpse of their own.

When not guiding Kindan in his storytelling, Master Zist was consoling Natalon, who was growing desperate for a dragonrider.

"What is taking them so long?" Natalon moaned. "How long can Aleesa wait?"

Zist shook his head. "I don't know. Fort Weyr would have dispatched a dragonrider on the same day, even if the watch rider couldn't land."

"Where would a dragon land here?" Natalon asked, eyes darting around the camp. "Is that the problem? Is there no suitable landing?"

"Dragons aren't so big that they couldn't land here, Natalon," the old Harper reassured him. "Only the bronzes or queens would have problems, and then they'd probably land up on the heights near the beacon."

"Would the dragonriders walk all the way down from there?" Natalon asked, somewhat astonished at the notion of a dragonrider walking the half mile that he made all the camp youngsters take at a run.

"I don't see why not," Zist responded with a grin. "They do have feet."

Natalon glowered at him, but the old Harper was unrepentant and kept grinning until finally Natalon smiled. "I suppose they do at that."

Zist slapped the Miner on the shoulder. "They do."

"What if they don't come soon? What if it's too late?"

With a sigh, Zist answered, "When you get to my age, Natalon, you learn to take things as they come."

Natalon laughed. "When I get to be your age, Master Zist, I'm sure I'll be able."

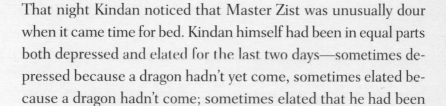

That night Kindan noticed that Master Zist was unusually dour when it came time for bed. Kindan himself had been in equal parts both depressed and elated for the last two days—sometimes depressed because a dragon hadn't yet come, sometimes elated because a dragon hadn't come; sometimes elated that he had been chosen, and a whole year of coal traded, to get a watch-wher egg, sometimes depressed for the same reason.

"A lot's being asked of you, lad, you know that, don't you?" Zist said to him.

"Yes."

"Your father taught you about watch-whers, right?" Zist asked.

Kindan shook his head mutely.

"You know how to hatch 'em, how to feed them, and how to rear them, right?"

Again Kindan shook his head. "My father used to say that I'd never be expected to do such things. I was too little to train, the older boys said."

Master Zist closed his eyes briefly. When he opened them

again, he smiled. "Well, you're a bright lad, I'm sure you'll find yourself able."

"I won't let down my Hold—er, Camp," Kindan said, despite his fears.

Master Zist pulled the blankets farther up and tucked them around Kindan. "I'm sure you won't, lad," he said firmly. Kindan noticed that the Harper had a troubled look in his eyes, something others likely wouldn't have seen.

"Is something wrong?"

Master Zist raised an eyebrow in surprise. "You've gotten far too good at reading my moods, youngster," he said. He took a breath and let it out with a sigh. "There is a problem, maybe only a slight problem, but it has me concerned."

Kindan gave him an encouraging look.

"Maybe it's just that I've mixed feelings about all this," the Harper muttered to himself. He looked at Kindan and said, "You know if you do this, you'll not be my apprentice much longer?"

Kindan nodded solemnly. The thought had been on his mind for the past several days. He was torn between his duty to the miners—Natalon and Zenor in particular—and his own dream of being a Harper. He had held the fancy that perhaps he could do both and hadn't tried to examine the idea too closely because, in his heart, he knew the idea was unrealistic.

"Well . . ." The Harper took a breath and plunged on. "Our meeting with Master Aleesa is set for tomorrow."

"Tomorrow?" Kindan sat bolt upright. "But what if a dragonrider doesn't come? What if they won't take us?"

Master Zist made soothing motions with his hands. "It may still turn out all right, even so," he said.

"How?"

Master Zist frowned, thoughtfully. "This is a craft secret, understand?"

Kindan paused, then nodded solemnly.

"And not a harpercraft secret, a— I suppose you'd call it a dragoncraft secret," the Harper explained. He continued, "You've proved you can keep your secrets, but this one especially you must not reveal."

Master Zist took another breath and plunged into his tale. "Long ago, when I was a journeyman, I was posted to Benden Weyr," he said. Kindan's eyes widened in amazement. "I made many a good friend while I was there. And used all of the poor healing skills I'd ever had and learned more."

He gave Kindan a frank look. "I was not all that good at healing—and still am not—so I was posted to copy their Records."

He smiled at his memories of long ago. "There was a Hatching the first sevenday I was there," he said.

Kindan couldn't help but gasp at the thought. Master Zist grinned at him and nodded, confirming that the event was just as amazing as Kindan had imagined.

"Twenty-five eggs on the Hatching Ground," the Harper continued. "And the last was slow to crack. Big, but slow to crack. The dragonriders said that it was probably a bronze and they were worried about it. The remaining Candidates were all gathered about it and I was high up in the viewing stands so I couldn't see all that went on, but finally the crowd opened up and one lad—the first one to greet me when I arrived at the Weyr—Matal, Impressed the bronze."

Kindan realized that he'd been holding his breath and let it out slowly, so as not to distract the Harper.

"I was so excited for my friend—M'tal, now—that I let out a

loud cheer," the Harper said, his face going red. "The sound must have echoed over by the hatchling, because it startled and caught its wing in its claws. Then it really started to get frantic and it seemed to take forever before M'tal and the others could calm it down. When they did, I could see that the dragon's wing was terribly mangled."

Kindan let out a gasp of shock and sympathy.

"It was all my fault," Zist said bitterly.

" 'Get help!' the Weyrleader shouted. I ran out as quickly as I could, hoping to find the Weyr healer only to run full tilt into someone coming the other way.

"I didn't recognize him. He pulled me up. He had a sack of supplies. 'It'll be all right,' he told me. 'It wasn't your fault. Do you want to help fix it?'

" 'Please,' I said. He grabbed my arm and spun me around, back to the Hatching Ground. Together we approached the wounded dragon—Gaminth—and M'tal.

"He had me put numbweed on the gashes. He had all the supplies that were needed, some thick fabric on which to lay the torn wing, and fine needles to sew the torn pieces together. We were done in no time.

" 'He'll be all right now,' the man said. M'tal looked up and started to say his thanks but stopped, looking from the other man to me and back again, gasping.

" 'You!' M'tal exclaimed. I didn't understand at the time, thinking that he recognized the healer.

" 'And you,' the man said with a smile. 'I've got to be going.' When I made to follow him, he held up a hand to stop me. 'I can find my way out, thank you.' And he left.

"Gaminth healed just fine, and M'tal has since gone on to become the Weyrleader of Benden Weyr," the Harper finished.

"And who was the man, then? Why did Lord M'tal say 'You!'?" Kindan asked.

Master Zist smiled. "Ah, there's a song in that answer," he said. Kindan raised his eyebrows. "I won't sing it for you, but I'll tell you the title. It's called 'When I Met Myself Healing.'"

Kindan mouthed the title to himself and looked up sharply at the Harper. "You met yourself? The healer was you? But older? How?"

"It's a craft secret," the Harper replied. "But maybe we can get the dragonriders to do it for us again."

Kindan pursed his lips in thought. "Dragons go *between* from one place to another—can they go *between* times?"

Master Zist smiled and nodded. "You'll make a good Harper."

"But I'm going to be a wherhandler now," Kindan answered sourly.

Master Zist's smile faded. "Yes, if that's your choice."

Kindan's face screwed up in anguish. "I can't let the others down," he said. "I'm sure I'll love being a wherhandler and I'll get to stay with my friends."

"There is that," the Harper said. "If you became a Harper, you'd have to apprentice in the Harper Hall and there's no telling where you'd be posted." He nodded to himself. "You're right to see the good in the situation."

Kindan nodded glumly.

◆

Kindan was awoken roughly the next morning. Zist was shaking him, a pitcher of cold water in his other hand.

"Up now, lad!" the Harper said gruffly. Kindan rushed out of bed, looking for his clothes. "No time for it, just throw this on." Zist threw a cloak at him. "And get your boots on."

Kindan worked as fast as he could but he was fumble-fingered in his excitement.

Master Zist growled at him, "All haste, too much waste! Take a breath and try again."

As soon as he'd finished lacing up his boots, Master Zist rushed the two of them out of the cottage and up toward the beacon heights.

It was pitch black outside and Kindan only made it up the cliff without stumbling because he knew the trail well enough to walk it in his sleep.

Three figures greeted them at the top by the beacon. And one was huge. Kindan looked up and up and finally found the face of the dragon. It peered down at him as though he were a mere trundlebug, blew a breath out its nostrils that turned to steam in the cold morning, and then looked away.

"Here they are," Natalon said. "This is Master Zist, lately of the Harper Hall, and Kindan, the son of our late wher-watcher."

The man whom Natalon addressed yawned pointedly. "You set a beacon for this?"

Kindan sensed Master Zist tense angrily beside him.

"We had hoped that we could ask for the hospitality of transport," Natalon replied. "We give fair tithe."

"The beacon and dragon pennant are for emergencies, Miner," the dragonrider responded, beckoning to his dragon and preparing to depart.

"Lord—?" Zist called urgently, stopping the irritated dragonrider in his tracks.

"I am Lord D'gan, Harper, lately Weyrleader of Telgar Wyer," the dragonrider replied, drawing himself up to his full height.

"We are most honored, Lord D'gan," Zist said, sketching a courtly bow. Hastily, Kindan copied him as best he could. "Camp

Natalon is a prosperous Camp with good prospects, my Lord. We have found much coal here which is greatly in demand—"

"Not by dragons or their riders, Harper," D'gan interjected. "If you were mining firestone, it would be a different matter. I care little if Holders are a bit cold this winter."

"We are mining Smithcoal, my Lord," Natalon said. "Our coal is of such quality that the MasterSmith himself has laid in a large order for it."

D'gan cocked an eyebrow at him. "I am very pleased for the MasterSmith."

"My Lord," Zist said, and Kindan could see signs of restrained anger in the old Harper's face, "that coal is used to make the steel that binds your fighting straps, strengthens your helmet, and buckles your belt."

"I am glad to hear it," D'gan replied. "We have had many complaints on the quality of steel coming from the Smith Hall. Now I know the source." He moved toward his dragon.

"My Lord!" Zist called. "Of old the dragonriders of Pern have been courteous in responding to the just requests of the Holders and Crafters."

D'gan stopped and whirled back, his hand on the dagger at his side. "Courtesy is much lacking in this Camp. Of old the dragonriders have been given more respect and have not been asked to provide frivolous thrill rides. Do not presume on my courtesy anymore!"

Kindan drew in an outraged gasp, covering his mouth quickly to hide his gaff.

But both Natalon and the Harper had also reacted to the accusation.

"Thrill ride?" Master Zist repeated, appalled, staring at D'gan.

"It is indeed to redress a serious problem at this Camp. We

have no watch-wher, and our mining efforts cannot continue without the aid of one," Natalon explained.

"We are to collect a new egg from Master Aleesa and time is of the essence," the Harper went on.

"Oh." There was studied insult in D'gan's manner as he inspected the three in front of him.

"Our Dask died leading us to a tunnel collapse," Kindan was bold enough to say.

Master Zist put his hand on Kindan's shoulder, a gesture more approval than rebuke.

"It enabled us to rescue the others," Natalon said.

"So, a watch-wher is your hero?" D'gan added.

To everyone's surprise, the dragon dropped his head toward their cluster and made a funny snort. It sounded a bit like a noise Dask might have made.

"He was, I gather, just doing his duty."

Stung, Kindan replied. "Had he rested, he would have lived. He did not rest while miners were trapped in a dark cave-in."

D'gan made a dismissive gesture with his hand. "You have only convinced me that Telgar's previous Weyrleader was far too accommodating. Asking a dragon to give transport to collect a watch-wher." He snorted again and smoothed his hair back. "Thread is coming again, as you should know, Harper. Do not presume on Interval courtesies anymore."

With that, D'gan turned and flung himself onto his dragon's back. In two chilling beats of its wings, the dragon was airborne and, in another, *between*.

Natalon turned questioningly to Master Zist, but the old Harper was too busy swearing to offer him any advice.

"What shall we do now?" Kindan asked after having learned enough new oaths from the angry Harper to dine on for a week.

Master Zist paused in his swearing, aware that Kindan had been listening intently. "You'll remember that I believe that any youngster who swears should have his mouth washed out with soap. And I shall remember not to swear in your presence."

"You were quite justified," Natalon said from behind them. "I have never met a dragonrider before—"

Zist held up a hand. "Do not say anything against dragon-riders until you've had a fair sample."

"And how will I get that?" Natalon snapped back.

"I have my ways," Master Zist answered. He looked at Kindan. "Put out the beacon and lower the flag. When you're done, meet me at the drums."

When Kindan had completed his tasks, Master Zist had pre-sented him with a message to beat out on the drums. The mes-sage had been simple: "Zist requests M'tal." Kindan had had to spell out both "Zist" and "M'tal," so the drumming was longer than he was used to. He waited until he got an acknowledg-ment from the two nearest drums and then reported to Mas-ter Zist.

"What are you doing here?" Zist bellowed when he saw the boy. "Get back up to those drums and wait for a response."

"Master?"

"What?" Zist bellowed again, clearly in a rare anger.

"Could someone send me some breakfast?"

The Harper drew breath for another bellow, saw the pale look of the lad, and let his breath out again. "Very well. And take this sweetroll up with you."

"Thanks!" Kindan answered, and trotted off back up the hill with the sweetroll in his tunic.

"I'll send some proper clothes for you, as well," Zist boomed after him. Unseen in the early morning light, Kindan turned bright red as he realized that he'd met his first dragonrider in his pajamas.

◆

Later in the day, Master Zist trudged up to the drum heights with another young lad beside him. Blond and brown-eyed, the lad was happy to hand his bundles to Kindan—Kindan's day clothes. Asking the Harper to carry such a bundle up to the heights by himself would be tantamount to insult.

Kindan tried not to look embarrassed as he took his clothes from the other boy and slid into them under his cloak but Master Zist must finally have noticed his discomfort for he charitably asked, "So, Kindan, what did you think of your first look at a dragon?"

The other boy gave Kindan a look of awe, but it was Master Zist who was surprised by Kindan's offhand answer: "Oh, they're pretty enough, but you'd never fit one in a mine."

◆

Someone shook Kindan awake and he jumped up with a start, aware that he had fallen asleep on watch. It was deep night. The beacon burned bright, still fueled by the last logs Kindan had piled on it earlier, so he figured he couldn't have been asleep more than an hour, two at most.

The person who shook him was dressed in leather—a dragonrider.

"My Lord," Kindan said, sketching a quick bow. Behind him he heard a gentle snort from way up high. Turning, he saw the dim outline of a dragon, its great eyes peering down at him with interest. "I am Kindan. Master Zist asked me to keep watch—"

The dragonrider smiled. He was nearly as old as Master Zist, Kindan judged. His hair sparkled with silver strands in the night. His eyes were amber, and he was all that Kindan had ever imagined a dragonrider to be—except, perhaps, older.

"Well, Kindan, please tell Master Zist that M'tal has responded to his request," the dragonrider said.

"No need," a voice called from the darkness, startling Kindan. "And do stop jumping, Kindan, you'll wear yourself out."

"He seemed quite worn out already," M'tal remarked.

Master Zist stepped into the light. "I'd noticed," he said lightly, "which is why I decided to keep him company for a bit."

"You were here, too?" Kindan asked in aggrieved tones.

The two men laughed.

"It's a habit of leadership, youngster," M'tal remarked. "It's always a good idea to check up on a sentry from time to time."

With a frown, the dragonrider turned his attention to Zist. "When I got your summons, I had expected to find you at the Harper Hall. I was sorry to hear of your loss."

"Thank you," Master Zist replied gravely. With a flick of his hand, he changed the subject. "Thank you for coming here. I was hoping to ask a favor of you."

M'tal's eyebrows creased in curiosity. "This—" He stopped with an inquiring wave around the campsite

"Camp," Zist supplied helpfully.

M'tal nodded. "This Camp looks to Telgar, does it not?" He looked at Kindan.

"It does, my Lord," Kindan said.

"Weyrleader D'gan did not consider our request a good use of his resources," Master Zist explained.

M'tal lips thinned as he considered Master Zist's response. "Ah, and what was your request?"

"Miner Natalon requested transport for himself, me, and Kindan here to meet with Aleesa the WherMaster," Zist replied.

"Kindan?" M'tal repeated, surprised.

"Miner Natalon has promised a winter's supply of coal to the WherMaster if she will give Kindan the chance of a watchwher's egg," Zist said. Seeing the dragonrider's interested look, he added, "Kindan's father was the camp's previous wherhandler."

"I see," M'tal replied. "And when is this meeting to take place?"

Master Zist's reply was an angry mutter. "Yesterday."

———◆———

"Yesterday?" Natalon repeated in astonishment later in the morning, banging his fists down hard on the table in the camp's main dining hall. "Yesterday? I've pledged a whole winter's supply to someone for a deal that ended *yesterday*?"

M'tal had lifted his mug of *klah* from the table at Natalon's first word, but Kindan and Master Zist were not as prescient— *klah* spilled from their mugs onto their tunics and ran to the floor below. At a wave from Master Zist, Kindan rushed off and found a couple of rags with which to wipe up the spill.

"There are certain Harper songs—" Master Zist began, only to splutter to a stop at the sight of Miner Natalon's face.

"My miners say they won't work if we can't get a watch-wher for them," Natalon said in dejected tones. "We've had two more near-disasters in the mines. Tunnel snakes have raided our stores. And I've promised a winter's supply of coal for—"

"For a chance at a watch-wher," M'tal broke in. "And you shall have that chance."

"How?" Natalon asked in disbelief.

"There are some old Harper songs," Master Zist began again.

Kindan's eyes danced, remembering their conversation several nights back.

"Which I hope will be quietly retired," M'tal said with a pointed glance at the old Harper.

Master Zist bowed his head. "I am sure, Weyrleader M'tal, that my old head is already having quite a hard time remembering them."

"Good," M'tal replied with a twinkle in his eye. "I shall return at noon, so that your lad can have some time to rest."

"I'm not tired, my Lord," Kindan lied stoutly.

———◆———

Minutes after lying down in a shuttered room, Kindan was fast asleep. He awoke to the sound of voices talking softly outside his room.

"They're not really like dragons, you know," M'tal was saying.

"So I gathered," Zist replied. "But they're not like fire-lizards either. There's not much lore about them, aside from a simple song or two."

"Perhaps you could learn more from Master Aleesa," M'tal suggested.

Zist snorted. "I'm sure I could, if Natalon would let me."

"I can't see why he'd stop a Harper."

"Aye, he probably wouldn't," Zist agreed. "But he'd be mighty curious—probably too curious—as to why I have to ask Master Aleesa when I'm supposed to have an expert sleeping in the room next door."

"The boy?" M'tal's voice was full of surprise.

"His father was the last wherhandler here," Master Zist reminded him. "Natalon's desperate, and he's convinced himself that Danil taught Kindan everything about watch-whers. Says that

Danil let the boy wash the watch-wher, and on the basis of that, he decided that Kindan must be special."

M'tal snorted. "Well, oiling a dragon is a big part of *my* job, so I could see that a wherhandler would spend a lot of his time washing his watch-wher—which might explain your miner's confusion." He shook his head as he caught Master Zist's somber expression.

"He'd be far too young to Impress a dragon, you know," the Weyrleader said soberly. "If the watch-whers are more like dragons or even like fire-lizards, I doubt he'll attach one."

Zist sighed. "He must. If he doesn't, then Camp Natalon will fail and he'll be blamed."

"That's an awful lot for one youngster to handle," M'tal noted.

"Well, he's got broad shoulders," Zist said. "They might bear the load."

To himself, Kindan swore that he would bear the load.

CHAPTER VII

Watch-wher, watch-wher in the mine,
Help save life, yours and mine,
Guide us in the darkest night,
With your keen unfailing sight.

"**B**etween only lasts as long as it takes to cough three times,"
M'tal told the others as he helped them up onto bronze
Gaminth's back.

"Cough three times?" Natalon repeated. He coughed experimentally three times. "Like that?"

Kindan was glad to hear the Miner ask the question; he had
been too afraid to ask it himself.

"Just like that," M'tal reassured him.

"It won't take any longer this time?" Master Zist asked with a
strange look in his eyes.

M'tal shook his head warily. "No, not longer. We'll be there in time."

"I don't see how," Natalon said sourly.

"Oh," M'tal replied airily, grinning at Master Zist, "dragons are faster than you think."

◆

When they were all settled on Gaminth's neck, M'tal made one last check of his passengers and called out to his dragon, "Let's fly, Gaminth."

The great bronze jumped into the air, swooped down toward the Camp, and with one beat of his wings soared high.

The dragon slowly flew higher. Master Zist knew that Gaminth was capable of much quicker ascents—in their youth, M'tal had been proud to illustrate his dragon's capabilities to those who were properly appreciative—so he guessed that the bronze rider was making this slow climb only to avoid upsetting his more nervous passengers. A quick glance assured him that Kindan, who was wide-eyed with an ear-to-ear grin, would never be considered a nervous passenger. Natalon, however, was quite pale.

M'tal turned back to them again. "We're ready to go *between*. Are you ready?"

"I still don't see how we can get there in time, my Lord," Natalon said, with only the slightest hint of nervousness.

M'tal grinned at him. "Trust me, we'll be on time," he answered. "You might find the effects a bit more draining than you'd think, but that's the price of the journey, as it were."

Natalon swallowed hard and nodded uncertainly.

M'tal took this for acceptance. "Good," he said. He turned to Zist and Kindan. "All ready?" When they nodded, he instructed them, "Take three deep breaths and hold the third one. Ready? One . . . two . . . three . . ."

And suddenly it was all darkness around them. Kindan felt a thrill of terror and excitement as he realized he could feel nothing but the press of the men before and behind him and the neck of the dragon beneath him.

M'tal's words came back to him: Between *only lasts as long as it takes to cough three times.* Kindan started coughing. One. Two. Three. *Four. Five.* He started to get worried.

We are almost there, a soundless voice said to him. Kindan was so surprised that he didn't react at all.

And then there was light. Or rather, lights. It was dark outside, as compared to the midday sun they'd left. Kindan could see a few twinkles spiraling toward them and realized with a start that they must be gliding steeply down to the ground. Unable to contain himself, he let out a whoop of pure joy. They had arrived—the day before they'd left.

"That's the spirit!" Master Zist shouted back over his shoulder.

"I think I'm going to be sick," Natalon moaned, his eyes squeezed firmly shut.

◆

"Do you understand what you're to do?" Aleesa asked Kindan.

"I think so," Kindan replied. His body felt tired and *stretched*— he wondered if that was from going back in time or because he was so nervous—but he was too excited to tell anyone.

Aleesa raised an eyebrow. "Thinking won't do, little one."

The WherMaster was much taller than Kindan. She was a lithe, slender person who spoke little. Kindan could tell by Natalon's manner that the miner was also awed by the WherMaster.

Kindan took a deep, calming breath. "I'm to bow to the queen and make my way toward the clutch. If she lets me, I'm to choose an egg and take it, bowing again and walking backward."

"She'd better let you," Natalon added in a hard voice. "There's a winter's coal gone either way."

Kindan gulped.

"Don't dawdle," Master Zist warned him.

"When you go in the cave," Master Aleesa said, pointing to a crevice in the side of the cliff, "bear right."

The crevice was wide enough for a watch-wher, and tall enough for Kindan—but just barely. It was also, Kindan discovered as he followed the way up and down, left and right, awfully twisty, like a tunnel snake's wiggle.

Kindan was amazed that Master Aleesa, who looked as if she had joint-ail, could possibly manage and then realized that she would have many to help her do her daily wher-caring. Still, as he entered the dark space, he knew her standards must be high because the place smelled very clean. He cleared his throat and murmured the soft chirps that his father had always used when entering Dask's lair.

Behind him he heard a surprised remark from Aleesa. "Well, at least the lad knows what to say to her."

Eyes opened up ahead of him, and in that light and the pale glow of light that filtered through from the crawlway, he could see the watch-wher, but not her eggs. Aleesa had said there were twelve, and he must make his own plea to the queen. She had refused two prospective handlers already. Kindan increased the intensity of his chirping, trying to sound kindly, as well as eager. He had to prove to Natalon that he was worth a whole winter's fuel coal—and some left over to keep the hatchling warm until its second, tougher coat came in. Remembering that, Kindan felt more confident. He knew more than he thought he did. Maybe blood *would* tell. Which reminded him of something else he had to do.

When he was close enough to the queen, he held out his right hand. There was not much of a scar left from where his father had slit his thumb pad to blood him to old Dask. He altered his sound to a reassuring tongue trill and showed her his palm. She ran her tongue over it. It was a nice, dry tongue. Sometimes Dask's had been slimy and not at all something you wanted licking you. He increased his trill to what he thought was a glad "Thank you."

She responded with a click of her own, and Kindan knew that he had performed an appropriate greeting. What should he do now? "May I please have one of your eggs?" His father had never had to ask such a thing, so he didn't know if there was a sound that was appropriate. He responded with a quizzical *brr*. He had been teased by his siblings because he could roll his r's and l's better than they did.

Although their family had done well by housing the mine's watch-wher, none of his brothers had aspired to their father's calling.

Well, he could be a sort of hero for the Camp, if he did get a watch-wher egg.

The men had been talking in fits and starts while they coasted a-dragonback down to the cliffside where Master Aleesa's hold was, reinforcing how important it was to rear a healthy specimen and maybe even breed a few themselves, if this new one met the Master's standards. Dask had been chosen to sire two clutches in his youth. Maybe that had been part of Aleesa's willingness to give Danil's family a chance, Kindan thought. He increased the intensity of his trill, making more complex noises, sinking into them his earnest entreaty. The watch-wher had opened her eyes wide at him now. Unable to control himself, Kindan yawned— he was still tired from all the recent early-morning rising.

"Excuse me," he said, deathly afraid that he had insulted her. "I'm tired. We went back in time to get here and—well, I'm afraid."

He bowed to her and formed the image in his mind of Gaminth and their journey back in time from tomorrow.

The queen gave a surprised *chirp*, and Kindan got the impression that she'd picked up the image from his mind. Her eyes intent on him, she twitched aside her wing. He gasped in astonishment at the pile of dimly glowing eggshells.

"Oh, how beautiful they are!" he exclaimed, leaning toward her hidden treasure and only recalling at the last moment that the queen would not permit just anyone to touch her eggs. He grabbed his hands back.

They were certainly not dragon eggs—at least according to all the Teaching Ballads Kindan had learned—being half the size and sort of rumpled, as if the layers of shell had been badly applied and the skin had wrinkled in forming. In fact, one egg had a distinct ring on one end, raised above the rest of the shell, like a necklace. But he had never seen anything like them. "How amazing they are!"

He almost fell into the eggs when she gave her wing a sudden flap and folded it against her backbone. Her spine did not have prominent ridges, as a dragon's would, so they'd be more comfortable to sit on. If one ever did. His father had ridden Dask, on some evenings when the air was heavier and easier for the watch-wher to fly in. Usually watch-whers didn't make the effort, especially with a rider, but Kindan *had* seen it happen.

Then he brought his mind back to the present and the realization that she had dropped her defensive posture. He made an interrogatory noise, and with a grace he hadn't expected she made a small gesture with her wing tip, from him to the eggs.

"I should choose?" he asked. Ever so carefully he extended his hand to her again.

She licked him, her tongue rasping his skin, before she inclined her head to him and then to her eggs.

"Oh kind one, oh gracious watch-wher," he said, trilling with his tongue when he finished speaking. He couldn't believe his luck.

"Shall I come rescue you?" Master Aleesa called.

"She's let me see her clutch," he called back over his shoulder.

"Then she means you to have one, young Kindan. Pick it, make your farewells of her, and leave. There are others here who want to try their luck."

Kindan shook his head in surprise, breathless with his success. Only which one should he pick? The children's selection chant popped into his head. Well, why not? Pointing his finger at each egg with each syllable, he chanted, "Eeny, meeny, tipsy teeny, ah vu bumberini. Isha gosha bumberosha, nineteen hundred and two. I pick you." His finger was pointing at the one with the odd ring.

He bundled it into his arms. It was heavier than he'd thought, and warm, but then the sands under him were warm as well. The shell felt hard enough that he could clasp it as tightly as he needed to and do no harm, which was fortunate, as he found it very awkward to clamber around on one hand and lurch forward. He turned back briefly and gave the loud trilled tongue sound of gratitude.

"Is the boy hurt?" someone outside asked.

"No, sir," Kindan said, ducking under the screen above the entrance to the lair. "Just happy."

Hands came under his arms and whooshed him out and onto his feet.

"All right, it's your turn, Losfir," Aleesa said, motioning for a short chunky man to enter the watch-wher's lair. She grinned at Kindan, her eyes twinkling with an expression of surprised approval. "Got the ringed one, I see. Good choice."

"Why? Why is it a good choice?" Natalon demanded.

"Just is," Aleesa said. "Knew how to talk to her, didn't you?" Grinning, she cocked her head at the lair from which only the sounds of scrambling could be heard. Then she chuckled. "That one hasn't a clue." She gave Kindan's right hand a look. "At least you knew how to talk and what to show for her favor."

"What? What?" Natalon demanded, irritated by all these cryptic remarks.

"Your lad here can explain at his leisure. Here come the others. You see that I get a delivery of that fine coal of yours by the next trader through Crom, or you'll never hear the last of it, Natalon. Away with you. You bore me."

Somehow Kindan knew not to take Aleesa's comment personally and helped stow the egg in the fleece-lined bag they had brought to protect it on the journey back to Crom.

"How long before it'll hatch?" he asked her, deciding that was a perfectly legitimate question.

She put a hand on the top of the egg in its bag. "Hmmmm. I'd say within the next sevenday. Possibly sooner. I'll have my drummer warn you if I hear others are hatching." She gave the egg a final proprietary caress.

"One more detail," Kindan said, as she began to turn away from them.

"Yes?" she replied, half-turning back to him. Her expression suggested he should not have to ask her details.

"My father raised Dask before I was born, so I just don't know what he ate right after he hatched."

He had phrased his query correctly.

"We've been experimenting, actually, on the best post-hatching meal. Watch-whers are not as insatiable as dragons, but they will gulp meat down and sometimes choke, as you know." She pinned Kindan with a fierce glare, and he nodded as if he knew exactly what she meant. "D'you have oats?"

Kindan nodded, glancing over at Natalon to be sure he was also listening to Aleesa.

"Then arrange to get fresh blood from whoever butchers at the camp. Make a porridge of the oats, using water, and add the blood as the oats thicken in the pot. I'd say a half-pail a day would be sufficient. If you keep the blood cool, a pailful should last over a day or two, no trouble. Most Camps or Holds slaughter every other day. Feed it as often as it wants, and some of the liver and lungs that might go to waste otherwise. Don't start meat hunks until three months, when it has enough back teeth to chew with. You can continue the porridge feeds in the morning until the hatchling starts to coat out."

Kindan nodded, mumbling something in his throat about being glad to start out this watch-wher with the best possible feeding in between his thanks for her suggestion. Then she turned back to deal with the newcomers.

"Well done, Kindan," Zist said, clapping him on the shoulder. "Well done, lad. What sort of soft talk did you employ?"

"Something learned from you, no doubt, Zist," M'tal said teasingly. "No matter, Kindan, well done. Let's get the two young-lings back home, and then we can all celebrate."

"And in time, please," Zist said with a bit of a bow to the dragonrider.

"No easier said than done," M'tal replied. "Come, lad, step up on Gaminth's knee and grab the safety strap. I'll give you a bit of a heave."

Keeping one hand firmly under his egg, Kindan made it to the dragon's back and settled down between two ridges with a sigh of relief. Curious, he glanced over at the lair just in time to see the man erupting out of it as if propelled by something strong and annoyed. He couldn't help giggling at Zist's remark about some folks not knowing when they weren't welcome.

"Didn't know how to sweet-talk her, I guess," M'tal added. "Proud of you, boy. Glad to have been able to help you out."

"This is just the beginning," Natalon remarked. "Are you up to it, lad?"

"Sir," Kindan said, swiveling around to speak to Natalon, "would you give Ima"—who was the main hunter and butcher for the camp—"the orders to let me get the blood I'll need? And to Swanee to allow me enough oats?"

"Of course I will," Natalon said briskly. "And loan you a big enough pot to make porridge for the watch-wher in. I doubt you'd have one large enough for the purpose."

The Miner looked a bit uncomfortable at the reminder that the lad was no longer living in his own home, where he would have had a good selection of pots.

"And I have some herbal candles to burn to get rid of the stench," Zist said, making a face as if he already knew how noxious the mixture would smell. "And you must promise me not to burn the oats."

"Yes, yes, of course," Kindan said and fixed his face forward just as M'tal warned them of their passage *between*.

When they returned to the camp, it seemed to Kindan as if they had only just left. It must have taken several hours to complete their mission, and yet not much had changed; the first carts, full of the black rock, still hadn't reached the top of the rail where their contents would be tilted over in the huge storage area. He shook his head as the dragon made a careful landing near the watch-wher's lair.

Natalon called out as the dragon settled to the ground. Tarik came rushing out of the shaft.

Natalon motioned for Kindan to descend first. "Help him down, Tarik," he ordered.

"You got the egg then?" Tarik asked, though it should have been obvious from the sack weighing down Kindan's shoulder that they had been successful. As Kindan swung his leg over the dragon's ridge, he was certain that Tarik had expected the journey to be fruitless. But he helped Kindan as if the boy had suddenly become fragile.

Politely, Kindan thanked Tarik, then made his way as fast as he could to the watch-wher's shed. He had prepared it carefully, with lots of straw. He felt the warm bricks he had placed under the floor of the small den. They hadn't cooled at all—which *was* odd, but he was just as glad that he didn't have to wrangle more in here just yet. Choosing a spot that he thought was just as warm as the hatching lair had been, he carefully took the egg out of the sack and set it down, piling the warm straw around it to approximate the cover and warmth of the queen's wing. He looked down at his handiwork and passed his hand over it, close to the straw. The heat felt sufficient. He was very hungry, though he had eaten a good breakfast just before the dragonrider had arrived.

Tarik and Natalon were talking together while Zist chatted with his old friend.

"Come, Kindan, we owe M'tal some hospitality. All that traveling made me hungry. How about you?" Zist held out his hand and, when Kindan reached him, waved in the direction of his cothold.

CHAPTER VIII

Watch-wher, watch-wher in the egg,
Grant to me the boon I beg.

M'tal begged off lunch, as he had to return to his Weyr soon.

"I don't want my stomach to get the wrong idea about what time it is," he explained with a wink at Kindan.

Kindan and Zist made a quick lunch of the bread and soup that had been kindly left for them in the Harper's kitchen. Kindan wished he'd asked Aleesa more questions, which he could have easily added when he explained that Dask had been a hatchling before he was born. When he mentioned this to Zist, the Harper frowned slightly.

"I shall see what I have here," he said, waving toward his small collection of hide-bound books on the shelf in the living area. "I don't recall there being much about watch-whers." He grimaced. "They weren't high on the Archival list when I did my time with the Master Archivist. Still, there might be some."

"I know my father—" Kindan faltered, still keenly feeling the loss of the one parent he had known. "—trained Dask with the other two Crom Hold watch-whers. They seem to educate each other."

"But you were talking to it," Zist said.

"I was talking to the queen, not the hatchling. Kids have to be taught to speak, you know."

"Yes, well, that is true enough," Zist admitted. "So you have to teach it to respond to the sounds. Do other watch-whers always use the same ones?"

"I don't really know," Kindan admitted.

The Harper stared into space, idly stirring the last of the soup. "Well, the important thing is that you got the egg, Kindan. We can wing anything else, somehow. M'tal's our ally, and they have watch-whers at Benden Hold. A few adroit questions— you'll have to think what you need to know—could be answered surreptitiously."

Kindan was more impressed than ever with his teacher and with the morning's incredible events. He mopped the rest of the soup from his bowl with a fresh piece of bread. Then he took his things to the sink and stacked them.

"I'll wash them when I get back from checking the bricks," he told Master Zist as he left the cothold.

That seemed to be all he did every waking hour. At night he slept in the shed, wrapped warmly in his worn fur; often he started from sleep to rise and make sure the egg was warm enough. He had increased the cothold's supply of oats, and had made a mess of porridge in the big kettle that had been placed on the back of the oven range. A pail of blood was already in the cooler. Natalon had quickly given the orders for Kindan to receive whatever he needed to tend to the watch-wher.

The first evening, after the day shift, Zenor popped in to see the egg. His expression of awe made Kindan feel warm inside. All right, it was only Zenor, but to receive such unalloyed approval alleviated some of his worst anxieties. He kept delving back in his memory for all references his father had made about watch-wher tending. He *had* remembered the right sounds and gestures. He *had* gotten the egg back to the camp. It was warm and it would hatch.

"When?" Zenor asked, his eyes glowing as he regarded the egg under its blanket of straw.

"Master Aleesa said in a couple of days," Kindan replied as nonchalantly as he could. "Would you mind getting me some more coal so I can keep the bricks warm?"

"No, no, of course not," Zenor said and darted out of the shed.

Kindan felt the shell of the egg, then started burrowing in the straw to find which bricks were cool enough to be reheated.

He was using the tongs to haul heated bricks out of the fire and filling in the spaces with cool ones when Zenor returned, staggering behind a loaded wheelbarrow. With an exaggerated sigh, Zenor upended it near the fire.

"Thanks, Zenor, I appreciate your help."

"Can you let me see the hatching, too?" Zenor asked wistfully.

"It's nothing like a dragon Impression," Kindan replied, rather wanting that moment to be private.

"Which I haven't seen anyhow, so please, huh, Kindan?"

"Well, I'll try, but I can't promise anything, especially as you may be on shift."

"If possible, please, Kindan? I'll bring all the coal you need."

"All right," Kindan said, relenting. Zenor was his very best friend. "Would you stay in the shed while I make another batch of porridge? I like to keep it as fresh as possible."

"Sure, sure," Zenor said.

Kindan had to scour the pot to remove the brown bits that had stuck to the bottom before he could start a fresh batch. He thought he'd be wasting a lot of oats, but he wanted to be sure he had porridge ready and waiting when the egg cracked. He knew how important it was for the hatchling to be fed as soon as possible after it emerged from its shell.

◆

Three mornings later, he was startled awake from a restless sleep by a loud noise. He sat up, momentarily confused, then opened the glow and carefully pulled the straw off the egg. A large crack almost bisected the center of the egg. He put a hand on it and felt something beat against his palm. He stroked the egg.

"Lemme get the porridge," he said, struggling to disentangle himself from his sleeping fur and dashing barefoot across the short distance to the Harper's cothold. He got the pail of fresh blood he had acquired that afternoon from the cooler, hauled the cookpot to the front of the range, and carefully poured in the blood, mixing it with the stiff porridge. He tried not to wake the Harper, but Zist heard the clink of the spoon against the side of the pot and, holding his fur about him, came into the kitchen.

"It's hatching?" he asked, rubbing sleep from his eyes and finger-combing his hair back.

"It's got one great crack across its middle," Kindan said. Carrying the pot, he returned to the shed, the Harper following him.

Kindan did remember his promise to Zenor but didn't dare leave the shed. Nor could he consider the effrontery of asking Master Zist to wake his friend.

The crack had widened, and a chip of the eggshell lay in the straw.

"I believe a watch-wher is born light-sensitive," Zist remarked, half-closing the glowbasket and turning it to face the back of the shed so as not to blind the creature on its emergence.

The oval rocked, and Kindan wondered if he should move it away from the bricks. Would they be too warm for the hatchling? He compromised by pulling his sleeping fur over as a carpet.

The egg gave one more lurch and fell into two sections. The hatchling reared up and tumbled out, landing on its nose on the fur.

Kindan chirruped encouragingly and reached out to touch the watch-wher. It managed to raise its head, open its mouth, and squawk.

"Feed it," Zist urged, and Kindan inserted his hand in the not-too-warm porridge mix and offered it to the watch-wher. Or, to be specific, dumped it on the hatchling's tongue. It gulped back the offering, swallowing instantly and opening its mouth for more.

Kindan used the spoon this time. Considering how the hatchling seemed to inhale the porridge, he could see why feeding it cubes of meat might cause it to choke to death. He continued feeding it until the pan was empty. The watch-wher cocked its head as if surprised its feeding was interrupted.

"I'll make another pot," Zist said, leaving the shed while Kindan stroked the hatchling and crooned encouragingly. Kindan guessed by the dim light that the watch-wher was green. Female, then. Wanting confirmation, he examined her carefully to be sure all the necessary parts were there. Yes, there were, and she was.

He worked the stumpy wings to be sure they functioned, and stroked the eye ridges and scratched her ears. The watch-wher butted at Kindan, squawking urgently and trying to take his fingers into her toothless mouth. Kindan remembered that watch-whers teethed, not unlike human babies, and with the same pain and discomfort. He made a mental note to get fresh numbweed, or some of the distilled spirits human mothers resorted to for teething infants. Not that any mother he knew would find the watch-wher lovable. It had a really misshapen, ugly kind of dragon face. Like its stumpy wings, which were sort of draconic, but not quite, so was this watch-wher, with eyes that blinked furiously until Kindan dimmed the glow to a thin sliver of light, earning a purr of pleasure from the hatchling.

Master Zist stumbled back into the shed, holding the pot in front of him. The hatchling made a snarling noise, smelling the proximity of food, and lunged in the right direction. Luckily, Kindan was able to seize the pot, grab the spoon, and dump a big glob into the watch-wher's open maw. This time, the moment Kindan felt the spoon scrape the bottom of the pot, he asked Master Zist to prepare a new batch. As Zist obeyed, it occurred to Kindan that maybe it wasn't proper for him to order his Master about like this.

When would this creature have eaten enough? Her belly was well rounded, and she still opened her mouth or nudged Kindan's body when she felt she had been unfed too long. Finally, though, she gave a monumental burp, emitting a sour, bloody smell, and crawled to a spot of straw that seemed appropriate, curled up, laid her head on her forepaws, and started to snore.

Zist got wearily to his feet and scrubbed at his mussed hair.

"I shall get properly attired and announce the arrival of . . ." He looked down at Kindan, who was lying back in the straw. "Did it give you a name?"

Kindan shook his head. "I didn't ask."

"Is it enough like a dragon to know its own name?"

Kindan shook his head. "I don't know. I wish we knew more about watch-whers."

"Is it male or female? Though I don't suppose it matters."

"It's a green. They're like dragons that way, so she's a female."

"Then I shall report that to Natalon." He reached over and tousled Kindan's hair. "You've done very well, lad. Very well indeed."

Master Zist left and wearily Kindan gathered up the odorous porridge pot and took it inside to the sink to clean. Then he started a new batch on a back burner, not knowing how long the current feeding would stave off the pangs of hunger in his new charge. While the pot simmered, he went back to the shed and settled down to await developments.

He roused somewhat to the sound of Zist's soft voice and Natalon's pleased remarks.

"And no idea what its name is?" Natalon asked Kindan.

"She didn't say . . . she was too busy stuffing her mouth and swallowing. Next time she's awake, I must blood her," Kindan said, giving a convulsive shudder.

"Is that essential?" Zist asked, wincing slightly.

"It's how watch-whers know who they answer to. And that tradition has already served me well."

Zist held out his hand. "Do you have a belt knife? I'll sharpen it for you. That way you won't feel the cut as much."

"I'll leave you to it," Natalon said, giving Kindan a sympathetic wave in farewell.

Kindan handed over his belt knife, murmuring a thank-you. He hated to tell the Harper that he was going to ask him to make the cut, as he wasn't brave enough to slash his own hand. He shuddered again as Zist left the shed. With nothing to do, Kindan settled himself on the warmest spot of straw he could find . . . and then remembered that he hadn't let Zenor know about the hatching. His friend would be topside by now from his shift, and maybe still awake.

Zenor *was* still awake but yawning mightily when Kindan called at his window.

"You were on shift, when the shell cracked," Kindan said apologetically.

Zenor muttered under his breath but slipped back into his tunic and joined Kindan.

"You actually didn't miss much. One single big crack woke me and then, it fell into two pieces. It's a green, so it's a female."

"Is that what you wanted?"

"I wanted a live, healthy watch-wher . . . and I suppose a female is as good as a male. Shards, does she eat!"

Zenor grinned. "My mother says my sisters eat more than I do."

"C'mon," Kindan urged, quickening his pace. "I don't know how long she goes between feedings and I still have to blood her."

They entered the shed, Zenor with a properly respectful attitude. He looked around.

"Where is she?"

A head rose instantly from the straw in which it had burrowed, the wide eyes blinking.

"She's not as big as I thought she would be," he murmured.

"Big enough to have the appetite of nine dragons," Kindan said, almost proudly.

The hatchling worked her way across the straw to where Kindan stood and, opening her mouth, made a noise that he instantly interpreted as a demand for food.

"I'll be right back," he said, giving the watch-wher a reassuring *chirp*.

When he got to the cothold, Master Zist had just put down his sharpening stone, and the new knife-edge glistened in the sunlight. Kindan gulped, thinking of that edge cutting into his hand, and stirred the simmering porridge.

"Hungry again?" Zist asked.

"Would you mind coming with me now so I can blood her?" Kindan asked. "And then start another batch?"

"Is there enough blood left in the pail for more?"

"I think so. I'll get more as soon as she's asleep again."

The Harper followed him out to the shed and greeted Zenor, who hadn't moved from the spot in which Kindan had left him. The hatchling had been trying to crawl up his legs, her hungry *bleek* more insistent.

Kindan put the pot down and turned to Zist, holding out his right hand. He pointed to the original scar, barely visible in the dimly lit shed. "Here, please."

He turned away so he wouldn't have to look as the Harper steadied his hand in his.

Neither had realized how quickly the hatchling would react. Just as the dizzying pain shot up Kindan's arm, a wet tongue was licking the blood from his hand—even before Master Zist had released it. The watch-wher mumbled a happy sound as she sucked at the wound.

"Isn't that enough?" Zist asked just about the time Kindan thought it was more than enough. The thin wound ached. Kindan disengaged the watch-wher and held her away from him as he lobbed a spoonful of porridge into her mouth. That did the trick—she was immediately diverted from Kindan's still-throbbing wound to sucking down the blood porridge.

"Here, Zenor, wrap this around Kindan's hand before the creature savages him," Zist said, passing Zenor the bandage roll. Kindan could feed the creature as easily using his left hand while Zenor wrapped up his right.

"You'll need some numbweed on that, as well as a healing salve," Zist said. "I'd no idea the hatchling would be so voracious."

Kindan hadn't either. "I wish we knew more about them."

Zenor gave his friend a surprised look. "You mean you don't—"

Kindan shushed him. "Not a word to Natalon, Zenor," he said imploringly. He exchanged looks with Master Zist, then continued with more assurance than he felt, "I'm sure I'll get it all sorted out when the time comes."

"Well, I'll help all I can," Zenor promised stoutly. Kindan grinned at him.

"And I," Master Zist added. "First, however, I shall get your things."

Kindan's brow puckered in surprise. "My things?"

Master Zist nodded. "Yes, you'll sleep here from now on. You'll need your things here, too."

"Here?" Kindan looked around the shed. It had not been built for warmth; Dask had had a notoriously thick hide that kept him comfortable.

"You need to be around the watch-wher," Master Zist declared. In a lower voice, he added, "And there's some that might not wish it well."

Zenor and Kindan both looked toward Tarik's house—not more than a dragon's length from the shed.

With a sigh, Kindan nodded. "But—"

"I'll have someone check on you regularly to see if the watch-wher needs food," Master Zist said.

"But—"

"I understand that it will be a hardship for you," the Harper went on. "But you made your choice when you agreed to raise the hatchling."

Kindan bit off any more objections and nodded dejectedly. "I suppose I've made my nest, now I'll have to lie in it."

Master Zist let out a hearty guffaw, drowning out Zenor's softer laugh. "Good one, lad! Good one."

"I could come and stay with you for a bit, after my shift," Zenor suggested.

"Thanks," Kindan said, shaking his head. "But I can't ask you to stay too long, you've got your own work and—"

"It'll be no problem," Zenor declared. "Especially if you let Miner Natalon know that you asked me."

◆

The new arrangements left Kindan exhausted by the end of the first sevenday. He was constantly fending off visits by the camp's children, the camp's miners, and Tarik, with his constant sour prophecies.

"It'll eat more than it's worth," was Tarik's first dour comment. Later, it was, "And how long before it's ready to go down the mines?

"When does that ugly creature reach its growth?" was the next snide remark. "Not much use as it is now, is it?"

And yet again, "Natalon paid *how* much coal for that bag of bones?"

Kindan's hatred of the head miner's uncle grew steadily greater with each return visit and insulting comment. He found himself afraid to leave the watch-wher unattended, not only for fear of what Tarik might do, but also for fear of what the watch-wher might do out of its own fright. The poor thing had already nearly bitten Zenor once when he arrived early one morning and threw back the heavy curtain draped down behind the door to protect the watch-wher's delicate eyes.

Kindan was frazzled and bone-tired every day, wondering how he would survive the watch-wher's fierce and frequent pangs of hunger.

Day by day, he grew more and more red-eyed, less able to stand the least cheerful comment and barely keeping himself civil in his dealings with the Harper. He found himself having the deepest respect for Zenor and could not understand how he could ever have been so thoughtless as to tease his friend when he had complained about losing sleep dealing with his younger sisters.

One morning, near the end of the second sevenday, Kindan woke groggily. Something was different. He looked around in the darkness.

Someone was in the shed.

"Ah, you're awake," a voice said. "It's about time. I think she's getting hungry. Why don't you go get her breakfast while I stay here?"

"Nuella?" Kindan said in surprise.

"Who else?" she replied. "Go on, get. She's stirring. Ahh, the lovely thing."

Kindan rushed out of the shed and up to the Harper's cothold. It was still dark, although there was a hint of dawn on the horizon. He let himself in, stoked up the fire, and began to heat the porridge.

"Who's there?" Master Zist asked irritably from the room beyond.

"It's me. Kindan. I'm just making breakfast for the watch-wher."

"Oh." Kindan heard the Harper rumble about in his room for his robe and slippers. "Wait a minute! Who's with the watch-wher?"

"Nuella," Kindan said.

"Ah," the Harper responded abstractedly, clearly still not entirely awake, "good."

Kindan grinned and rooted about the cabinet for *klah* bark. "I'll put on some *klah*," he shouted.

"Good idea," Master Zist boomed back, entering the kitchen. Then he blinked. "Did you say Nuella was with the watch-wher?"

Kindan nodded.

"Mmm. That's not good. What if something happens?"

"She can hide in the shadows," Kindan suggested.

"But what if she has to raise the alarm?" Master Zist returned.

Kindan started to make a number of different replies before he finally stopped and shook his head. "I see what you mean."

"I'm glad you do," the Harper replied testily. "Go get the blood from Ima, the porridge is nearly hot."

Kindan was nearly frantic by the time Ima delivered his pitcher of blood. He raced back to the Harper's cothold, nearly spilling the pitcher in his haste. Panting, he made the mix and ran down to the watch-wher's shed.

"Where were you?" Nuella asked testily when he returned. "You took forever."

"Sorry," Kindan gasped.

"You sound as if you've been running all over the place."

"I have," Kindan replied, pouring the noxious mix into a bowl for the wakening watch-wher.

Nuella crinkled her nose at the smell. "You know, it's really surprising that something as pretty as her would eat something as awful as that."

"Pretty?" Kindan exclaimed.

"Yes, pretty," Nuella repeated emphatically. "You see pretty with the heart, not with the eyes, you know." She paused, giving Kindan a chance to argue and, when he didn't, reverted to her original topic. "Wouldn't meat scraps make more sense?"

"But Master Aleesa said—"

"She's the one you got the egg from, right?" Nuella asked.

"Yes," Kindan agreed.

"What did your father's watch-wher eat?"

"Well," Kindan considered, "mostly meat scraps. But Dask was much older, and she's still young."

Nuella cocked her head at the watch-wher, who had already begun to eat, and stroked the soft neck gently. "Hmm," she muttered to herself. She clucked at the watch-wher, diverting the creature's attention long enough to dip a finger into the bowl. Nuella sniffed at the blood-porridge mix on her fingertip and then, much to Kindan's astonishment, licked it clean. She made a face at the taste and then said, "If I were you, I'd try meat scraps. It'd be much easier all around."

"I suppose it wouldn't hurt to try," Kindan admitted.

"And what are you going to call her?" Nuella asked impatiently.

"Well, I was hoping her name would suggest itself," Kindan said.

Gingerly Nuella ran her hands over the watch-wher. Kindan was surprised and a little abashed to realize that he had not yet done so himself.

"She's beautiful," Nuella said.

Kindan grinned. "She is, isn't she?" The watch-wher was an

ugly lump of muscle scantily clad with skin, her oversized eyes looking even bigger in her young head—but she was his and he wouldn't trade her for anything.

"So what's her name?"

"I'll tell you this evening," Kindan promised. "Or the next time you come here."

Nuella nodded. "It might not be this evening, but I'll see what I can do." She rose, feeling her way toward the curtain and the shed door.

"The sun's up," Kindan told her warningly.

"That's why I borrowed Dalor's clothes, silly," Nuella replied. "Help me put his hood on right. It's cold enough this morning that no one will think it odd if I'm wearing it."

Kindan rose and helped her settle the hood on her head. Nuella pushed her long hair back out of sight and rubbed her face with her hands, dirtying it.

"How do I look?" she asked him.

"Dirty," Kindan told her.

She frowned at him.

"You don't look like Dalor when you take on that sour look," he commented. "And you won't be able to play at being a boy too much longer."

"I know," she said softly, lips downcast. "I've heard Father talking to Mother late nights when they think I'm asleep, wondering what will become of me." She raised her head and gave Kindan a determined look. She was about to say more when they heard voices outside the shed.

"You'd better go," Kindan said. "Do you know the way?"

Nuella snorted. "Kindan, I'm blind, not stupid." And before Kindan could apologize, she slipped through the curtain and headed out into the early morning light. Spurred by the watch-wher's alarmed squeals, Kindan hastily pulled the curtain back in place.

After his eyes readjusted to the darkness, he returned to his watch of his watch-wher. Sated with the morning feed, the little green had curled up again, but she was happy to lay her head in his lap before falling asleep once more.

Idly, Kindan used the width of his hand to measure her length. She measured about ten hands-widths from nose to tail—slightly more than a meter—as near as he could make out, and she would stand about three hands high at the shoulder. He grinned down at her sleeping head, feeling full of pride and a little awed that she seemed to trust him so much.

"What are we going to call you?" he murmured to her as he stroked her ungainly head. The small watch-wher raised her head and peered straight at him intently. Kindan stared back, feeling as though he could almost *hear* her talking to him. After a long moment, the watch-wher let out a little murfle and laid her head on his lap again.

"Kisk," Kindan said. The watch-wher opened one eye, shook her head, and closed the eye again. "Your name is Kisk." The watch-wher shifted her weight, once more oblivious to everything around her. But Kindan *felt* Kisk's acceptance of her name.

◆

Kisk was quite happy to try some meat scraps with her next meal. Master Zist fretted that it might be too soon, but Kindan made sure the scraps were all small and contained no bone or gristle, and he could *feel* how happy Kisk was with the new diet. Her rubbing her head against his leg contentedly and making small *merrble*-ing sounds only confirmed his opinion.

Certainly Ima was much happier to be asked to make ready a

supply of scrap meat instead of fresh blood "at all hours of the day." Supplying the growing watch-wher with scraps was much easier on everyone than the time-consuming blood-porridge.

In fact, as the watch-wher reached her first month, Kindan found himself wondering how much Master Aleesa really knew about the raising of young watch-whers—or whether the whole blood-porridge idea had been a joke on the part of the cranky "WherMaster."

Master Zist came down to the shed every spare moment he had. He insisted that Kindan learn all the songs there were about dragons on the principle that because dragons and watch-whers were related, the songs about dragons would provide insights into raising watch-whers.

"But there's not all that many songs about raising dragons, is there?" Kindan said after several days.

Master Zist frowned, shaking his head. "You're right. Most of the songs are about fighting Thread and chewing firestone." He scratched his head thoughtfully. "And there's the bit about how they grow—"

"And when a dragon's old enough to ride," Zenor, who had joined them earlier, added.

"Well that should be about the same for watch-whers, shouldn't it?" Nuella asked.

Nuella, Zenor, and the Harper had established a routine of meeting in the shed just after the end of the day shift. Zenor would arrive at the Harper's, and he and Kindan would escort Nuella down to the shed, keeping her well hooded and away from probing eyes.

"That seems likely," Kindan agreed.

"That would be a Turn and a half," Master Zist said. Kindan groaned.

"That long!" Zenor exclaimed.

"But how long until you can start training her?" Nuella wondered.

"I don't know," Kindan confessed.

"Well," Master Zist said consideringly, "she's too young to start training right now. It'll be months before she's ready, I'm sure."

"Is it just me, or is she more active at night?" Zenor asked.

"She should be, she's nocturnal," Nuella snapped before Kindan could respond.

"I wonder if I should take her out at night," Kindan said.

Master Zist shook his head. "Not yet. I think when she's ready to leave her lair, she'll let you know."

Nuella cocked her head thoughtfully. "You might want to put a collar on her, with bells. I'd hate for you to be asleep the first time she decided to go for a stroll."

"Isn't that what happened with you?" Zenor asked Nuella. "I mean, when we first met."

Nuella smiled impishly at him. "I wasn't wearing a collar, but I *did* manage to go for a stroll."

"You're lucky Cristov didn't catch you," Kindan remarked.

Nuella shook her head. "I'd smell him at least a dragonlength away—he wears that awful scent his mother likes." She frowned in thought. "I wonder how good Kisk's sense of smell is."

The others considered her comment silently.

"I imagine we'll find out," Master Zist answered finally. He rose and stretched. "But not tonight. Nuella, it's time for your lessons."

"We could do them here," she suggested hopefully.

"No, Zenor's got to get some sleep," the Harper replied. "I can't ask him to stay here the extra hours it would take to finish your lessons before he walks you home."

Zenor grimaced. "Master Zist is right. Mother needs me even now that Renna's gotten big enough to look after the others some more."

"She's doing most of the work Kindan used to do, isn't she?" Nuella remarked. Master Zist cleared his throat warningly. Nuella frowned at the noise and turned back to Kindan. "It's not as though you could do all your old work *and* look after a new hatchling, too, you know."

"I suppose," Kindan agreed morosely. "But it seems that *all* I do is look after the hatchling."

Zenor gave him a commiserating look. "She'll grow up before you know it, Kindan. And then you can help us in the mines."

With that bit of encouragement, they left. Kindan curled up in a warm spot, and Kisk draped herself over and around him with a series of chirps and squeals. But she didn't sleep. First she twitched one way and then she twitched another way. Kindan moved away from her, but Kisk moved back toward him and curled up again.

Kindan was finally drifting toward sleep when a warm tongue licked along the side of his jaw. Kindan blearily opened one eye and saw that Kisk was lying next to him, her head raised to look him in the face. He made a soothing sound and closed his eye.

He was licked on the other cheek. He opened both eyes. Kisk cocked her head at him and, with a chirp, darted her tongue out to lick him on the chin.

"Hey! Stop it!" Kindan shouted grumpily. Kisk recoiled at his tone and made a sad click. "I'm tired, it's time to sleep—oh, no! Don't tell me that you're not tired!" Please don't tell me you're not tired, he thought to himself.

Within five minutes Kisk had made it abundantly clear that she wasn't tired at all. In fact, she wanted to play. She found one of his shoes and grabbed it in her mouth, tossing it in the air and catching it with a claw, and then tossing it back to catch it with her jaw again.

"Hey, that's my shoe," Kindan complained, grabbing for it. In a moment, as the little watch-wher tossed it out of his grasp, he realized that he'd made a big mistake. He had taught Kisk the fun game of finder's-keepers. It took him ten minutes and a handful of scraps to get his shoe back.

And still Kisk showed no signs of sleepiness. Instead, she started rooting around the shed. She grabbed the curtain with a claw and played at flipping it back and forth, pausing at first when the outdoor light startled her. She hissed and turned her head away hastily, but after a moment, she turned back to the dim night light and stuck her head under the curtain.

Kindan found himself leaping to his feet to grab Kisk's tail before she could dart out. As it was, it took all of his effort to get her to hold still long enough for him to hastily rig a halter out of some old rope before she tugged him outdoors—no mean feat for a creature that was barely up to his kneecaps.

"Okay, okay!" Kindan said as the watch-wher pulled him down toward the lake. "We're going to the lake, Kisk, is that what you want?" He remembered how Zenor had talked to his littlest sister, always telling her what she was seeing and what was happening. So he began a narration of their journey down to the lakeside where Kisk sniffed at the water and, after a few daring darts of her tongue, lapped up a good several mouthfuls of fresh water.

"Were you thirsty, then?" Kindan asked. "Did you want to get a drink?" Kisk looked up at him, blinked her big eyes, and gave a little cheep that Kindan couldn't interpret.

"Apparently not," he muttered to himself when the watchwher yanked her head around and nearly pulled Kindan off his feet.

"Those are the cots, Kisk, you don't want to go there," Kindan told her. "People are sleeping and they aren't much fun."

But Kisk wasn't interested in that; what had caught her attention was the forest just beyond the line of cabins. She sniffed about at the smaller plants, tried and spat out any number of bushes—fortunately Kindan knew of none in the vicinity that were poisonous, or he would have been more worried—and worked her way up alongside the pathway that led back toward Kindan's old, now Tarik's, house.

"Are you ready to go to sleep?" he asked, keeping his voice low and soft in hopes of inspiring his charge. Kisk looked up at him and gave him a wide-awake *chirp* which was anything *but* reassuring. She started sniffing toward Tarik's cothold, and Kindan grew alarmed at the notion of attracting Tarik's attention and, doubtless, wrath.

Somehow Kisk must have guessed his feelings, for she made another little inquisitive noise, sniffed at him, snorted at the house, and turned her attention elsewhere. She bounded toward a bush and hissed angrily at it.

It was then that Kindan realized they were not alone.

"She won't bite, will she?" whoever was hiding behind the bush asked nervously. It was Cristov.

"She bit me," Kindan said irritably, lying to impress him. Kisk looked back at him and snorted. "But that's because I was blooded to her, you see."

Cristov stepped out from behind the bush. "She's pretty small," he noted. "Were her teeth sharp?"

Kindan held out his bandaged hand. "See for yourself."

"You'd better leave it wrapped until it's healed," Cristov said, pushing Kindan's hand away.

"Suit yourself," Kindan said brusquely. He and Cristov had barely said two words to each other in the past Turn, and before that they'd either fought until dragged apart or ignored each other contemptuously. "What are you doing out—skulking?"

Cristov's hands balled into fists and he looked angrily at Kindan.

Kindan frowned. "I'm sorry. That was mean. But honestly, what are you doing out tonight?"

"I—well—" Cristov found himself tongue-tied, searching for an answer. At last he blurted out, "Mother says that watch-whers are nice. I wanted to see for myself."

Kindan's eyes widened in surprise. Kisk gave a surprised noise herself and craned her neck up to peer at Cristov, pointing her tail nearly straight back for counterbalance. Kindan was surprised to see how high she could lift her head on her long, sinuous neck—it almost reached his neck.

"I know my father doesn't like them," Cristov continued breathlessly, holding out a hand palm up to the watch-wher, "but my mother says we should respect them. She says, 'A grown-up makes their own decisions.'"

Kisk darted her tongue out and licked Cristov's outstretched hand before he could pull it back. She made a sad, don't-you-like-me noise at Cristov.

"She gets scared by sudden moves," Kindan warned him. Honesty compelled him to add, "I think she likes you. I haven't seen her try to lick many people."

Kindan forebore mentioning Nuella's tart remark about the scent Cristov wore.

Encouraged, Cristov put his hand out again. At his sudden move, Kisk ducked her head behind Kindan's back, but slowly she peered around again. In short order she licked his palm, muffled a sneeze, and darted her tongue quickly around the boy's face.

Kindan smiled at Cristov. "She likes you."

"Cristov!" a voice shouted from inside the house. It was Tarik.

"I'm here," Cristov shouted back. Before Kindan could back away, Tarik appeared.

"What are you doing?" Tarik demanded, his lips pursed tightly.

"I just wanted to see the watch-wher," Cristov replied, but Kindan could hear the fear in his voice.

Tarik stepped out of the house and joined the boys. He looked down at Kisk, eyes narrowed suspiciously.

"So this is the watch-wher that will save us all?" Tarik said derisively. "It's smaller than a wherry. Ima's been saving her best scraps for *this*?"

"She's nice," Cristov responded quietly.

"She's a waste of time," Tarik said with a snort. "They all are." He gave Kindan a dismissive look. "And so are those who care for them."

Kindan stood up to his full height and glared at Tarik. "Miner Natalon thought her worth enough to pay a whole winter's coal for her."

Tarik barked a laugh. "My nephew's a fool. A winter's coal! What a waste!"

"Tarik!" Dara called from inside the house. She peered out the door. "You've found Cristov. Good. Now the two of you come in for dinner." She saw Kindan and smiled at him. "Ah, Kindan!

Good to see you. Is that the new watch-wher?" Kindan caught the narrowed look she gave her husband. "A green? Has she given you her name yet?"

"Kisk, ma'am," Kindan replied politely.

Dara nodded. "A good name," she judged. Then she said, "You'll have to forgive my men, their dinner's ready."

"It's quite all right," Kindan replied using his best Harper-trained manners. With a frown he added, "I think Kisk has gotten bored again, anyway."

He was right: The watch-wher had started tugging on her lead. However, to Kindan's dismay, Kisk was not ready to return to her lair. In the end, he was certain that he had heard the first of the dawn chorus before Kisk emitted a huge yawn and nearly curled up where she was. It took all Kindan's charming to get her back to the shed, where they both fell into a deep sleep before the first cock crowed.

CHAPTER IX

Walk, baby, walk, come you to me.
Soon, baby, soon, you'll walk away from me.

"Well, I've given up." Master Zist sat back on his haunches with a disgusted look. "I've read everything I could, got Tarri to bring me references up from Crom itself, and we still don't know anything more about our voracious friend here than what we've learned ourselves in the past three months."

Kindan, Zenor, and Nuella all nodded in agreement.

"They're smarter than fire-lizards," Zenor said stalwartly. One of Tarri's traders had a fire-lizard, and Zenor had observed it closely the last time the caravan had come.

"And Kisk, at least, can sense when I'm sad or happy," Kindan said, his voice breaking as he spoke. Zenor grinned at his discomfort, earning a scowl from Kindan. He was glad that the

Harper had not commented on Kindan's voice—which seemed all squeak and growl, either too high or too low. He remembered with deep regret how horribly he'd teased Kaylek when the older boy's voice had broken.

"I'll bet you'd be happier if she could understand when you're sleepy," Nuella murmured.

"Oh, not to worry, Nuella," Master Zist said with a wave of his hand. "Kindan's just turned twelve, and as soon as he hits his growth, he'll find himself a night owl just like Kisk, here."

Zenor, who had shot up in the past several months, nodded glumly. "Growth spurts hurt, Kindan," he said. "But at least you won't worry about your sleep schedule."

Zenor had teased Nuella when he'd passed her height, but she had ignored him. However, when Kisk grew tall enough to butt her head, Nuella had been quite startled.

"Well, it's only fair," Zenor had joked in his new, deep voice. "You started growing earlier and have been taller all this time. It's about time you got a dose of your own medicine."

Kindan, whose height was still less than Nuella's, wisely kept quiet. In fact, if he didn't grow soon, Kisk's shoulders would be level with his.

She was twelve hands high at the shoulder, and nearly forty hands from nose to tail. She had all the size of a near-grown workbeast like those pulling the drays.

"She's filled out a fair bit, too," Master Zist commented, patting Kisk firmly on the side of her neck. Her muscles, always visible under her skin, were now tight and well formed, firm with strength. "I think she'll reach her full height in another two months or so."

"Is that earlier than dragons?" Kindan asked.

"Hmm, there's one way to find out," Master Zist said. He

stood up. "Kindan, why don't you leave Kisk in our care while you go to the watch-heights? I'm sure M'tal would like to see how well your watch-wher's grown."

"You're going to send for a dragonrider?" Nuella asked in amazement.

"He's an old friend of mine," Master Zist confided.

"But I thought that Telgar wouldn't answer the call."

"Weyrleader M'tal," Kindan said, pausing to savor his friends' astonishment, "leads Benden, not Telgar."

"Benden!" Zenor and Nuella gasped in unison. Both of them had been born and raised in Camp Natalon. Crom Hold was an unimaginable distance to them, Telgar Weyr a place only in the rarest of dreams. They couldn't begin to imagine a place as distant as Benden Weyr.

"All right, Kindan, now that you've seen their jaws drop, you can run off and drum out the call," Master Zist said drolly. "You do remember it?"

"Zist requests M'tal," Kindan recited easily.

◆

Kindan knew that it would take some time before M'tal would even get the drum message and probably longer still before the Weyrleader could find time to respond.

Winter had come again to the Camp. Toldur and his evening shift had finished cutting the new shaft into the mine. There had been a special Gather at Natalon's hold to celebrate. Because there were no traders, Nuella couldn't attend. It had looked like Master Zist would have to handle the evening's entertainment by himself, but Nuella, with Zenor's connivance, had volunteered to watch Kisk.

"She'll need exercise," Kindan had warned.

Nuella had dismissed that with a toss of her head. "You can exercise her when you get back. I'll keep her here, thank you."

"How will you get back to the hold?" Kindan had asked.

"How else? You and Kisk will escort me," Nuella had replied. "Honestly, don't you think everyone will be too tired to notice or, more likely, asleep?"

Kindan had cheered up. "Thanks, Nuella. I appreciate this."

Nuella smiled at him. Then she added, "Don't think I won't remember it, you know."

"And I'll keep Zenor out of trouble," Kindan had added.

"*That* goes without saying," Nuella had responded, shoving him out the door.

"You're lucky she was willing to take the risk," Master Zist had commented later. "I'm afraid this is the last time we'll be able to perform together."

"What?" Kindan had been aghast.

"Think about it," Master Zist had said. "Your watch-wher is getting bigger. She's almost old enough to start training. And then she'll start work. Watch-whers work—and train—at night. There will be very few Gathers during the day until the thaw. And then you'll be working full-time."

Kindan had been thunderstruck. He had known that becoming the wherhandler had meant that he couldn't remain Master Zist's apprentice, but he had hoped to always be able to find time to perform with the Harper. Master Zist had seen the look on his face and had worked carefully to cheer Kindan up before the Gather, finding dainties for him and talking encouragingly about the watch-wher and Kindan's sacrifice for the good of the miners.

Kindan was sad when he returned to the shed after the Gather. He found Kisk and Nuella curled up together in the straw. He woke Nuella, and Kisk stretched luxuriously in what appeared to be the beginnings of a long, active night.

"What's wrong?" Nuella asked on the silent walk back up to the hold. Kindan told her. "It has to happen, Kindan," she said. "The night shift only sees a Gather on a restday. You can't be at Gathers and in the mines at the same time."

"I know," he replied sadly. He looked at Kisk, whose great eyes whirled green and blue in her love for him, and sighed. "But I liked singing and playing."

"You're not much good for singing, with your voice going up and down like that," Nuella remarked. Kindan grunted sourly.

"You know," Nuella said after an uncomfortable silence, "that new mine shaft's awfully close to Father's secret passage."

"Secret passage?" Kindan repeated.

"Yes, the one that I used to get Master Zist back to his cottage before you the first day he came," she answered. She smiled in memory. "You should have heard the way you reacted! All panting and then gasping in shock. I nearly burst when I heard you."

Kindan stopped, struck by a sudden inspiration. "Nuella, can you show me that passage?"

◆

It had taken very persuasive talk on Kindan's part to finally get Nuella to agree to let him see the secret passageway.

"You'll wait until after dark, of course," Nuella told him. "Then meet me on the second-floor landing."

"I want to bring Kisk," Kindan objected.

"Well, of course you do," Nuella said. "You told me that it'd be good training for her. Although I think it'd be more for you—*she* can see in the dark."

Kindan shrugged. "We have to work together."

"I understand," Nuella said condescendingly. "So meet me tonight, after I've finished my lesson with Master Zist."

"After?"

"Well, you can't expect me to go along and miss my lessons, can you?" she asked with a touch of exasperation.

"You're coming?"

"How are you going to find your way about without me?" she asked, tapping her foot impatiently. "It's not as though you'll be able to *see* in the dark, you know."

Kindan gave in with a reluctant sigh. "Fine. I'll see you tonight." Then he frowned. "But why do you want to meet on the second floor? Why not by the kitchen?"

"Because the entrance to the secret passageway is on the second floor," she told him simply.

———◆———

From the very start, things did not go the way Kindan had planned. He found himself at the end of a line with Nuella leading Kisk.

"Why am I back here?" he complained as they reached the first turn in the passageway. He stumbled and caught himself.

"That's why," Nuella replied calmly. "You want Kisk to learn how to lead people safely in the dark, don't you? Well, how can she do that if all you can teach her is how to stumble around?"

"But it's dark in here," Kindan said, defensively.

Nuella snorted. "It's no darker here than it is anywhere else for me," she said. "Honestly, Kindan, have you never tried walking with your eyes closed?"

"No," Kindan replied, stumbling on a rock and going down hard on his knees—again.

"Well, it's time you learned," Nuella said. She added conversationally, "It was the first game I learned to play with Dalor."

"Really?"

"Well, he used to tease me so much and it really got to me," she admitted. "But my mother asked me one day why didn't I play a game that showed my strengths, not my weaknesses. So we started playing in the dark." She added with a laugh, "It got so that I used to move the furniture around to make Dalor trip."

Kindan, feeling the smart from his shins, still couldn't understand why he was behind Kisk and Nuella was in front of her. Nuella's explanation was that she could show Kisk where to go, and it made no sense for the two of them, who could "see" well enough in the dark, to have to halt their stride just because Kindan couldn't. But it was a pity the passageway wasn't quite wide enough for Kindan to travel side by side with Kisk.

"How much farther is it?" he asked when he felt that they'd gone on forever. He regretted letting Nuella convince him that they should leave the glows behind. What if something happened to her? But, Kindan reflected ruefully, everything so far had happened to *him*.

"I told you," Nuella's voice carried back in a whisper from somewhere up ahead, "there are two turns, this last one and another gentler one. The sharp turn comes about one third of the way along, and the gentle turn comes about three-quarters of the way along. Of course, it's just the opposite on the way back."

Kisk turned her head back and blew a soft reassurance at Kindan.

"Hey! I can almost see her eyes," he said excitedly.

"Almost?" Nuella repeated. "How can you *almost* see something?"

"Well, it's hard to explain. Like maybe I can, maybe I can't," he replied, trying to recall the image now that Kisk had turned her head back.

Nuella's reply was thoughtful. "Sometimes I think I can see things that way, too. It's like when I dream. My eyes worked fine until I was about three, you know. Mother thinks that's why I see things when I dream. It's rather confusing, to be honest."

Kindan, whose light-starved eyes were reporting all sorts of strange lights, nodded in understanding.

At least the air was cool and clean, he noted. He brushed his fingers against a wall, as Nuella had advised him, and corrected his course slightly. Originally he had tried holding on to Kisk's tail, but the watch-wher had flicked it away from him impatiently.

The sound of Nuella's breathing and the lighter, faster breathing of the watch-wher were reassuring in the darkness. Kindan stopped feeling wrong-footed—blind—and started feeling more comfortable in the darkness. He strained his ears, hoping to hear with Nuella's ease, but admitted after a while that it was hard.

"You're thinking too much," Nuella's voice piped out of the darkness. "Just listen. Don't try so hard."

"How did you know what I was doing?" he demanded, eyes bulging in surprise.

"Your breathing changed," she said simply. "You took a really deep breath, then a couple of short ones, and then you started breathing in spurts."

Kindan sighed.

"And just then you sighed because I guessed what you were thinking," Nuella went on. She giggled. "I used to play this game with Dalor, too. It really infuriated him."

"I can understand," Kindan said feelingly.

"Okay," Nuella said, "I'll stop now. But just listen, okay?"

Kindan nodded, not worrying whether Nuella could "hear" him or not, and the three continued on in unlit silence.

After a while, Kindan noticed that his right hand was brushing against the wall. He moved to the left, but noticed a short while later that his hand was brushing the wall again.

"Is it curving now?"

"Very good," Nuella said. "I was wondering if you'd notice."

"So we're almost there?"

"Yep. About fifty more paces," Nuella told him. That had been another surprise to Kindan, being told he had to keep count of the number of paces he took. He'd forgotten to keep counting, too, and wondered if Nuella had or if she had just memorized the distances.

"Wait," she called. "Listen."

Kindan strained his ears. He felt Kisk turn her head this way and that.

"Can you hear it?" Nuella asked after a long moment.

"No," Kindan confessed.

"It sounds like they're putting up the entrance for the second shaft," Nuella said. "It's just through the rock on the right here."

"How far?" Kindan wondered.

"Not more than half a meter, probably less," she answered promptly. "I heard Father talking. I'm sure he had it made that way on purpose, so that this passage could be connected to the two shafts before the next Pass."

That made sense. When Thread started to fall again it wouldn't be safe to have people going outside to get into the mines; with the passage, people would be able to go straight from the Hold to the mine without venturing outside at all.

Perhaps, Kindan mused, Natalon had also thought of building a special enclosure so that all the mined coal could be safely stored without worrying about Thread.

Thread was voracious—Kindan knew that as well as any child in the camp. The Teaching Ballads said it would eat anything organic—flesh *or* coal. He was glad that the next Pass, when the Red Star drew Thread down on the planet, would not be for another fourteen Turns. Kindan realized that he'd be really old by then—twenty-six Turns.

"That'll be a good thing for the next Pass," Kindan said aloud.

"Only if the Camp is proved," Nuella responded. "Otherwise it'll all be a waste, like Uncle Tarik's Camp."

"What do you know about that?" he asked, intensely curious.

"Shh!" Nuella hissed. She added, in a whisper, "We're getting near the end of the passage. I'll tell you later."

Nuella had explained, when she had first shown Kindan the entrance to the passage, that the exit was in a pocket toward the back of the mine entrance, close to where the shaft's huge pumps were placed.

"Father had it built to look like part of the supports," she had said.

Kindan could well imagine that no one would guess about the existence of the passage: It had been expertly concealed at the back of the upstairs hall closet in Natalon's hold. What had looked like simple round trim at the top and bottom of the back wall had turned out to hide carefully crafted latches that slid back top and bottom on one corner when Nuella moved them. Only someone who had known how they worked would have had a chance of discovering them.

On the other side were protruding dowels: When pushed in,

they caused the door to close neatly, so that no one, even someone who knew about the secret passage, would know they had entered.

The doorway to the exit was much the same. Kindan guessed that Cannehir, Crom's itinerant woodsmith, must have made the doors. Kindan wondered how many other people knew about the "secret" passageway. He made a mental note to ask Nuella later.

He felt a change in the air in front of him, and a lighter spot showed ahead.

"What are you doing?" he whispered.

"Opening the door," she answered. "You didn't think we'd come all the way here without going into the mines, did you?"

"Are you mad?" Kindan shot back, thinking that it was becoming the most common question he asked this uncommon girl. "We'll be seen."

"By who? Toldur's crew are still working on the other shaft," she replied, unperturbed. "Dalor told me that you can't see here from the pumps, and that's the only place people would be."

"Dalor told you?" Kindan whispered back, eyes wide.

"Sure," Nuella said. "You don't think this is the first time I've come here, do you?"

"Of course not—you were here at least once before, with Master Zist."

"Exactly," she agreed in a tone that told Kindan she had been here many more times than just that once. "How is Kisk here going to learn the mines if she doesn't explore them?"

"But we might get caught," he responded, sweat beading on his forehead. "And no one's supposed to go into the mines without the shift leader knowing. What if there were a cave-in? We'd be trapped."

"I suppose you're right about that," she admitted after a moment's silence. "I hadn't thought about it before."

Kindan snorted, remembering how he had had to remind Nuella to put on a hard hat—there was a shelf of them behind the secret door into the passageway. Everyone who ever went into the mines was taught to wear a hard hat as a matter of reflex.

"Well," she said reluctantly, "I suppose we could turn back."

Kindan sighed. He was as reluctant as Nuella to turn back, but he had heard too often about the dangers in the mines—and he could still remember the cave-in and Dask's bleeding body— to be willing to take such a grave risk. "Yes. Next time we can tell someone—maybe Dalor?"

"Dalor would be perfect," Nuella agreed. "Maybe Zenor. I don't know about Master Zist."

"Seeing as you're in front," Nuella said after they'd retreated through the door and closed it, "why don't you lead us back? It'll be good practice for you."

It was. When they came across the gentle turn a quarter of the way back, he walked right into the wall.

"I told you to count your paces," Nuella commented unsympathetically when she realized what he'd done.

Kindan groaned, rubbing his sore nose.

Nuella smothered a laugh. "Well, maybe it hurts enough to keep you from making that mistake again. Clearly, my telling you isn't enough."

Kindan started counting his paces. His pace was shorter than Nuella's, who was still taller than him, but he corrected for the difference and was delighted when he accurately made the sharp right turn two-thirds of the way back to the hold's entrance.

"I think we're at the door," he said not long after, when his pacing told him they should be there.

"Yup, I can smell it," Nuella confirmed.

Kindan felt for the dowels at the top and bottom of the door, and slid them back.

"Wait!" Nuella whispered cautiously. "Listen first. You never know when someone might be out there."

A sudden rush of fear and anger at his own foolishness swept through him, and for a moment he could not hear anything but the sound of his blood pounding in his ears.

Nuella laid a comforting hand on his shoulder. "I just don't think it'd be easy to explain you and a watch-wher suddenly appearing from our closet." She listened some more and then said, "All clear."

Kindan slowly opened the door to reveal the still-dark closet. He cautiously opened the closet door and peered around before beckoning Kisk to come through. Nuella followed behind and they closed the door.

"I'll lead you down to the kitchen door," she said.

"Is this light too bright for you, Kisk?" Kindan anxiously asked the watch-wher, wondering if he could shield her eyes with his hands.

Nuella flicked open the closet door and pulled something out. "How about this?" she asked, handing him a robe.

Kindan, who had been watching Kisk closely, shook his head. "She seems okay. Glows don't seem to bother her all that much."

"Well, I'll bring it anyway," Nuella said. "It might be cold outside."

But they needed it before they got outside. In the kitchen, Kisk skittered away from the open hearth and its roaring fire, making anxious noises in the back of her throat. Kindan quickly grabbed the robe from Nuella and shielded Kisk's eyes from the fire. Her anxiety diminished immediately, and she gave Kindan a thankful noise.

"You know," Kindan said thoughtfully, "we'd never get away with this in a proper Hold. There'd be a guard or something."

"Well, this is more like a house, isn't it?" Nuella said. "And Milla only comes down to feed the fire when she gets chills."

Coming outside into the cold evening air, Kindan felt as though he'd awoken from a dream.

"Well, thanks," he said to Nuella as she stood in the doorway. "We'll be going back to the shed now."

"You're welcome," Nuella returned with a small smile. Shyly, she asked, "Do you want to try again tomorrow night?"

"Maybe," Kindan said. "We're hoping M'tal might come tomorrow."

"Could I meet him, do you think?" Nuella asked.

"I don't know," Kindan said hesitantly. "What would your father say?"

Nuella dismissed his objection with a wave of her hand. "Who cares? It's not like the Weyrleader of Benden is going to tell on me, is it?"

Kindan was still not sure. "Master Zist says that the more a secret is shared, the less it is a secret. Soon everyone knows."

" 'Secrets like to be free,' " Nuella quoted in agreement. "My mother always says that."

"That sounds right," Kindan agreed. "Why don't we talk about this tomorrow?"

"All right," Nuella said. But she sounded as if she expected to be disappointed.

As Kindan drifted off to sleep that night, he couldn't help wondering which would disappoint Nuella more—not being able to meet a dragonrider or not going into the mine. As he considered the question, he imagined that Nuella rarely had a chance to stretch her legs or get out and about, until he realized that she'd probably spent a lot of time navigating around the hold. She'd certainly done enough exploring to find and memorize the secret passageway. He fell asleep wistfully remembering the ease with which Nuella had navigated the dark corridor.

◆

"She's really grown," M'tal said as he examined Kisk in the darkened shed. The Weyrleader had come the third day after Kindan drummed out his message. They were lucky to catch him, as the snows had settled in on the high mountains, including Benden Weyr. While snow was no deterrent to dragons and dragonriders— M'tal told an envious Kindan that the Weyr was naturally warm during winter—it could cause problems for holders and crafters caught unawares. M'tal and his Weyr had spent the first sevenday after the snowfall rescuing people trapped by the cold or isolated without needed supplies.

Kindan's eyes had widened when he heard that—for he'd never heard of any Telgar dragonrider bothering to check up on the holders or crafters during foul weather. And, after his encounter with D'gan, Weyrleader of Telgar, he could understand why. The two Weyrleaders were clearly cut from very different cloth.

"And you say she sees in the dark?" M'tal mused now. "Dragons can't, you know."

"Yes, she's—" Kindan stopped, not wanting to break Nuella's secret about the passageways. "I think she's almost ready to go in the mines," he added hastily.

M'tal patted Kisk gently and rubbed his hands over her body.

"Not quite a dragon in miniature," he commented. "She's got more muscles—at least that I can feel. She feels well grown. And you say her skin never itched or cracked?"

Both Kindan and Master Zist shook their heads and said in unison, "Never a bit."

M'tal sighed feelingly. "I wish I could say the same with Gaminth."

"What we were wondering, old friend," Master Zist said to the dragonrider, "is whether there is any lore gathered in the Weyrs that might help us in training Kisk, here."

M'tal stroked his chin thoughtfully. Then he grimaced. "Not at Benden, as far as I know. What about the Harper Hall?"

Master Zist shook his head ruefully. "My request to the Harper Hall for any information on watch-whers crossed *their* request for all the information I had on watch-whers."

"Apparently watch-whers have become forgotten on Pern." M'tal frowned. "I don't like that. They were clearly bred from the same source as dragons, so there must have been a need for them. We shouldn't have lost that lore." Gently he extended Kisk's vestigial wings. "I can't imagine how she could fly with these."

"My father once flew Dask," Kindan reported.

M'tal looked up. "Really? How?"

"It was late at night," Kindan replied. "I don't think they went up too high," he added. "I think my father was afraid of heights."

"They fly at night?" M'tal mused. He continued thoughtfully. "And they see in the dark, don't they? Perhaps they were bred for night."

"So it would seem," Master Zist agreed. "Kisk is much more active during the night—definitely nocturnal and not just light sensitive."

"She's certainly smarter than a fire-lizard," M'tal noted. "I wonder . . ." He trailed off, frowning.

Suddenly, Kisk's body jerked, and she gave a questioning chirp.

M'tal patted her soothingly. "That's just Gaminth, my dragon," he reassured her. He turned to the others, eyes alight with excitement. "Gaminth can speak to her!"

"Really?" Master Zist said.

"Wow!" Kindan exclaimed, glancing at Kisk admiringly. Then he asked her, "Can you talk to Gaminth, too?"

M'tal's eyes widened with the possibilities. "That is certainly worth exploring, Kindan."

"If watch-whers could talk to dragons, send messages . . ." Master Zist murmured, imagining all the ways in which such communication could benefit people, dragons, and watch-whers.

"I must think about this," the Weyrleader said, still lost in thought. He slapped his hand against his thigh decisively. "Zist, if you don't mind—and you, too, Kindan—I'd like to mention this to some acquaintances of mine. Perhaps we can help each other in learning more about watch-whers."

"Sure."

"Certainly."

M'tal nodded his thanks. "In that case, I must be off. I shall return as soon as I can, maybe in company."

And with that, he departed.

◆

"And you didn't even tell me!" Nuella shrieked at Kindan the next morning. Kindan was still groggy from the late night—Kisk had remained excited for most of the evening and it was only when the first light of dawn could be seen that she became even remotely tired.

"It was all so sudden," he protested. "Lord M'tal arrived and came straight into the shed, examined Kisk, and then—he was gone."

"Hmmph!" Nuella was not in the least comforted. "And now you want me to help you into the mines? Why should I?"

"Because you offered," he replied, wishing that somehow Nuella would retreat from her anger.

Kindan's wish was granted. The head miner's daughter drummed her fingers on her leg for a moment, flared her nostrils in one last spat of anger, and sighed. "All right," she agreed. "But only because Kisk needs the training. And only if you tell me *everything* that dragonrider M'tal said last night."

Kindan did so, his narration interrupted constantly by Nuella's questions. Kindan realized as he answered her that Nuella was very good at illuminating every detail of a conversation. Her questions reminded him of things he'd forgotten and brought nuances of the conversation to light for him that he otherwise wouldn't have seen.

"All right," she said at last, standing up and dusting herself off determinedly. "Meet me at the hold this evening after my classes with Master Zist."

"This evening?" Kindan was surprised. Nuella, despite her eagerness, had had to postpone their sojourn the past three nights.

"Yes," she said. "Dalor will meet you and bring you upstairs."

"Ah, so you convinced him, eh?" Kindan muttered.

"Not so much convinced as blackmailed," she admitted. "I happen to know who he's sweet on, you see."

Kindan's eyes widened in surprise, then narrowed again thoughtfully. Dalor was growing steadily and thickening out into a strong-muscled young man. Kindan himself was in that awkward stage of adolescence where his voice was neither fish nor fowl. In some ways it was a relief that he had Kisk to train; he would have hated the disappointment his breaking voice would doubtless have given Master Zist.

"And he's gotten taller than me," Nuella added in an aggrieved tone. "I can't use him as a double anymore."

"You've changed, too," Kindan countered. "You couldn't pass as Dalor even if he hadn't gotten taller."

"What's that supposed to mean?" Nuella demanded. "Oh, I suppose his voice is different, but if he kept silent, no one could tell."

"Nuella, we're all growing up," Kindan responded. "I've noticed it, you've noticed it, and I'm sure Zenor's noticed it."

"Oh." Nuella paused. "Do you think so?" she asked, her tone wistful.

"Yes," he replied firmly, relieved that he'd managed not to burst out laughing at her response. It seemed he knew who Nuella was sweet on, too!

"Don't you dare tell him," she warned him icily.

This time, Nuella made a point of letting Kindan lead the way through the secret passageway from the hold to the mine. He had to reassure Kisk that he would be right back before the watch-wher would let him leave them. Quickly he scouted out the area around the pumps, making certain that it *was* possible to get from the secret door to the lifts. Then he came back for Nuella and Kisk.

He led them to the lifts without alarm, although his heart raced as they clambered onto the platform and he began to lower them down. The mine lifts were built to operate in parallel: When one was lowered, the other was raised, so that there was always a lift at the top and the bottom of the mine shaft. Kindan was sure that the noise of the lifts would be heard throughout the mine on such a still night.

As soon as they reached the bottom, he hustled them off the lift and over into a spot unlit by glows. When his pulse had slowed enough for him to think, he peered around to see the lay of the land.

"Come on," Nuella said impatiently, pushing past Kindan and turning to the left.

"We're heading south," Kindan observed quietly.

"I know," Nuella replied testily. "South is where Father's shift is digging the new street."

Natalon had adopted the convention of calling tunnels dug through the length of the coal seam "streets," and the tunnels dug through the width of the coal seam were called "avenues." In Natalon's mine, "streets" ran east-west, while "avenues" ran north-south.

There were already two streets dug into the coal seam, both north of the main mine shaft. Natalon's new street was being dug one-third of the way between the current mine shaft and the newly dug shaft that Toldur's crew had just finished. What the miners called "main avenue" had been dug following the edge of the coal seam north and south of the first mine shaft. It met and went beyond the new mine shaft toward the very edges of the coal seam. Natalon had ordered the tunneling southward to stop short of the end of the seam as he wanted to avoid the chance of tunneling into water under the lake.

The coal seam was thick, nearly two and a half meters. In

making the streets, the miners had to dig out coal. As they progressed in their mining, they would divide the huge coal seam into "rooms," leaving pillars of coal to support the rock above the seam. Now that the surface seams were all depleted on Pern, this "room and pillar" mining was the only method practical with the tools and manpower available.

Each of the east-west running streets followed the sloping coal seam as it angled deeper into the mountain range. Kindan knew that there were several north-south avenues cut between the older streets, but the miners had not yet started on a connecting avenue to Natalon's newest east-west street.

"The glows are dim around here," he said, looking at one flickering glow mounted on a joist.

"Really? I'd hardly noticed," Nuella replied with a grin. Kindan snorted.

"How come you're in front?" he asked a few paces later.

Nuella raised her arms slowly to either side. She shook her head. "I don't know, the tunnel's wide enough for all of us."

Kindan bit back a tart reply, shook his head ruefully, and caught up to Nuella's left side. Kisk poked her head between the two of them.

"Here's the turn," he said when they reached the new street.

"I know," Nuella said.

Kindan didn't bother to ask her how she knew; he had been around her long enough to guess that she'd either heard the difference in the sound of their footsteps or felt a breeze, or smelled new air, or something. There were times, he admitted to himself, when he had a hard time believing that she was blind.

Nuella turned right, into the new street.

"Wait!" Kindan called.

"Why?" she demanded.

"These supports," he said. "There are an awful lot of them."
He ran a critical eye up and down the thick timbers that held the
huge supporting beam overhead. There were three such joists
in close succession, spaced within a meter. He walked past the
opening to the new street and saw that there was a matching set
of three joists on the far side of the new tunnel. "There are three
joists on either side of the entrance."

"I heard Father say he always puts in extra support when he
starts a new tunnel," Nuella said. She added, "He and Uncle
Tarik were arguing at the time, actually. Uncle Tarik said that Father was being too worried and that a single joist would do just as
well, but Father said you can never be too careful. Uncle Tarik
said that there was no point in taking in all the extra time and effort so it was a waste."

"I'll bet he did! Him and his talk of people being 'lazy'!"

Kindan noted as they went down the new street that there
were three more joists on it, too, about two meters beyond the
entrance. The glows were slightly brighter there, no doubt because Natalon and his shift would have wanted fresh glows to
work with.

Kindan kept pace as he walked down the new street. Just as
on the main avenue, tracks ran down the center for the coal
carts. Nuella stumbled once on a poorly driven stake but recovered quickly. Her look dared Kindan to say something. He kept
quiet.

The tracks ended when they had gone forty-eight meters
down the new road. Kindan could clearly see the pick marks in
the wall facing them just a few meters beyond.

Nuella continued forward, her right hand held up, palm out.

She stopped when her fingertips stroked the still-trapped coal. She felt the entire length of the wall, grimacing when she couldn't reach the top.

She turned toward Kindan. "I always wanted to know what it was like where my father works," she told him shyly. Then she grinned. "It's not bad!"

Kindan, looking at the dimming light and the dirty coal of the walls, shook his head in disbelief.

Nuella took in deep lungfuls of air. "Smell anything?" she asked after a moment.

Kindan sniffed. "Nope. The air's a bit stale, maybe."

"Well, Father said that part of the reason he wanted to make this new road was to see if there might be more of that bad smell Dask mentioned," she told him. "He was afraid that if there was, it would show that the mine was too dangerous to work. Uncle Tarik said that's what happened to his mine." Nuella's tone clearly showed that she didn't believe him.

"But the accident was on Second Street," Kindan protested. Second Street was the northernmost tunnel through the coal seam.

Nuella nodded. "That's what Uncle Tarik said. But Father said that if the problem was at the west end of the field, it would probably stretch the whole way. If it was only at the northwest end of the field, then we could still work the southern part, unless we got too close to the lake."

"Well, I don't smell anything," Kindan repeated.

"What about Kisk?" Nuella asked.

"What about her?"

"Well, isn't she supposed to notice those sorts of things?" Nuella suggested.

"I suppose."

"So," she replied testily, "why don't you ask her what she smells?"

Kindan finally understood that Nuella planned to start the watch-wher's education there and then. With smelling.

"What can you smell, Kisk?"

The watch-wher made an inquiring noise.

"Come on, smell the air. See what you can smell. I smell coal and stale air, how about you?"

"Less talking, Kindan, more thinking," Nuella snapped.

"What do you know about it?" he snapped back.

"I know just as much about training a watch-wher as you," she responded. "More, in fact."

"More?"

"Yes," she replied, raising her head. "I've been playing with Larissa, teaching her."

"What can you learn from a baby that you can teach a watch-wher?" Kindan demanded angrily.

"Manners, for one thing," she said bitingly. "And it seems to me that Master Zist needs to work on yours."

The two traded more barbed comments before Kindan cooled off. He paused, looking shyly at Nuella, whose nostrils were still flaring in anger—until he realized that his breathing was labored.

"Nuella, the air!" Kindan said. "It's bad. Really bad, not just stale. We need to get out of here."

Nuella looked up at him, took a deep breath, and nodded. "You're right. I've got this terrible headache and it's not just from your shouting." She grinned. "Talk to Kisk."

"What?"

"Tell her about the air—get her to remember what it smells like," she said. "I'd been hoping this would happen."

"Hoping?"

"Yes, so we can teach Kisk," Nuella said. "Oh, do talk to her. Or must I do that, too?"

Kindan patted the watch-wher on the neck. "Do you smell the air, Kisk?" He took a deep breath by way of example. "It smells stale, doesn't it?" He took another breath. "Stale."

The watch-wher took a breath and let it out with a rasp. She looked up thoughtfully at Kindan and chirped, *Errwll*.

"Stale," Kindan repeated, taking another breath.

Kisk took another breath. *Errwll*.

"You've learned a word!" Nuella exclaimed.

Kindan gave her a look and was glad that she couldn't catch it. "I can't see how you can say that *errwll* sounds like stale."

"I didn't say that. I said that *you've* learned a word. Now you know that when Kisk chirps 'errwll' she's telling you that the air is stale."

A look of comprehension dawned on Kindan's face. "You mean, she's teaching me her language?"

"I doubt watch-whers have a language. Even the dragons don't have a language—they make noise for emphasis but they don't speak. They don't need to, they use telepathy," Nuella said. "But that doesn't mean that the two of you can't work out ways to communicate together." She stretched a probing hand out toward the watch-wher and, when she found it, gently rubbed Kisk's nose. "What a good little girl."

"We'd better go," Kindan said. "My head is killing me."

"See? And you've learned that your head aches when the air gets stale," Nuella added triumphantly.

"I knew that already," he replied. "My head ached for days after I pulled you guys out of your house."

"Oh," Nuella said, crestfallen, "right. I'd forgotten."

Silently, Kindan turned back down the street. A moment later Nuella's hand crept shyly into his and squeezed it. "Thank you," she said softly.

Kindan could think of nothing to say.

CHAPTER X

Hot air rises, cold air falls;
These are thermodynamic laws.

Zenor was furious with them when he found out two days later. "You went down there by yourselves! You could have been killed. What if something had happened to you?"

"Dalor knew," Nuella replied just as hotly.

"I wasn't talking to you," Zenor said to her.

"Well, I was talking to you," Nuella snapped back.

Kisk gave a worried *cheep* and nudged Kindan.

"Stop it, both of you," Kindan said, his voice quiet, his pitch—thankfully—deep, and his tone firm. It had, he realized as Nuella and Zenor both gave him startled looks, the tone of command to it. He suppressed a smile and continued with his momentum, saying, "Zenor, we were as safe as we could be, maybe even safer because we had Kisk with us."

"An untrained watch-wher makes you safe?" Zenor cried in disbelief.

"And how do you expect her to *get* trained?" Nuella inquired in a tight voice. Her hands were balled into fists at her sides.

Kindan started to say something, to try his "command voice" again, but Kisk nudged him with her head, stood up off her front legs, and flapped her tiny wings at him, making a throaty *chirp*. Kindan cocked an eyebrow at her. Kisk repeated herself, complete with *chirp*.

"You two, we're going to have company," Kindan said.

"What?" Zenor said. "How do you know?"

Kindan gestured. "Kisk told me. A dragonrider." The watch-wher shook her head firmly, unmistakably. "Two dragonriders?" Kisk nodded vigorously.

"You've been practicing!" Nuella exclaimed delightedly. "What's it like?"

"Well," Kindan said, consideringly, "it's *almost* like I get images from her—but it's not. And I guess it's more like communicating with a fire-lizard than with a dragon. Or maybe somewhere in between. Whichever way it is, she *tells* me until I understand her.

"Zenor, would you run and warn Master Zist?"

Zenor glanced at Nuella. "What about her? Shouldn't I get her back to her room?"

"No way!" Nuella cried. "I'm staying right here." She stalked over to Kisk and wrapped her arms around the watch-wher's neck.

Zenor flushed with anger, but Kindan gave him a quick calm-down gesture. "Please, Zenor, I'm sure the Harper will want to know."

Zenor's mouth worked angrily. "Well at least hide, Nuella. Don't let them see you." Nuella's response was to bury her head in the watch-wher's shoulder with an audible *hmpph*. Zenor grimaced again but left.

"It's not my secret anyway," Nuella muttered softly into Kisk's tough hide.

"What?" Kindan had been distracted, wondering what *two* dragonriders could want.

"I said, it's not my secret," Nuella repeated. "It's Father's. He's the one who doesn't want anyone to know about me.

"His mother was blind too, you know. He's afraid it's passed on, that any daughter we kids have will be blind, too. *And* he's afraid that it makes him look weak—as if anyone would care. It's not like he's the one who's blind."

Kindan sensed that Nuella was telling him because she just *had* to tell someone. He also guessed that she felt she couldn't tell Zenor— or was afraid.

He tried to say something comforting. "But Larissa—"

"It's too early to tell, still," Nuella interjected. "I could see just fine until my third Turn and then, over the course of a year, everything got blurry and dim."

"Does Tarik—"

"I think that's why Father keeps him around," Nuella said. "He's afraid Tarik will spread tales. He's afraid about what'll happen to me, if I'll ever get married—"

"Zenor—"

"Him!" Nuella snorted. Kisk curled her neck around to butt Nuella gently on the shoulder with a soothing *mrrrgll*.

Kindan, whose ears had gotten much better under her tutelage, asked, "Nuella, are you crying?"

"No," Nuella said, but Kindan could hear the tears in her voice. "Why should I be? I'm fine. I'll be just fine. I don't *need* to get married, you know. I'll take care of myself. I have plans, you know."

"Plans?" Kindan repeated. "What sort of plans?"

"Secret plans," Nuella said. "I'll be okay, don't you worry about me."

Kindan was rather sure that Nuella's plans were secret even to her. He tried again to comfort her. "Nuella, I'll always be your friend. Kisk and I will always be there for you."

"How?" Nuella asked, turning away from Kisk's side and wiping her eyes. "How can you say that? What happens if there's a cave-in or something? What if you're killed, both of you? What then? What are you going to do then?"

"We won't be killed," Kindan said firmly. "If there's a cave-in, Kisk and I will dig ourselves out. And then we'll dig the others out, too. Zenor and Dalor and everyone."

"Don't put yourselves out over Zenor," Nuella said grumpily. Kindan reached out tenderly and brushed the tears off her face. She caught his hand in one of her hands and wiped her tears with the other. "Thanks," she said softly. "I'm okay now. It's just sometimes . . . I wish I could see." She made a rueful face. "I wish I could see Zenor's face when I get him angry. Oh, I can feel the heat of his blush—who couldn't?—but I don't know if it's the same . . ." She trailed off and her face took on an abstracted look. "I've just had a thought," she said slowly. "If I can feel the heat off Zenor's face, I wonder if Kisk could?"

"Well, I—"

Nuella shook her head briskly. "No, I don't mean like that. I mean like maybe her eyes *see* heat."

"See heat?" Kindan repeated blankly.

"Well, her eyes are huge, aren't they?"

"To see in the dark," Kindan objected.

Nuella shook her head in disagreement. "Or maybe it's not the light that she sees, but the heat. And everything is so much hotter during the daytime that it'd be like looking at the sun to her."

"An interesting theory," a man's voice said behind her.

Renna was on watch duty that night. She had been so proud of herself when Kindan had had to give it up so that he could raise the watch-wher. "It's not because you're Zenor's sister, you know," he had said when he'd told her. "It's because you're the most responsible. I'm sure you'll do an excellent job."

Renna was sure that she had. It was hard being the one to set watch, and she had had to do a lot more to make sure that everyone else did their jobs. She would wake up in the middle of the night and check up on the younger watchers. Sometimes, she found one asleep. She usually had a lot of fun sneaking up on the laggard and shrieking in his—it was mostly the boys who fell asleep—ears.

Tonight she was spelling Jori, who was taking extra long over her dinner. Renna didn't really mind, though; she liked the late evening up on the watch-heights. Her ears were good and she could hear almost every word spoken as it rose up from the valley below, echoing off the hard cliff walls. She also had a great view of the lake under the night stars.

When two dragons popped out over the lake, she jumped with delight. They were huge, larger than anything Renna had ever seen—certainly larger than Kisk, Kindan's growing watch-wher, and far prettier. She watched in awe as they glided over the houses and landed on the hillside that led up to the mine entrance.

A man's voice drifted up to her. "J'lantir, are you sure?"

She watched the two dragonriders dismount. The dragons rose again, flew toward the lake, and then plunged with frightening abandon into the water. Renna was afraid they'd drowned, until they popped back up again, bobbing like large wooden rafts on the water. She shivered. It was a cold night—dragons must have tough hides to like that water. Or maybe they'd just come from a hot place.

"Lolanth felt a strong presence," the other dragonrider, J'lantir, replied. "J'trel would know for sure, M'tal, but my guess is that there is a young girl here who could ride gold . . . only—"

"What?"

"Well, Lolanth tells me that this girl is in constant darkness," J'lantir replied in a puzzled tone.

"Trapped? Is she in danger?" M'tal pressed.

"I don't know. Lolanth seemed to think that the girl had been that way for some time," J'lantir replied.

"You don't suppose she's blind?" M'tal wondered softly.

"Maybe that's it," J'lantir agreed. "What a pity, to be so gifted and not able to Impress."

Their voices grew fainter as they headed down toward the watch-wher's shed.

"This Camp looks to Telgar—and D'gan won't Search," M'tal said after a moment. "I think we shouldn't mention this to anyone."

"I think you're right," J'lantir agreed.

"Ah! We're expected," M'tal said with a laugh. "Gaminth tells me that Kisk is curious about your Lolanth and wants to come out."

"Well, at least we know she can talk to dragons," J'lantir replied with a chuckle. "I've told Lolanth to say 'later' to her."

The two dragonriders ducked into the shed and their faint voices were cut off from Renna's hearing. She ignored the sounds of the dragons splashing in the lake below as she recalled the conversation. For one thrilling moment, she'd hoped that perhaps they had been talking about her, and that she might be the one who could ride gold. Did they mean a gold dragon—a *queen* dragon? Wouldn't that be marvelous, Renna mused. But then she'd heard M'tal saying that maybe the girl was blind. Renna ran through the list of girls in the Camp. She knew of no blind girl. Perhaps they were thinking of a baby or something. But if they were, she mused, wouldn't their dragons be able to tell them? Maybe the girl was hidden someplace—but who would keep a person hidden away? Anyway, where could anyone hide someone here? In the mine? She shook her head. That would be too dangerous. But she couldn't think of anywhere else, and she'd been *everywhere* in the Camp! She creased her brow in thought. Everywhere . . . except the second floor of Natalon's hold.

Renna spent the rest of her watch in thoughtful silence. She didn't even grumble when Jori arrived back half an hour late.

◆

"Nuella, this is Lord M'tal, Weyrleader of Benden Weyr," Kindan said as the two dragonriders entered the shed. He looked at the other one. "My Lord—"

"J'lantir, rider of Lolanth, Wingleader at Ista Weyr," the second dragonrider supplied deftly.

"You must be Kindan," he went on jovially, holding out his hand. Kindan shook it quickly. J'lantir turned and held out his hand to Nuella. Kindan started to sidle unobtrusively over to her, to give her a nudge but stopped when he saw J'lantir and M'tal exchange a thoughtful look.

Before the silence grew too large, Nuella raised her hand. J'lantir quickly moved to grab it.

"I'm Nuella," she said. She quirked an eyebrow at him and then her face fell. "You moved, didn't you?"

"I did," J'lantir admitted. "How did you know?"

"I can feel it in the angle of your hand," she replied. She moved closer to him, letting go of his hand and raising her own. "Would you mind if I touched your face?" she asked very nervously. "That's the way I get to know people."

"Not at all," J'lantir replied gallantly.

Nuella raised her hand up, hesitantly. Her fingertips touched his chin, then traced his jaw, his lips, his nose, eyebrows, and forehead.

"You're sunburned," she said with surprise. "Is it still warm at Ista, my Lord?"

"Sometimes the sun can burn worse on cloudy days," J'lantir admitted. "However, in my case it comes from flying above the clouds, where the sun is still shining. At Ista the clouds sometimes gather very low."

"You fly above the clouds?" Nuella repeated, awed.

"I do," J'lantir affirmed.

M'tal stepped beside him. "I am M'tal," he said to Nuella, reaching out to her. She found his hand and shook it and, with his permission, traced his face.

"Do you have a good Harper at Benden Weyr, my Lord?" she asked when she had finished.

"A good Harper?" M'tal mused. "Why yes, we do. Why do you ask?"

"It seems to me that your face laughs a lot," Nuella answered. "I thought maybe that was because your Harper was funny."

"He is," M'tal replied with a laugh. "I'll be sure to tell him you said so; I think he'll be very pleased."

Nuella dipped her head in acknowledgment, only partly hiding her blush.

"Nuella," J'lantir said after a moment, "you had an interesting theory about how watch-whers see."

"I think they see heat, my Lord," Nuella responded.

M'tal said to Kindan, "J'lantir has been asked by his Weyrleader, C'rion, to learn all he can about watch-whers. I suggested that it might be a good idea if you and he pooled your knowledge."

Kindan nodded, looking at the other dragonrider with increased interest.

"How could we test it?" J'lantir wondered aloud.

"I've been thinking about that, my Lord," Nuella responded. "I thought maybe if we got a hot stone and a glow—"

"What a marvelous idea!" J'lantir exclaimed. "I think I would go with more than one glow, one dim and one bright, and maybe the same thing for the stones." Very soon he and Nuella were engrossed in designing a complete test of the watch-wher's sight.

"We could just ask her," Kindan said to himself.

M'tal smiled at him. "But then it'd take away all their fun."

"No, it wouldn't," Nuella said with her usual lack of deference. She put a hand to her mouth. "I'm sorry—I meant, my Lord."

"She's like that with everyone," Kindan murmured.

"She's got good hearing, too," M'tal agreed, with a twinkle in his eyes. He turned to Nuella. "Nuella, I think that we all will be working together quite a great deal, so I think it best if we dispense with formalities and just get on with things—what do you say?"

Nuella's eyes got very big. She nodded, speechless.

Kindan was no less amazed. "Do you mean you want me to call you by your name, my Lord?"

"It only seems fair," J'lantir told them. "Besides, I'm not used to all this 'my Lord'-ing."

"J'lantir is usually either flying upside down or is off somewhere reading," M'tal said, clapping the other dragonrider on his shoulder. He leaned down to Nuella and whispered, "I heard once that he lost his whole wing for a week without noticing."

"Only three days," J'lantir corrected unflappably. He winked at Kindan. "It was quite peaceful."

Kindan's eyes widened at the thought of the dragonrider losing his wing of dragons, but then he grinned back, realizing that he was being let in on a joke.

"That couldn't happen," Nuella said, mostly to herself. "Dragons are telepathic!"

J'lantir smiled and wagged a finger at her; then, realizing that she couldn't see it, he gently tapped her nose. "Very astutely observed, my Lady."

The curtains of the shed rustled and Master Zist entered. Zenor followed, carrying a pot and some mugs.

"Ah, Master Zist, I have heard a lot about you," J'lantir said, whirling to face the Harper. "J'lantir, rider of Lolanth, Wingleader of Ista Weyr."

Master Zist bent his head and said, "My Lord."

J'lantir waved away the honorific. "I was just telling your Nuella that I prefer simply to be called J'lantir by my friends," the dragonrider said. He looked earnestly at the Harper and added, "And I hope we'll be friends."

"I'm sure we will," Zist replied with a grin. He looked over at Nuella. "Your father will be coming down shortly to greet the dragonriders."

"He doesn't want anyone to know about me," Nuella told the dragonriders. "Please, let me hide until he's gone."

Both M'tal and J'lantir reacted with grave, concerned looks.

"It's a secret he wants to keep," Kindan added. "Master Zist tells me that some people need to keep secrets."

M'tal looked grave. "A secret is never a good thing," he said.

"Please?" Nuella begged. "It would hurt him a great deal, and he would be very angry with me."

J'lantir gave M'tal a look. Unhappily, M'tal nodded. "We will keep your secret for now, Nuella," he said. He cocked an eye at the Harper. "I will want to talk to you about this later, Master Zist."

The Harper nodded. "I am not happy with this secret," he said, "but I think it is not too harmful for the moment."

J'lantir made a shoving motion toward Nuella, then stopped, a rueful expression on his face. "Go! Hide!" he said to her. "We'll let you know when he leaves."

"You won't need to," Nuella said as she turned to burrow into a thick pile of straw in one of the corners of the shed. "I'll hear him leave."

Natalon arrived not long after and stayed long enough to ensure courtesy all around. Then, sensing that the dragonriders wanted to work with Kindan and Kisk alone, he withdrew as soon as etiquette allowed.

"I could send something down from the kitchen, if you'd like, my Lords," he offered as he was leaving.

M'tal shrugged a question to Kindan, who replied with a fervent nod.

"That would be excellent, Miner Natalon," M'tal said. "Whatever you have—we don't want to put you out."

"Could you have some hot bricks sent down?" J'lantir asked.

Natalon frowned. "If you're cold, my Lord, I think there's a grate here someplace. We could start a fire."

"No, I don't think that's necessary," the dragonrider said. "Just some bricks, if you don't mind."

"I could carry them," Zenor offered.

"You're supposed to be asleep," Natalon said, shaking a finger at him. "You've got work tomorrow, and I don't need you all worn out."

Zenor looked so crestfallen that Natalon grinned at him, shaking his head. "Besides, I think you might be imposing on Kindan's hospitality."

Zenor shot Kindan a pleading look.

"I'd be happy if Zenor could stay, my Lord," Kindan said instantly.

Natalon glanced at the men. "If it wouldn't be an inconvenience, it might be a good idea to have someone else be familiar with the watch-wher," he suggested.

"Of course!" M'tal said, waving the issue aside. "Besides, another body would add to the warmth in here."

J'lantir nodded vigorously.

"Very well," Natalon said. "But no more than an hour, Zenor—unless my Lords say otherwise."

"All right," Zenor said, looking both very pleased and somewhat unhappy at the same time.

"Well, come along," Natalon said to him. "You've volunteered to carry those bricks back down."

Zenor nodded and turned to follow the head miner back to his hold.

"You know, you could just ask her," Kindan repeated after Zenor and Natalon had left.

"Ask her what?" Master Zist inquired. Kindan started to relay Nuella's observation, but was interrupted with a correction from Nuella, which then opened up a general conversation.

"You know," the Harper said, rubbing his chin thoughtfully, "the human body generates a lot of heat."

"Are you thinking to perform a simple experiment with human bodies and glows?" J'lantir wondered.

Kindan pulled a glow out of its holder and held it up.

"Kisk, which is brighter to you, me or this glow?"

The watch-wher hesitated, then butted her head at Kindan's midriff.

"There, I think we have our answer," M'tal said.

"Hmm," J'lantir murmured, lips pursed thoughtfully. "Well, we know one thing—a watch-wher is much smarter than a fire-lizard."

"More patient, too," Master Zist added drolly. "I hope Zenor brings back some food for her."

"She just ate," Kindan told him. He looked at the Istan dragonrider. "J'lantir, do you know how much they should eat?"

"Well, actually, I've only just started my investigations a fortnight ago," the dragonrider confessed. "I met Master Aleesa"—his tone conveyed how the encounter with the prickly WherMaster had gone—"and decided that perhaps I should pursue other avenues."

Master Zist bit back a laugh. J'lantir rewarded him with a pleasant nod.

"I have, of course, spoken with the wherhandler at Ista

Hold," he continued. "And I was surprised"—he cocked an eye at the Harper—"to discover that the Harper Hall had very little information on watch-whers."

"None at all, from what I've found," Master Zist agreed.

"C'rion decided that seeing as we're getting nearer the next Pass, it would be a good idea to gather every scrap of information that might help us tending dragons during times of Thread," J'lantir said. "I was assigned to learn about watch-whers."

"When I told J'lantir about Gaminth being able to communicate with Kisk," M'tal said with a wave at the attentive watch-wher, "he asked if he might be able to work with us."

"I don't know if I'll get another chance to work with a watch-wher hatchling," J'lantir said.

"Oh, she's hardly a hatchling at this point," Master Zist said.

"She's over four months old now," Kindan put in.

"She'll be five months in a fortnight and three days," Nuella corrected with precision.

"The youngest watch-wher I've seen is over three Turns," J'lantir said. He asked M'tal, "You think they mature faster than dragons?"

M'tal nodded. "That was my guess."

"I'd say you're right," J'lantir agreed. He walked up to the watch-wher and put a hand out, palm up and open, for her to sniff.

"It's okay, Kisk," Kindan told her. Kisk cocked her head toward him, then sniffed J'lantir's hand again and licked it shyly.

"May I touch you?" J'lantir asked the watch-wher with a polite half-bow. Kisk whuffed back at him. J'lantir looked at Kindan. "Was that a yes?"

Kindan nodded. "Although maybe your dragon could talk to her," Kindan suggested as an experiment.

"She'd like that," Nuella agreed.

J'lantir brightened. "That's a good idea," he said. His face took on the abstracted look of a dragonrider talking to his dragon. Kisk watched him appreciatively, then gave a slight start and a chirp, and then a second gleeful chirp. She walked right up to J'lantir, positioning her shoulder under his hand, her neck craned back toward him to see if her position was satisfactory.

The group chuckled.

J'lantir dutifully ran his hands over her body, checking every muscle and gently exploring the shape of her back, belly, head, and tail. "Alike, yet unalike," he commented to himself. He looked over at M'tal. "All the watch-whers seem much more muscled than dragons."

"I've noticed that, too," M'tal replied.

J'lantir touched Kisk's wing, gave her an inquiring look, and then said, "Lolanth, please ask Kisk to spread her wings."

Kindan realized that the dragonrider had spoken out loud in order to warn everyone that Kisk would be moving.

The watch-wher chirped happily and ruffled her wings.

"The wings are awfully small," J'lantir noted. He looked at Kindan. "Your father actually flew his?"

"Late at night," Kindan affirmed.

"Amazing," J'lantir exclaimed. "No one, even Master Aleesa, claimed that watch-whers could fly."

"It appears that harpers aren't the only ones who have forgotten about watch-whers," M'tal said with a teasing glance at Master Zist, who just shrugged. The dragonrider turned back to J'lantir, saying, "What I was wondering was if we could teach watch-whers to talk to our dragons."

"But didn't Kisk here just talk to your Lolanth?"

"Indeed she did, but she was responding to being spoken to.

Can she address one dragon by name? Say, in an emergency?" M'tal said.

J'lantir pursed his lips in thought. After a moment he looked at the Benden Weyrleader with widening eyes. "So watch-whers could alert us to Threadfall? What a marvelous idea! Perhaps that's why they were bred—"

"It won't work," Nuella interrupted.

"Pardon?" J'lantir was taken aback.

"Watch-whers are nocturnal," Nuella said. "They could hardly send a warning during the day."

"Perhaps in an emergency . . ." J'lantir suggested.

M'tal shook his head. "No, I suppose not," he said.

"But they could still call for aid in emergencies at night," Kindan pointed out.

M'tal nodded. "That could be useful. They could tell us about the weather, too."

"An excellent idea," J'lantir agreed.

"Merely being able to tell a dragon that help was needed would be a great boon to some of the outlying minor holds," Master Zist said.

"Some of the minor holds that were snowed in had watch-whers," M'tal said. His eyes grew sad. "If the watch-whers had been taught how to reach our dragons, lives would have been saved."

"Well, then," J'lantir said briskly, "this sounds like a worthwhile endeavor. When do we start?"

"I'd like to start as soon as possible," M'tal said, with a nod to Kindan. "If that's okay with you, Kindan. I know you need your sleep—"

Kindan burst out laughing. "I don't sleep at night, not anymore."

M'tal nodded, looking somber. "Ah, but I do. And my night comes to my Weyr hours before yours."

"So does mine," J'lantir added ruefully. "But I can probably arrange a chunk of time to work with Kindan and Kisk without causing too much of a disruption at Ista Weyr."

"And you cannot," Master Zist said to M'tal.

"But spring will be upon us soon enough," M'tal protested. "If we can teach the Benden watch-whers before then, many lives will be saved."

"Very well, then," J'lantir said. He glanced around at the others. "It seems that we must learn not only how to teach Kisk here to talk with dragons, but learn how to teach the same to other watch-whers and their handlers."

"She seems to do well already," Nuella said. "I mean, she told Kindan that you were coming and how many of you—"

"And how did Kindan know what she was saying?" J'lantir asked curiously.

"Well, it just seemed right," Kindan said.

"Fire-lizards are like that," Master Zist said. "At least with some of their owners."

"Yes," J'lantir agreed. "And watch-whers seem to be smarter, more able. What I'm thinking of is training the watch-wher— and Kindan—so that they know and agree exactly on what they're saying to each other, and to the dragons."

"That would be excellent," M'tal agreed fervently.

"And then taking that training and bringing it to other watch-whers and their wherhandlers," J'lantir added.

"I imagine a harper should be involved," Master Zist commented wryly.

"I'll help," Nuella put in eagerly. Kindan shook his head, totally unsurprised.

◆

Over the course of the next several days, Nuella and J'lantir engaged in countless discussions about the best ways to train the watch-wher, and the vocabulary that was needed to communicate meaningfully between wherhandler and watch-wher. They agreed that Kisk would need to tell a dragon who she was and where she was, that she'd have to know how to communicate with a particular dragon, that she would have to know how to say such things as "emergency," "fire," "help," "healer," and "flood." They argued over whether it was more important for Kisk to be able to use numbers than to say "avalanche."

Kindan felt almost unneeded as the two would argue and then agree, move on, and start to argue again. They would stop to ask Kindan to get Kisk to do something or, worse, to ask Kindan's opinion on their disagreement—Kindan learned early on to be diplomatic—and then the arguing would start up anew.

Often the evening would end with Nuella curled up asleep beside Kisk, J'lantir quietly departing before the first cock crowed, and Kindan too weary to think straight.

At the end of the third evening, J'lantir announced that he had to stay at his Weyr for a time, to report to his Weyrleader, check on his wingriders, and get some rest. Nuella looked so crushed that J'lantir gave her a hug.

"Don't worry, I'll be back," he reassured her.

Kindan figured that Nuella was so sad because she had had so much fun and excitement working with Kisk and J'lantir. He imagined that she would be very bored—not to mention grouchy—until the dragonrider returned.

"J'lantir," Kindan asked just before the dragonrider departed, "do you suppose we could teach Kisk to go *between* like a dragon?" The thought had been on his mind for a while.

"Hmm," J'lantir murmured consideringly. "Fire-lizards can do it, so I can't imagine that watch-whers could not."

"It won't work," Nuella said sleepily. Kindan started: He had thought she was asleep. "They have to see where they're going, and they see heat," she explained.

"So?" Kindan said.

"Ah, I see what she means," J'lantir said. "A dragonrider has to give the visual reference for his dragon. So only a wherhandler who could *see* heat could give a watch-wher a proper visual reference."

"And no one can see heat," Kindan agreed glumly.

"I can imagine it," Nuella murmured from her perch on Kisk.

"Why did you want to know?" J'lantir asked Kindan.

"If watch-whers could go *between* they might be able to rescue people, to bring them out of cave-ins and such," Kindan explained.

"An excellent idea, Kindan," J'lantir agreed. "Truly excellent. It's a shame that it won't work."

"Goo' 'dea," Nuella agreed sleepily. She yawned and rolled over, facing away from them.

"Well, thanks anyway," Kindan said, turning to join Kisk and Nuella on the shed's straw floor.

J'lantir reached out and tousled the youngster's head. "It was a good try, Kindan."

◆

Kindan was correct in his assessment that Nuella would be grouchy until the dragonrider returned. He spent several days cheering her up, enduring endless barbed comments from her, before he got her to agree to go back into the mines for more training.

"But only if you agree to explore every bit," Nuella demanded. When Kindan agreed, she said, "We can go down when the shifts are off."

The miners worked in the mine only three days in every sevenday. Two other days were spent grading and bagging the mined coal, felling more timber for shoring and supports, and general work around the camp. The last two days were left free for the miners, with the exception that *everyone* had to help on Camp matters, like quarrying for stone, repairing the road, or making furniture and crockery.

The pumps were the only parts of the mine that were constantly manned. Natalon would never allow a build-up of bad air. Not only would that make it impossible for the miners to return, but it would also allow any gas that leaked out of the exposed coal to accumulate in pockets large enough to cause an explosion, like the one that had killed Kindan's father and brothers.

"Let's start with the street Tarik's working on," Nuella suggested once they were in the mine and a peeved Dalor was on watch at the hold's entrance to the secret passageway.

Kindan readily agreed and they turned north from the mine shaft to walk toward Second Street. Kindan had learned how to keep his pace count going while he was thinking or even talking—mostly through painful thumps from Nuella when he forgot.

"You're even more blind down here than I am, Kindan!" Nuella had cried the last time he'd been forced to admit that he'd lost his count. "That's it! From now on, you're going to wear a blindfold," she had declared. "You'll have to rely on Kisk and your pace counts to avoid banging into things."

She'd handed him a dirty scarf that she'd brought along to use as a mask against the worst of the mine's dust. "You can put this on."

When Kindan protested, she had told him, "Look, what if there's a cave-in or something and all the glows are out? What will you do then? If you know your paces, and you're comfortable in the dark, you won't panic. And if you don't panic, you'll be able to help others."

Kindan had been convinced. From then on he had donned a blindfold the moment they had safely exited the lift at the bottom of the mine shaft. And, apart from some truly amazing bruises on his shins, Kindan had walked unscathed. The bruises had faded as he learned to keep his count and to trust his memory. But privately he admitted to himself that his mental map of the mine was nowhere near as detailed or accurate as Nuella's.

Now Kindan felt for joists by delicate touch—having removed several splinters after the first attempt—and walked with something approaching Nuella's flowing grace.

When they came to Second Street, the tunnel down which Tarik's shift worked and hauled out coal, Kindan checked for supports on either side of the junction. Nuella waited patiently after her own cursory inspection.

"I'm ready," Kindan said, turning back around with his right hand trailing along the tunnel wall. He found the turn onto Second Street and started counting the paces to the street's joists. After fourteen paces—ten meters, the usual interval for the first set of supporting joists—he grew puzzled. After twenty-one he grew alarmed.

"Did you feel any joists?" he asked Nuella, who was walking up the street on the left-hand side, opposite Kindan.

"No," she said, sounding concerned. "Should we go back and check again?"

Kindan struggled with the desire to remove his blindfold and won, remembering Nuella's sharp hearing. She'd know if he took off the scarf—the sound of rustling fabric would be a dead giveaway.

"Yes," he told her, lowering his hands.

Nuella giggled. "You were going to take your blindfold off, weren't you?"

Kindan let his sigh answer her. He counted his paces back to the entrance, turned, and carefully walked forward, searching for the joists. He stopped at nine paces.

"I feel something here, but it's not like a proper joist," he said. The wood was thin, and as he stretched his hands to touch the ceiling above him, he could only make out a thin beam of wood overhead.

"It's not thick enough," Nuella agreed. "Or wide enough."

"It's like half or even a quarter the usual," Kindan said.

It was like that the whole way down the tunnel, they discovered. Kindan's alarm grew as they made their way down. There were numerous side avenues dug off the street, more than he would have guessed.

"It's almost as though Tarik has started mining this street," he said. He knew from discussion around the Camp that the mine was supposed to be thoroughly explored before full mining would commence—and that the "room" mining would begin at the far end of the mine, away from the mine shafts so that any cave-in wouldn't block rescuers. "This is bad," he said.

"Yes," Nuella agreed. "Father must not know—he wouldn't allow it."

They completed their exploration of Second Street and all its adjoining avenues with their nerves on edge. Nuella did not object when Kindan suggested that they change their exploration to First Street the next time they entered the mine.

Kindan hadn't forgotten his notion about watch-whers rescuing people. Every chance he got, he tried to arrange an experiment to test Kisk's capabilities, or to teach her something new.

But when he said he wanted to see how she might excavate a trapped body, Nuella would not allow him to try.

"Look, all I want to do is cover myself with some coal and have Kisk dig me out," he'd protested when she'd first vetoed the idea.

"What if you get hurt?" she demanded. "What will we do then?" And, despite all Kindan's arguments to the contrary, she absolutely refused to go along with it. What surprised him was that Kisk backed her up—he had expected that the watch-wher would accept his direction without dissent.

"Okay, okay, you two ladies win," he grumbled in the end. His comment earned him a swift jab from Nuella.

"It's not that we're ladies, you fool, it's that we're being sensible," she snarled at him. She sighed and added, "If you're determined to practice this, let's do it up in Kisk's shed first before we try it underground."

Reluctantly, Kindan agreed.

———◆———

Kindan and Kisk returned to the shed, having seen Nuella safely back to her second-floor room in the hold. Kisk was still playful. Tired, but resigned to the need to wear Kisk out, Kindan decided to teach her a modified form of hide-and-seek. He would hide under the straw, which let him lie still, quiet, and almost asleep, while she would search for him.

Kisk was excellent at finding him. Kindan made sure that

she turned her back while he was hiding and told her "Don't listen!"—with little real hope that she wouldn't. As the game progressed, he took to gathering small stones and tossing them in different directions to try to confuse her hearing.

The flaw with that plan, of course, was that even properly buried, he'd still have to tell her when to start searching for him, and the sound of his voice would give his location away. After some experimenting, he discovered a solution: He would throw a final rock at the curtain covering the doors. When Kisk heard that, she was allowed to start looking for him.

The game got more interesting then, as Kisk took longer to find him.

On the second attempt, having tossed the last stone at the curtain, Kindan squeezed his eyes tight, reduced his breathing to the barest trickle, and tried to think of nothing but blackness, doing his best to imitate the ground beneath the straw.

As he lay there, tired and sleepy, he started dozing off.

It was then, just on the edge of sleep, that Kindan thought he saw something—a glowing shape, like someone curled up in a tight ball just like he was. No, he corrected himself in amazement, it *is* me!

He heard the soft padding of Kisk's feet as she made her way over to him. In his mind's eye, he saw the shape get closer, saw the head become more resolved—not a face, but a sort of smudged oval-shaped rainbow—and then become obscured as bright jets, the orangeish-yellow color of flame, came streaking over it. He felt Kisk's warm breath blow gently through the straw over his face, seeming to perfectly match the flame he was imagining.

Kisk *bleeked* happily.

Laughing, he opened his eyes and burst from under the straw

to wrap his arms around the watch-wher's head. "You found me!" he said. He hugged her tightly. "You great girl, you!"

———◆———

"Describe it again," Nuella demanded the next evening. "Tell me exactly what you saw."

"I can't, really," Kindan replied. "It was like everything was the color of flames—"

"What's that mean?"

Kindan pursed his lips, trying to think. "Did you ever look at something really bright—um, when you were little?"

"Like what?" Nuella asked, making a face at his question.

"Like the sun," he said with sudden inspiration. "Or a flame."

She shrugged. "Maybe."

"Well, I've done that," he went on. "And afterward, I've closed my eyes and I still have the image in them. It starts out as bright white and then slowly fades to yellow, orange, red, green, blue . . . and out."

"Go on."

"Well, it was like that except that all the colors were there with the white bit being the smallest, in the center, and surrounded by different rings of color from yellow to blue."

Nuella suddenly looked wistful. "Do you do you suppose I could see Kisk's images?"

"We can try," Kindan said. "How about it, Kisk? Can you show Nuella your image when you find me?"

Kisk looked from one to the other and *chirped* a cheerful assent.

"Could you?" Nuella asked in a voice full of wonder. She closed her eyes tentatively, then squeezed them shut firmly

"I'll hide," Kindan said. Kisk dutifully turned away from them. Shortly after Kindan threw his stone against the curtain, he heard Nuella gasp.

"Kindan, put your arm over your face," she said. Kindan complied, casting aside his cover of straw as he did so. "Oh! Now the other one."

Kindan obeyed, then impishly raised both arms over his head, clasped together.

"You put your arms up!" Nuella exclaimed. "You're grabbing your hands—by the Egg of Faranth, I can *see* you!"

Kindan sat up and stared at her. Tears were rolling down her cheeks from her closed eyes.

The next day, he and Nuella started teaching Kisk how to find people buried under rubble. At Nuella's suggestion, they started with having Kisk simply find individual people. Kisk loved this game and found Nuella, Kindan, Zenor, Dalor, and Master Zist— even though Dalor and Master Zist were in their respective cotholds, and Dalor was tired from his shift work.

"Dalor doesn't get into the mine any more than I do," Zenor grumbled before heading off to sleep. "We're both on pumps."

"I'll bet Tarik would let you come into the mine," Nuella said.

Kindan gave her a startled look.

"Maybe you could ask to change shifts," she went on.

"Tarik?" Zenor repeated, shaking his head. "I don't know . . ."

"Well, suit yourself," she said. "Either stop grumbling, or switch to Tarik's shift."

"What was that all about?" Kindan asked after Zenor had left.

"Remember how worried you were about the supports on

Tarik's street?" Nuella asked. When Kindan nodded, she explained, "Well, *we* can't say anything about it to my father, because then we'd have to admit that we've been down in the mine. But if Zenor goes down with Tarik, then he can *see* the shoddy supports that Tarik's been putting up and warn Father."

———◆———

Kindan and Nuella were pleased when Zenor announced joyfully that he'd switch shifts. "Best of all," he'd said, rubbing his hands gleefully, "I won't have to do the morning feeding! Regellan even thinks *he's* getting the best of the deal, can you imagine?"

"There, that's sorted then," she said complacently to Kindan when she entered Kisk's shed that evening. Kindan looked beyond her to the curtains, which had rustled closed behind her.

"Didn't Master Zist bring you down?" he asked.

Nuella brushed aside the comment. "No, I came down on my own."

Kindan's eyebrows rose. "Isn't that dangerous? What if someone saw you?"

"Well, they'd either say something or ignore me," she said impatiently. "Seeing as no one said anything, I suppose they ignored me." She patted her cloak and pulled off her hood. "It's not like everyone isn't dressed this way in this weather."

Nuella was right: So far the winter had been particularly bitter and cold, and they were only just in the middle of it.

"Spring will be here soon," Kindan said by way of consolation.

"Soon! And what good are we doing?"

Kindan was taken aback by her vehemence.

"We've been waiting here over a month and haven't heard anything—and spring is coming," she went on. "What about all those people? The ones Lord M'tal was worried about? The ones that might be flooded in the spring thaw?" She checked her anger with some effort. "I thought maybe I could help, you see."

Then she frowned. "But nothing's happened. And I'm no help at all."

"You've helped me," Kindan told her softly. Kisk gave her a reassuring *chirp* and walked over to butt Nuella's shoulder with her head. "And Kisk. We wouldn't know half what we know if it hadn't been for you. Soon we'll be ready to go into the mine and—"

Nuella's derisive snort cut him off. "Sure, you'll go into the mine and then what? What will I do then? 'Thank you, Nuella, you've been a big help, now you can go back to your room. And don't get caught!' " Her voice choked on the last word and she buried her head between her knees.

Kindan didn't know what to say and the silence between them stretched out interminably. Finally he opened his mouth to speak, only to see that Nuella had held up a hand and cocked her head in the direction of the curtains at the doorway to the shed.

"You may as well come in," she said out loud. "You've heard too much already and I just don't care anymore."

After a moment the curtains rustled and a small figure could be seen in the dim glow light.

"You look just like Dalor," the figure exclaimed. It was Renna.

Nuella sniffed, breathing in the scent of the newcomer, and nodded her head in comprehension. "You must be Zenor's sister," she answered. "He has some of the same smells."

"It's Renna," Kindan confirmed. He looked back and forth between the two. "Aren't you supposed to be on watch?"

"Yes," Renna said, "but Jori owes me." She looked at Nuella. "I saw someone coming down from the hold and—"

"You followed me because you thought I was Dalor, didn't you?"

Renna's blush showed that Nuella's guess had hit the mark. Kindan remembered that Nuella had once blackmailed Dalor into helping them get into the mines because, as she'd said, "I happen to know who he's sweet on." From Renna's blush, Kindan guessed that the feeling was mutual.

Suddenly Kisk raised her head, chirped, and butted Kindan. He closed his eyes in concentration, accustomed now to passing images with Kisk.

"It's J'lantir and Lolanth," he said a moment later. Kisk chirped at Kindan again. Obligingly, he closed his eyes once more, concentrating on the images the watch-wher was trying to form. The images were a quick series: a heat-rainbow shape being pulled backward by an arm, the same heat-rainbow shape running so fast that the legs were a blur, the same shape banging its head repeatedly, bowing low, and, finally, running again. With a smile, he told the others, "He says he's sorry he's late. He'll be here as quick as he can."

"A dragonrider?" Renna squeaked.

Kindan nodded.

"Here?"

Kindan nodded again.

"Now?"

"Right now, in fact," J'lantir agreed as he stepped into the shed. His cheerful look changed to startlement when he realized that the speaker was not Nuella. Then he cheered up again, looking at Nuella. "Your secret is out. Good! I was afraid—"

"Her secret is *not* out," Kindan said, shaking his head. "Just compromised."

J'lantir's face fell. "Well, that may make things more difficult," he said. "You see, the reason I've been gone so long—no, rather the reason why I'm back *now* is because things aren't going well."

"What do you mean?" Nuella asked.

"Wait a minute," Kindan said, forestalling her. He turned to Renna, whose eyes were as big as saucers. "Renna, please go inform Master Zist that J'lantir is here. He may want you to bring refreshments, too, but please tell him that I've asked you to come back. Don't say any more to him—tell him we'll explain later."

"I'll be *all* ears," Nuella murmured, her face gleaming with her usual humor.

CHAPTER XI

Watch-wher, watch-wher, guard us all
With your dragon-summoning call.

"...And Renna was already here when J'lantir arrived," Kindan finished explaining to Master Zist. The Harper's color had returned to a more normal shade from the bright red of rage it had been when he had first found Renna in Kisk's shed.

He had been ready to tear Kindan's head off for letting Renna in on the secret—he had a few hot words for Nuella, too—but Kindan had managed to get the first word in and refused to be silenced until he'd finished telling the full tale. Master Zist let out a long sigh. "J'lantir was just about to tell us why he had come when I sent Renna off to get you."

"Hmmph," the Harper said at last. "My Lord J'Lantir, first let me apologize for delaying you in delivering your message—"

J'lantir waved aside the apology. "No need, Master Zist, no need at all," he said graciously. Then he wagged a finger at the Harper, adding, "And I thought we'd agreed to dispense with the formalities."

"But you call me Master," the Harper protested, "I could hardly not return the honor."

J'lantir laughed. "I only do *that* because your young charges here all go blue in the face if I don't." He added conspiratorially to the Harper, "You must tell me how you do it, someday. It's a trick I'd like to use on some of my riders."

Master Zist chuckled appreciatively. "I'm afraid it comes from all my years at the Harper Hall, intimidating young scamps worse than Kindan here." Then he frowned. "Well, maybe only just as bad as him."

Renna returned at that moment, bearing a pot and several mugs. "They sent me down with some hot *klah*," she told the group. She glanced apprehensively at Master Zist, then looked to Kindan and Nuella for comfort. Kisk butted at Kindan and gave Renna a cheerful *mrrp*, at which point the girl visibly relaxed.

"Well, pass the cups around, child," Master Zist barked at her. When she jumped and nearly dropped the pot, he added calmly, "I've heard the whole story now and I won't bite. But I'm sure I need a warm cup of *klah*, and I wouldn't doubt our dragon-rider friend here is still chilled from *between*."

Kindan and Nuella both moved before Renna's panicked reaction spilled the pot. Kindan retrieved the pot and mugs, while Nuella put a reassuring hand on the girl's shoulder and pulled her out of the way. With a flourish, Kindan poured *klah* for the dragonrider and the Harper.

Nuella held her hand out, saying, "I'm more parched than

anything, but I'll also be glad for the heat." Kindan filled a mug and carefully guided her hand to it.

Shortly they were all settled on the straw floor, gathered in a semicircle facing J'lantir. Renna had been as polite as her awe of the dragonrider permitted when she had been introduced, and J'lantir, for his part, had gone out of his way to make her feel more comfortable.

"So," he said at last, "you probably want to know what's been happening." He paused. "I apologize for not getting back to you sooner, but things got rather out of hand. Weyrleader M'tal had hoped that I could train the watch-whers that look to Benden the same way that we've managed to train Kisk here."

He nodded politely to the watch-wher, who blinked happily at him and nodded back. J'lantir and the others chuckled at her behavior. Kisk reared her head and chirped mournfully to Kindan until he reached up and scratched her eyeridges, saying, "It's all right, they're just proud of your good manners." Kisk glanced around at all of them, decided that Kindan was correct, and settled back down, making noises of self-satisfaction.

"Such a well-behaved watch-wher," J'lantir agreed. Then he drew a breath and continued, "Sadly, we did not get the reaction we had expected. Many of the wherhandlers could not believe that their watch-whers would talk to dragons, and still others refused to believe that there was anything that any dragonrider could teach them about *their* friends."

He shook his head sadly. "And the truth of it was that they were right," he told them. "For all that I tried, for all that Lolanth tried—" He smiled fondly at the mention of his dragon. "—we couldn't get any of the watch-whers to work with us."

"Whyever not?" Nuella wondered. "You had the scrolls Master

Zist wrote for you, and the training is fairly straightforward. Were they just too simple to understand?"

"I think that the underlying problem was that there was too much *telling* and not enough showing," he replied. "M'tal and I had several long talks on the topic, and we came to realize that the best way to teach wherhandlers was to have someone who hadn't Impressed a dragon but who *had* taught a watch-wher show them how to do it. Someone who wouldn't intimidate them."

He looked straight at Nuella.

"He's looking at you, Nuella," Renna whispered.

"Of course," Nuella agreed. "He wouldn't be looking at Kindan because he has to stay with Kisk, and it's not like she'll be able to go *between* to follow him."

But then Nuella proceeded to marshal all the reasons why it wouldn't work. "J'lantir, I'm afraid that that's not a good idea. I'd love to do it, but my father—"

"Nuella, this is your chance to *do* something," Kindan interrupted her. "Training the watch-whers will help save lives, Weyrleader M'tal said so."

Nuella ducked her head in acknowledgment but persisted, "My father doesn't want anyone to know about me. He's afraid that once they find out I'm blind, no one will want to marry Dalor or Larissa and—"

Kindan had been watching her with narrowing eyes ever since the dragonrider had made his proposal. Closing his eyes in thought while Nuella spoke, he reached a hand casually to rub Kisk, only to stop as he felt a jolt of fear travel from the watch-wher to him. He gave Nuella a look of surprise, whispering in awe, "You're afraid!"

Kindan's announcement stopped her cold. She groped for

words, trying to deny his accusation, but couldn't say anything. Kindan reached across and grabbed her hand.

"Nuella," he said sincerely, "you have never been afraid of anything."

Uncontrolled tears spilled from her eyes. "They'll talk! They'll laugh at me and they'll—"

Kindan grabbed her in a hug and patted her back awkwardly. "No," he said softly. "No, they won't."

"But I won't know where to walk. I'll stumble and trip over things, and they'll *know* I'm blind!" she wailed. J'lantir exchanged a distressed look with Master Zist.

"No, they won't," Kindan said again. "It'll be night. Watch-whers are awake at night. You'll stumble no more than anyone else."

"Zenor never said you were blind!" Renna broke in. She had listened patiently while Kindan was talking, but she realized that for all his good intentions, he didn't *get* it. She turned to Nuella. "He never used your name, but I knew he was sweet on someone. He would talk about all the things he wanted in a girlfriend, and he'd smile that secret smile of his, like he knew something I didn't." She snorted, shaking her head at the foolishness of her brother trying to keep a secret from her. "I knew it had to be you the moment I saw you, Nuella. You are *everything* he was talking about."

Nuella looked puzzled.

"Don't you see?" Renna asked. "He never talked about your sight. It doesn't matter to him." She paused. "And I think it doesn't matter to him because it doesn't matter to you. You just get on with living, don't you?"

Nuella nodded reluctantly.

"If it doesn't matter to you," Renna continued fiercely, "and it doesn't matter to my brother, why are you being so *blind* that you can't see that it doesn't matter to anyone else?"

Nuella sniffed a final sniff and wiped her eyes. She pushed herself away from Kindan and faced Renna. "Do you really think he likes me?"

Renna nodded, and then said, "Of course. He'd be a fool not to." Thoughtfully, she added, "Sometimes I don't think he's all that smart, but he can't be *that* stupid."

Nuella smiled. "But my father—"

"A secret that causes harm is a bad secret," Kindan said.

"I think we can still keep your father's secret," J'lantir offered. "I rather doubt that Telgar Weyr will want to train watch-whers to talk to dragons. And if that's the case, then no one in Crom will ever meet you."

"Rumor travels fast," Master Zist pointed out.

"Of course, if we don't tell him . . ." Kindan suggested.

"No, I think there are too many secrets already," Master Zist said firmly. He looked at J'lantir. "Natalon is a good man," he said, "and while he may err on the side of caution, I do not believe he would do anything to hinder you in this worthy cause."

"Once he calms down," Nuella corrected, her normal sense of humor having returned. She turned to Renna and said, "You *will* keep the secret, won't you?"

Renna made a sour face. "I will," she agreed. "But I think it's a bad idea." She looked squarely at J'lantir. "I think people should tell the truth. All the time, no matter what the consequences."

J'lantir gave her a shocked look. Then he grew thoughtful, brows furrowed.

"I think that some youngsters should mind their manners," Master Zist said tightly. "Particularly with dragonriders."

Renna dropped her eyes and nodded unhappily. "I'm sorry."

J'lantir waved the apology away. "No harm done," he said. Renna looked up. J'lantir grinned at her. "And perhaps some good." They shared a look for a moment, before the dragonrider continued, "Food for thought, at least."

Master Zist looked up at that. "Food is an excellent idea, J'lantir," he said agreeably. "Perhaps you and I should head up to Miner Natalon's hold in search of some."

J'lantir nodded in enlightenment. "That would allow me to pay my respects," he allowed.

Master Zist laughed. "And bring up any matters of import at the same time." With a groan he uncoiled himself from his cross-legged position on the straw. "You know, Kindan, you must really see about getting some chairs in here sometime. All this sitting on the floor is hard on us older people."

"Not to mention cold," Nuella added. She looked up at Master Zist. "Should I—?"

"I don't think there's any reason for you to accompany us," he said.

She looked ready to accept, but thought better of it and shook her head firmly. "No," she said slowly, "Renna's right. There have been too many secrets. This concerns me; I should be there."

"As you wish," J'lantir said, rising to his feet "Perhaps you could lead the way?"

Master Zist turned to Renna, who had started to get up, and looked thoughtfully at her. "Aren't you supposed to be on watch?"

"I traded with Jori," Renna said. "She owes me."

He wagged a finger at her. "Then," he intoned, "you are up far too late and need some sleep. I expect you in my class bright and early."

"I could bring some *klah* to help wake you up in the morning," she suggested impishly.

Master Zist drew breath to scold her, paused, then let it out, nodding his head. "I'm afraid I'll be needing it," he agreed wearily.

◆

"Are you all set, Nuella?" J'lantir called over his shoulder as they prepared to go *between*.

"I'm a bit nervous," she admitted, clutching the dragonrider tightly.

You'll be fine, Lolanth reassured her.

"Remember it will take no longer than it does to cough three times," the dragonrider added.

"All right," Nuella said. For a moment, nothing changed. Then she felt cold and detached from anything and everything. This is strange, she thought. She savored the moment and then it was gone. Nuella took a breath, then carefully sniffed the air. It was different from home.

"We're here," J'lantir said. "You did just fine."

"It was great!" Nuella exclaimed.

J'lantir laughed. "That's not the normal reaction people have the first time they go *between*."

Nuella clutched the dragonrider tighter as Lolanth banked and started a steady spiral down to the ground. The sensation startled her, but she recovered before Lolanth said, *We are landing, it's all right.*

"Nuella, you're here," M'tal called, rushing up to greet them. "Welcome to Lemos Hold."

When she felt his hand grip hers, she swung her leg over Lolanth's neck. Getting down was easier than getting up, particularly with M'tal's strong arms to hold her.

She felt J'lantir's hand on her shoulder as he landed beside her.

"Permit me to lead the way," M'tal said, deftly catching her hand and placing it on his elbow, just the way Master Zist had assured her that all the great lords escorted their great ladies. Nuella blushed at the thought, but followed M'tal gratefully.

"Harper Inrion has managed to convince the Lord Holder to let young Lord Darel and his sister, Lady Erla, stay up with Lemosk to get your training," M'tal explained as they walked up the steps to the Great Hall of Lemos Hold.

"But it's old Renilan and his watch-wher Resk that you'll really need to train," J'lantir added. "If you can convince him . . ."

Nuella nodded. Her father had agreed readily enough when J'lantir and Master Zist had presented the facts to him, but he had insisted that if, for any reason, Nuella couldn't train other watch-whers, she be returned immediately to her hold. Nuella understood, and even agreed with his thinking: It would be bad enough if she failed, but utterly unbearable if she was asked to repeat her failure time and time again.

"I want to start with the most stubborn person," she had said. When J'lantir had protested, she dug in her heels until Master Zist dryly informed the dragonrider that it would be very hard to find someone more stubborn than she was. Nuella wasn't so sure, but she wanted to find out as soon as possible.

In the days between her father's consent and M'tal's news that he'd set up a class at Lemos Hold, Nuella and Kisk had trained hard together, going over everything it was felt watch-whers and their handlers needed to know. Nuella marveled at how helpful and patient Kindan was, even when he mostly had to stand aside and let her work directly with Kisk.

"She's just a girl!" a gruff old voice exclaimed as M'tal led her into a large, echoey room. A younger voice—that of a girl Nuella judged to be younger than Renna—giggled nervously. Nuella made a note to ask everyone's age beforehand next time. If there *was* a next time.

She paused, taking a deep breath. She could smell a fire burning on the hearth and turned her head slightly toward its warmth. A pleasant scent, not perfume but a nice soap, came from where the girl's voice had originated. A sharper, woodsy smell came just faintly from her right, away from the fire.

Nuella turned toward it. "You must be Renilan," she said, letting go of M'tal's arm and raising her right hand in greeting.

She heard the old man's sharp gasp and figured that he was still a meter distant. Then she heard him walk slowly toward her and felt his gnarled hand grasp hers firmly.

"My wife lost the use of her eyes three Turns before she passed on," he told her softly. He sighed. "She had the most beautiful eyes. Like yours, lass."

Nuella smiled. "Thank you."

"You've a pretty smile, too," he added.

"And I'm stubborn," she told him.

"I think you must be," Renilan agreed. "And I can tell by the way you said it that you've been told that I'm stubborn, too." He gripped her hand tighter. "My Lord Holder asked me to meet you. He said you could teach me what Lord J'lantir couldn't. How to talk to my Resk, here."

Nuella shook your head. "I can't teach you that," she said. "All I can do is help you *learn* it. If you're willing to do that, then the next time there's an emergency at your cothold, you'll be able to get Resk to call for help. From dragons."

She heard the surprised gasps of the two youngsters on the other side of her and knew that they were drinking in every word.

"Ah, that'd be a good trick indeed, lass," Renilan said. "If it could be done. But I've tried already with Lord J'lantir—tried for nearly a month, and the only thing I've got to show for it is a bare larder and hungry wee ones to feed."

Nuella nodded in understanding. "Could you introduce me to your watch-wher, please?"

"I don't know if that's a good idea, lass," Ranilan said with a trace of nervousness in his voice. "Resk and I are well bonded and he's not one for strangers. I'd hate it if he bit you or anything."

Nuella stepped around the older man and toward the sound of the watch-wher, her right hand held out, palm up.

"Lolanth, would you ask Resk if I could greet him?" she said out loud. She heard a surprised snort from the watch-wher and then a quieter *chirp*.

"Resk, my name is Nuella," she said in soft, soothing tones, still walking slowly toward the sound of the watch-wher. "You just heard Lolanth, J'lantir's dragon. He's a nice dragon, I just rode in on him. He's a relative of yours from back in ancient times. He's a very friendly dragon. He wants to help. He helps like you do. I know you can hear him. Can he hear you? I can teach you how to talk to him. I can teach you and Renilan how to call to the dragons. Would you like that?"

Warm, moist air blew softly across her outstretched palm. Nuella moved her hand up, slowly, to touch the hard hide of the old watch-wher. Resk started and moved back, but Nuella waited patiently. Slowly, she heard him return. Presently she felt his hot breath on her palm again.

Concentrating on calm thoughts, she stood still, trying to get a *feel* for the old watch-wher.

After a moment, she turned back to Renilan. "May I touch him?"

"I don't see why you're asking me, lass," the old man said with a snort. "You're practically touching him now."

"Manners," Nuella replied tartly.

Renilan let out a bellow. "Ha! Put me right in my place, you did!" he said, still laughing. "Very well, on your head be it. At least you seem to know what you're doing."

"Thank you," Nuella said. "But could you please tell Resk that it's okay?"

Renilan sobered up. "Ah, I see what you mean. Good one, lass." To his watch-wher he said, "Resk, let the lass touch you, there's a good lad."

"I just want to get a feel of you, Resk," Nuella said calmly. "You can feel me, too, if you wish." Slowly she raised her hand to follow the line of his jaw and up toward his neck. She felt the watch-wher's shock and alarm, and his growing calm as she moved her hands down his neck. She stopped.

"Are you itchy? Can I rub your eyeridges? The dragons love that, you know." She stretched her senses until she felt that the watch-wher had acquiesced. "Okay, let me do that now."

Slowly she reached up and scratched the watch-wher's left eyeridge. After a moment the watch-wher lowered his head so that she could reach more easily. Nuella kept scratching.

"That's a good lad," she crooned.

Resk turned his snout toward her and butted her with it. Nuella laughed. Resk gave a sweet chirp and butted her again. Then Nuella felt the watch-wher's slivery tongue slide along the line of her jaw and he gave another happy chirp.

"I don't believe it!" Renilan exclaimed.

"It's just the salt on my skin," Nuella said, turning her head to the old man.

"Ha!" Renilan snorted. "If that were so, I've much saltier skin than yours—he'd be slobbering all over me."

She giggled. "Then you might try washing more."

The two holder children gasped at her cheekiness, but Renilan just guffawed. "Washing!" he said between laughs. "Oh, I'll try that for sure."

Nuella heard him walk over to her and felt him clap her on the shoulder. "You're a good one, lass," he said approvingly. "You're a good one."

"Thank you, sir," she said, reaching up to pat Resk again. "I hope you'll still say that when I'm done."

"Weelll . . . let's say that I'm willing to listen," he admitted.

Nuella shook her head. "Listening is not enough," she said firmly. "*Learning* is."

She heard poorly stifled groans from the children behind her. She turned to them and smiled. "Lord Darel, Lady Erla, M'tal tells me that you work with the Hold's watch-wher, Lemosk. Is that right?"

"Yes," Erla admitted after a moment's hesitation and some whispered consultation with her older brother.

"Well, I don't think that you can learn all that much without Lemosk here," she said. "And it seems to be awfully late. Would you prefer me to teach you another day?"

"I'm not tired," Lord Darel insisted over his yawn.

"Very well," Nuella said tactfully. "However, I think I should work with Renilan and Resk first, so that they can get back to their people, don't you?"

"Yes," the two youngsters said in chorus.

Nuella smiled. "Great. You can watch if you like," she told them. "But there won't be all that much to see. In fact, the first thing we'll do is close our eyes. I'd like you and Renilan to close your eyes and turn toward the fire in the hearth. Can you do that?"

She heard Renilan's stubborn hiss and turned to him with a smile and an inquiring look. The old man sighed reluctantly. "There. Now what?"

"What do you see?" Nuella asked. "No, don't open your eyes. With your eyes closed, what do you see?"

"I don't see anything," Erla said crossly.

"Really? Don't scrunch your eyes, my Lady, just close them, like you're asleep."

"It's lighter toward the fire," Darel reported.

"What color is it?" Nuella asked. "Is it gray or some color?"

"Sort of orangey-red," Erla said. "And I can feel the heat on my face."

"Very good," Nuella said encouragingly. "Renilan, how about you?"

"Well," the old man said slowly, "I'm farther away, but I can see a lighter spot where the fire is and feel the heat, of course."

"Good. Now keep that image in your mind. My friends tell me that it's blurrier than looking at a fire with your eyes open. Do you agree?"

"Well, it's not the same at all, really," Renilan said thoughtfully. "It's like it's hottest in the middle and cooler on the edges."

"That's how your watch-wher sees it," Nuella said. "Try keeping that image in your mind and asking Resk if that's what he sees. Keep your eyes closed, please."

"Can we ask Lemosk?" Erla asked.

"She's not here, silly," Darel said. "She's outside by the gates."

"Is there a fire or a torch near her?" Nuella asked. "If so, you could ask her to think about that."

Renilan gasped and Resk made a startled noise at the same time. "By the First Shell, you're right! That's what Resk sees."

"Watch-whers see heat, you see," Nuella explained. "That's the way their big eyes work."

"So that's why they can see tunnel snakes when there're no glows!" Lord Darel exclaimed excitedly.

"Exactly," Nuella agreed. She turned to Renilan and said for his ears alone, "You felt him, didn't you?"

"Yes," Renilan said in a hushed voice. "I could feel him. I've always sort of known how to talk to him but now . . ."

"Now the hard part's over," she said. "Now that you can imagine how Resk sees, you'll be better able to understand the images he sends you. Now you and Resk can build up a vocabulary, come up with agreed sounds and images that mean something. And then we can teach Resk to use your 'words' to talk to the dragons."

"They can see heat," Renilan repeated, more to himself than anyone. He raised his voice for Nuella's ears, "Can they see people buried in snow?"

"Or coal, or mud, and even a bit in water," Nuella told him.

"That's why my Lord M'tal wants to train us," Renilan said in an awed voice. "We lost three cotholds with all their families in an avalanche last winter."

"My friend lost his older brothers and his father in a cave-in at our mines two Turns ago," Nuella said by way of agreement.

"They should have had a watch-wher," Renilan said firmly. "I hear they're good in mines."

Nuella turned a bittersweet smile into a full smile. "If they're trained properly."

"Very well, Lady Nuella, let's start training," Renilan said with a voice full of commitment.

"It's just Nuella," she replied, shaking her head at the honorific.

"Not to *my* way of thinking," Renilan said fervently.

Nuella laughed. "Let's see if you still say that when the cock crows in the morning!"

◆

"My Lord M'tal, I cannot thank you enough!" Renilan said the next morning, pumping the dragonrider's hand greatfully. "This will save so many lives."

"I'll be sure to have my sweep riders stop by and get acquainted with Resk," M'tal told the old wherhandler. When Renilan's eyes widened, the dragonrider added, "Well, it wouldn't do any good to have your Resk know how to summon just one dragon."

"I suppose it wouldn't at that," Renilan admitted in awed tones. "And you can be sure we won't abuse the privilege; we'll only call in direst emergency—"

"Not even a Gather?" M'tal asked plaintively.

Renilan accepted the teasing with a nod. "And Gathers."

M'tal clapped him on the shoulder. "We dragonriders are here to protect Pern and its people, Renilan. I'm just glad that you and your watch-wher can help us do our job better."

"Much better," Renilan agreed, "now that Lady Nuella has taught us how."

"Do you think you could teach others yourself, now that you know?" J'lantir asked, stifling a yawn. He had been quite surprised to wake in a soft bed that morning. The last he remembered he had still been in the Great Hall. The mystery had been cleared up when he learned that Nuella had asked to have him moved there after he'd fallen asleep at one of the Great Hall's tables.

Renilan pursed his lips thoughtfully. He gave Nuella a sideways look, then replied, "I think I could. I might not be quite as good as my Lady here, but I would do my best."

"Resk can talk to the other watch-whers, you know," Nuella said. "That's half the battle already."

"Half the battle?" Renilan asked.

Nuella nodded vigorously. "Sure. Resk can tell the other watch-whers how to talk with the Benden dragons he's met. And they can tell him about the ones they've met."

"They can?" M'tal and J'lantir said in chorus.

"Dragons can, can't they?" Nuella said. "If a dragon can, why can't a watch-wher?"

"I'd never thought of that," M'tal admitted in a tone of admiration. He cocked his head thoughtfully. "Renilan, has your Resk ever met Breth, the Weyrwoman's dragon?"

"Why, no, my Lord," Renilan said.

"Would you then, kindly," M'tal continued, "ask your Resk to ask Lemosk how to talk to Breth?"

"If you wish, my Lord," Renilan agreed. "He's a bit sleepy, I'm afraid. It's just dawn. He might not be too good at it."

"Just try," M'tal said. "We can try tonight or another night if this doesn't work."

Renilan nodded. He closed his eyes in concentration. Resk was sharing Lemosk's lair for the day and so too far away to hear his handler speak out loud. After a moment Renilan looked up again. "I've done it, my Lord. I think Resk knows now."

"Could you ask Resk to send a message to Breth?" M'tal asked.

Renilan looked dubious. "I can try, but I'm still learning, as you know." He took a quick look at Nuella and straightened up, determined. "Let me correct myself—we'll do it, my Lord. Maybe not this time but we'll try until we do. What is the message?"

"Could you ask her to contact Gaminth?" M'tal said.

"Oh, no, make it Lolanth," J'lantir suggested gleefully. "That would be a much better test as they're not in the same Weyr."

"Very well, could you ask her to contact Lolanth, then?"

"I'll tr— I'll do it now," Renilan answered, closing his eyes again. "There. Although Resk is awfully tired—"

"By the Shell of Faranth!" J'lantir shouted, jumping with excitement. "It worked! It worked! It worked!" He bounced around the others in glee.

Throughout the waking Hold, heads turned and Lolanth and Gaminth bugled from their cliffside perches.

"That's fine, J'lantir, but you'd better tell my Weyrwoman what we are up to," M'tal replied drolly. He turned to Nuella and bowed deeply. "My Lady, on behalf of Benden Weyr, I thank you."

Nuella blushed scarlet from her head to her toes.

CHAPTER XII

Harper, harper, sing me a song.
Give me a tune that lasts all day long.

When Nuella returned home, it felt like she had been gone a lifetime, even though it was only a fortnight. She had smelled the sea. She had tasted exotic fruits. She had drunk the best Benden wine—watered down, just the way it was served to the young Lord and Lady; she wasn't sure she liked it but she had kept that to herself. She had been introduced to fire-lizards and found them charming but too flighty. Watch-whers were much more her sort of person. And dragons, of course. Beneath her, Lolanth rumbled in amused agreement.

She simply had *not* gotten used to being called "my Lady." And the people who had said it to her! It was bad enough that M'tal, Weyrleader of Benden Weyr, had said it, but the Weyr-leader and Weyrwoman of Ista Weyr had also called her that.

C'rion had even presented her with a gold necklace especially made just for her!

It was formed of links in the shapes of dragons, fire-lizards, watch-whers, and dolphins. Seeing the latter, Nuella had fearfully entertained the notion that the Istan Weyrleader might want her to teach watch-whers to talk to dolphins, too. Fortunately, as she hadn't the slightest idea how to go about it, that wasn't the case—C'rion had merely wanted to give her something as a mark of the Weyr's gratitude.

The training had been easy after Renilan. And Nuella had loved every exhausting second of it. The warmth of amazement from both watch-wher and wherhandler as they learned to communicate with each other and with the dragons of Pern was something she would cherish in her heart forever. And she admitted to herself that it was an accomplishment no one could take away from her—and no one else could have done. She *had* to be blind to see the way the watch-whers did.

Nuella realized how much she had learned herself. As she worked with new watch-whers, it had become easier, much easier, to create a rapport with them, to get a feel for what they were feeling and "see" their images.

She had also learned an incredible amount of watch-wher lore. She couldn't wait to tell Kindan that Kisk's name had been predetermined—that watch-whers picked a name that matched their human's, and that their names always ended in "sk". Or that the watch-whers of the major Holds always named themselves after their Holds and always bonded with someone of the Hold's bloodline. Or that watch-whers sometimes outlived their humans and could re-bond with another human—or maybe she wouldn't tell him that, she thought with a frown. It might upset Kindan too much to realize that if he had only known better he might have saved Dask. Well, she decided, perhaps not. From all she'd heard, Dask had been too injured to re-bond and was too determined to carry out Danil's wishes to obey anyone else.

She wondered if Zenor would be there to greet her. They were arriving late, but not too late for him to be up for a special occasion. She wanted to show him her necklace. She wanted to show her father, too. And her mother. Her mother, whose faith in her had never flagged, who had never allowed Nuella to feel held back in the least by her blindness, who had always shown her ways to make it into an asset, to use it to her advantage. And little Larissa. Maybe—Nuella crinkled her nose— she could get out of having to change the baby's diapers for a bit, perhaps two or three days.

She felt the impact as Lolanth landed softly on the meadow outside the first mine shaft. She'd asked J'lantir to land there so that her arrival wouldn't be noticed. She hoped her father would appreciate her thoughtfulness.

She felt J'lantir hop down. "Come on down, my Lady," he called from below.

"It's lucky it's night and there's no one about or we would have had to use the watch-heights to avoid the coal carts."

Nuella threw her leg across Lolanth's neck and slid down off his side into J'lantir's waiting arms. She had gotten quite fond of that drop, falling free, knowing that someone would be there to catch her. J'lantir twirled her around once and then lightly set her on her feet.

"All back, safe and sound," he announced gaily. Then he added in a slightly puzzled tone, "Although the welcoming party seems to have become somewhat mislaid."

Eagerly, Nuella sniffed the night air, hoping to catch a scent of new arrivals before J'lantir's eyes saw them. She listened, drinking in the night noises, sifting through them for the sound of approaching feet. With a triumphant smile she found them— a pair approaching, just coming into view about—

"Ah, there they are," J'lantir announced. "Not quite as many as I would have expected, but perhaps it's the late hour."

"No," Nuella said, suddenly feeling chilled. "Something's wrong."

"Nuella?" Zenor called out in the night.

Nuella took a relieved breath. "Zenor, what is it? Where's Kindan? Kisk?" Nuella reached out for the familiar wispy touch of her favorite watch-wher and got back saddened darkness. "What happened?"

"There's been an accident," Renna said, walking up beside her brother.

"It's all my fault!" Zenor cried in a tear-choked voice.

"A cave-in," Renna said.

"Kindan? Kisk? Are they okay?" Nuella asked in panic.

"They're in the shed," Renna said. "Kindan tried to go but Tarik forbade him and punched him when he tried to get in anyway."

"Tarik?" Nuella repeated blankly.

"He's no miner," Zenor snarled. "I told Natalon when I saw their joists. He—your father went to look for himself. He was furious when he saw the state of Second Street. He made Tarik switch with him." He took a deep breath and said in a rush, "I think they were shoring up the tunnel when it collapsed."

"Father?" Nuella cried.

"And Dalor—all their shift," Renna told her tearfully.

"Tarik," Zenor said venomously, "said that the cave-in was too long to dig them out."

"Toldur tried anyway," Renna added. "But they couldn't get

more than a meter. Toldur said that at least ten meters of the tunnel's caved in. That'd take weeks to dig out."

"Tarik put guards on the shaft after Kindan tried to bust in," Zenor said. "There's only a pump crew there now, trying to get clear air into the mine."

Nuella started walking down the hill toward the camp.

"Nuella," J'lantir called after her, "what are you going to do?"

"I'm going to see Kindan," Nuella shouted over her shoulder. "I'm going to rescue my father."

◆

Kindan's eyes snapped open as someone nudged him awake. He hadn't meant to fall asleep, but the day's events had left him battered, bruised, and more frazzled than he had realized. A soft hand felt his forehead and pulled away quickly from the large bump and half-dried scab.

"He hit you hard, didn't he?" Nuella asked as he sat up. "Can you walk?"

"Nuella . . ." Kindan groped for words.

Nuella shushed him with a finger on his lips. "Zenor told me."

"I *tried*, Nuella," Kindan said with new tears rolling down his cheeks. "Kisk and I tried."

"I know," she said, her throat tight with pain. "I know." She felt her warm tears run down her face and hugged Kindan tightly, and for a moment both of them were lost in their grief. After a long while, Nuella felt the tightness in her chest ease and she drew back from Kindan. "Can you try again?" she asked after a moment.

The curtain at the entrance rustled and someone stepped into the shadows.

"I have an axe." It was Cristov.

◆

"Cristov?" Nuella said in surprise. Her mouth hardened. "You can't stop us."

"Nuella," Kindan began, warningly.

"I won't stop you," Cristov said with a grim smile. "I want to help."

Nuella gasped in surprise.

"I won't stop until we get them out," Cristov said fiercely. "Alive or dead." He looked at Kindan. "Your father taught me that. A miner never leaves his friends." He added dejectedly, "Only, I don't know how to get past the guards."

"I do!" Nuella sprang up from the floor. Kindan stood up with her. Kisk rose and, with a cry of support, rustled her stubby wings.

◆

They met Zenor and Renna at the shed's entrance. Kindan spoke quickly in low tones to Zenor to explain the situation with Cristov and then they all headed up to the hold.

"Where are we going?" Cristov asked. "This is the path to the hold."

"Exactly," Nuella said. "Didn't you ever wander around it when you lived there?"

"Well, yes," Cristov admitted reluctantly.

"Did you ever try the closet on the second floor?" Kindan asked.

"I knew there had to be another entrance!" Cristov exclaimed. "But the closet?"

Kindan enjoyed Cristov's look of amazement as they made

their way up to the second-floor landing, but his own jaw dropped when they topped the stairs.

"Toldur!"

The big miner grinned down at them. "You're late," he said, hefting an axe to his shoulder. "I thought I was going to have to come find you myself."

He nodded to Kindan. "I figured you were your father's son. I knew you'd try again." He caught sight of Nuella and frowned; his frown deepened when Renna reached the top of the stairs.

"This is Natalon's daughter, Nuella," Zenor said, stepping forward deliberately. "She's going to rescue her father."

"And I'm helping," Renna added in a voice that brooked no argument.

"There are enough hard hats for all of us through that door," Nuella said, pointing beyond Toldur's back.

The big miner grinned. "Don't I know it? Who do you think checks on 'em to make sure they're still safe? How do you think I found out about you, anyway? Although I'd always thought the blond hair was Dalor's."

"My brother," Nuella admitted.

"Can we go now?" Renna asked.

Toldur nodded. "Just let me get some glows."

"No time," Nuella said brusquely. "I'll lead. I know this passageway like the back of my hand."

"You can't see the back of your hand," Zenor muttered.

Nuella's hand shot out, super-quick, and accurately whacked Zenor on the side of his head with the back of her hand.

"Who said anything about seeing it?" she asked sweetly. She walked into the closet and quickly slid open the secret door at the back.

"That's got to hurt," Renna added with no trace of sympathy for her brother.

Zenor grinned at her, still clutching his wounded head. "At least she's not sulking anymore."

"I heard that," Nuella shouted back from the darkness.

◆

Inside the passageway, they quickly picked up hard hats and put them on. Nuella led the way, with Kisk and Kindan close behind. Toldur brought up the rear, grumbling under his breath about missing glows.

"Shut the door," Nuella called over her shoulder. "Kisk sees best in the dark." After she heard the door close, she asked Kindan, "Do you remember how many paces it was to the new mine shaft?"

"One hundred and forty-three after the first turn," Kindan replied without thinking.

"You lead then," Nuella ordered, bracing herself against the wall to let him and Kisk pass.

"Why this passage?" Renna asked. "Who built it and why?"

Toldur answered her. "We did—Natalon, your father, Kindan's father, and myself when we first came into this valley, half a Turn before the rest of you. Natalon wanted to be sure that the rock was strong enough for a hold. We used all the rocks we excavated to build Natalon's hold, the Harper's hold, and the bridge over the river.

"It took us nearly two months," he added. "But it was worth it because we learned a lot about digging through this sort of rock. It really helped when we sank the main shaft."

"How long would it take to dig through from this passageway to the new shaft?" Nuella asked as she started forward again.

"Three, maybe four hours," Toldur replied at once.

"That's too long," Zenor muttered.

"Could Kisk help?" Kindan wondered. "If we broke through in a couple of places, could she push hard enough?"

"It's solid stone, Kindan," Toldur objected.

"Is that for a full-grown man?" Renna asked. "Because I'm not full-grown; so maybe I could get through sooner."

"We have to get Kisk down there, too," Nuella pointed out.

"Here's the turn," Kindan called. He started counting his paces, trying not to let his pounding heart interfere.

"We could carve out a crawlway," Cristov suggested.

"In an hour, maybe less," Toldur agreed. "I'll start."

"You'd better be right about the position of that shaft," Nuella muttered softly to Kindan.

Kindan took a ragged breath and nodded in the darkness. One twenty. One twenty-one.

"Are we there yet?" Renna called from the rear.

"Nearly," Kindan called back. One thirty. "About ten more paces."

He counted the final paces and stopped. "Right here." He marked the spot with his hand. "Nuella, find my hand and put yours there," he said. "I'm going to measure off the far side."

"I'll come with you," she said. "Toldur, can you find my hand?"

In a few moments the big miner had marked out a crawlway with a few taps of his pickaxe.

"Okay, everyone put your fingers in your ears," Toldur warned them. "This is going to get mighty loud."

The big miner swung fifty times at his spot and then inspected his work. "Cristov, come here," he called. Toldur got Cristov oriented and then the young miner went to work for another fifty blows. Zenor took over after that, then Kindan.

"My turn," Renna declared when Kindan had counted fifty.

"This is not the time to learn to swing an axe," Zenor swore at her.

"There'll be plenty of work later," Toldur promised, relieving Kindan of the axe.

"All right," Renna allowed grudgingly.

A short while later, Toldur broke through. "How long did that take us?" he asked the group.

"Nineteen minutes," Nuella responded promptly, "I timed it in my head."

"Good," Toldur said enthusiastically. "Let's see if we can get a crawlspace done in the next twenty."

In the end it took them twenty-three more minutes to clear a space wide enough for Kisk.

With Kindan's encouragement, the small watch-wher poked her head through the opening. "Where are we, Kisk?" he asked her. The others waited silently.

Nuella felt for Kisk's response. "We're right behind the pumps," she said.

"How'd you know?" Kindan asked, just about ready to say the same thing.

"I've gotten a *lot* better at feeling watch-wher's thoughts," she told him.

"Come on, let's get going," Renna urged from the back of the group.

"Let's go, Kisk," Kindan said to the watch-wher, giving her a push.

"Everyone be quiet," Toldur whispered.

"Quiet?" Zenor repeated incredulously. "After all our digging?"

"That might not be noticed over the noise of the cave-in settling," Toldur explained. "But voices will."

The group crept silently around the unused pumps and over to the new shaft's lifts.

"Two groups," Kindan whispered over his shoulder. Nuella passed his message on. Kindan, Kisk, and Nuella climbed onto the lift at the top of the shaft. Kindan and Nuella worked as a team from months of practice.

"Shards, it's noisy," Kindan hissed as the thick ropes creaked and the pulley at the top of the shaft squealed.

"Don't go too fast," Toldur whispered from above.

"Don't go too slow," Nuella hissed at Kindan.

She fidgeted nervously while they waited at the bottom of the shaft for the others to lower themselves down.

"We weren't that loud," she whispered to Kindan.

"How do you know? We were too busy trying to be quiet to listen," Kindan countered.

Finally, just when she thought she couldn't take it anymore, the noise stopped. The others joined them.

"There won't be anyone at the bottom of the old shaft, will there?" Zenor wondered aloud.

"No," Toldur replied. "It's too risky for anyone to stay down here."

After a moment, Nuella said, "Kisk could see anyone before they could see her, anyway."

"Let's go, then," Zenor said.

Nuella and Kindan had already started moving, with Kisk between them.

"No blindfold this time," Kindan murmured to Nuella.

"Which is a pity, because I could have used it for a dust mask," Nuella replied.

"Hang on," Toldur whispered from behind them. The group paused. "Yup, I thought so," he said after rustling a hand about in his hard hat. "There are scarves in the hard hats. Pull them out, but make sure you keep your hat over your head—there could be loose rocks anywhere along here jostled from the cave-in."

"Not that it'll do much good," Nuella grumbled as they set off once more.

"Then why'd you mention it?" Zenor muttered back.

Nuella sniffed and increased her pace.

"You are keeping count, aren't you?" Kindan asked her after a moment.

"Yes," she said immediately. "Aren't you?"

"Third Street is twelve paces ahead," Kindan said by way of confirmation.

"Nuella," he asked as they passed Third Street, "what if we're too late?"

"We won't be," she said fervently, wishing it to be true. "When did it happen?"

"About an hour before sunset," Kindan said. In agony, he confessed, "Kisk was still asleep. There was too much light for her until the sun went down. We got to the mine as quick as we could after that."

Kisk gave Nuella a disconsolate *bleep*.

Instinctively, Nuella reached out and patted the watch-wher's side. "Not your fault, sweetie, you did your best."

Beside her, Kindan took Nuella's words to heart, as well.

"That's nearly twelve hours ago," she said after a moment. "How long can their air hold out?"

"It depends on the size of the tunnel that survived," Toldur answered from behind them. "No more than a day, though. Maybe less."

Maybe a *lot* less, Nuella guessed. Desperate to avoid thinking about it, she said to Kindan, "Did you know that a watch-wher takes its name from its human?"

"Really?" Renna asked from the rear of the group, rightly guessing that Nuella was trying to distract herself.

"Yes," Nuella affirmed. "And that the more bonded a watch-wher is with its human, the more closely the watch-wher's name matches the human's."

"Oh," Kindan said. "So I would've been better off to pick Kinsk over Kisk?"

"I don't know how much it's a question of *your* picking as it is of *her* picking," Nuella corrected. "And it's not to say that a short name won't mean a long bonding. Renilan and Resk have been bonded now for over thirty Turns."

"Oh," Kindan said more cheerfully. Then he nearly tripped on a rock. "Rocks ahead!" he called over his shoulder. "Everyone mind your step."

"Everyone start counting your paces," Toldur ordered. "We don't want to get lost."

Nuella called out from the left, "First Street," at the same time that Kindan called out from the right, "Main shaft."

"Eighty-three meters from here," Toldur said quietly.

"Do you feel that?" Cristov asked. "I feel a draft—it must be the pumps."

"In or out?" Zenor asked. "It feels to me like it's blowing in."

"Everyone freeze!" Toldur hissed.

"What's wrong?" Nuella asked.

"Tarik's blowing air into the mine," Zenor replied in a dead voice.

"We'll have to turn back," Toldur said.

"Why?" Nuella cried. "We're almost there! We can't stop now!"

"Nuella," Zenor said slowly, "with the air blowing in—it's like adding coal to a fire."

"No, it's exactly like adding air to coal-gas," Renna corrected. "It could cause an explosion."

"He's not doing it on purpose is he?" Kindan asked. No one wanted to answer that question.

"Come on, we have to turn around," Toldur repeated.

"Wait!" Nuella cried desperately. "If we can get the pumps to suck the air out, could we go on?"

"It won't work," Zenor said. "You'd have to get crews on both the old and the new shafts or it'd have pretty much the same effect."

No one knew what to say.

"We tried, Nuella," Kindan said as the silence dragged on.

"I'm not quitting," Cristov announced. "I won't leave them."

"We can come back when it's safe," Toldur said.

"For the bodies?" Zenor cried.

"Wait!" Nuella hissed. "If we *could* get the pumps on both shafts to suck the air out, could we continue?"

"It'd be too risky," Toldur said after a moment. "The air has been pumped in here for hours now. At any moment it could meet a pocket of gas and . . ."

Everyone shuddered at the thought of the fireball that would result.

"We could leave our picks here," Cristov suggested. "That way we couldn't possibly make any sparks."

"We'd have to move the rocks by hand anyway," Zenor agreed.

"We still don't have any way to get the pumps manned," Toldur pointed out.

"Oh, yes we do," Nuella said, her heart lifting. "Kindan, can I borrow Kisk for a moment?"

"Sure," Kindan said instantly. "Where are you going?"

"Nowhere," Nuella said in a tone that discouraged further questions. She put her hands on Kisk. "Kisk, I need you to talk to Lolanth. Tell Lolanth to talk to me, please. It's an emergency."

Kisk nodded her head and blinked her eyes slowly. Then she chirped a happy acknowledgment and butted Nuella in search of affection. Nuella gave the green watch-wher a quick pat on the neck.

"Thank you Kisk," she said. Then she continued, "Lolanth, please tell J'lantir that I need the pumps on both mines manned to suck the air out of the mines. Ask him to get the MasterMiner. Tell him I'm trying to save my father."

J'lantir asks if you're in danger, the dragon relayed.

"Only if we don't get the air sucked out of the mine," Nuella said aloud.

J'lantir says he will do it, Lolanth answered. *He is very worried. I am very worried. We are calling Gaminth. M'tal comes. Islu comes. The miners have been told.*

"If Tarik complains . . ." Kindan said, guessing what Nuella was doing.

"Are you talking to a dragon?" Zenor asked in amazement.

"Dragons will talk to anyone if they want to," Kindan told him.

"Really," Zenor muttered in amazement.

From above, they heard a chorus of dragon bugles loudly in the night.

The MasterMiner is here, Lolanth informed Nuella. *He has started the pumps the right way. He is very angry with someone.*

I am here, Nuella, the gentle voice of Gaminth called. *M'tal wants to know where you are.*

"We're down here, in the mine," Nuella answered aloud.

MasterMiner Britell is very worried, Gaminth informed her. *He says you should come up immediately.*

"I can feel the pumps," Cristov said. "They're pulling the air out."

"The MasterMiner is here," Nuella told them. "He says we have to leave."

"We're not going!" four voices responded in unison.

"Well, I can't drag you all out by myself, and I won't leave you," Toldur said slowly. He said to Nuella, "If you can get a message to the MasterMiner, tell him what we're hoping to do and ask if he has any suggestions."

Nuella relayed the message. *The MasterMiner says you should hope your luck holds,* Gaminth reported.

"He says good luck," Nuella told the others.

"Okay, let's get going," Kindan said. "It's another eighty-six meters to Second Street."

◆

In silence, the group trudged past the mine shaft and the vigorous sound of the pumps. The rocks on the floor of the tunnel grew more numerous, and larger.

"We cleared a path on the tracks," Toldur said. "If you walk in the middle of the road, you shouldn't have to worry."

The air was thick with dust. Occasionally they passed a glow, its light doing little other than illuminating the thick clouds swirling around them.

The darkness grew worse. Kindan realized that he had come upon another glow only because he'd insisted on keeping his fingers touching the sides of the tunnel and had felt the frame of the glow basket.

Shortly after that he barked his shin on a huge, irregularly shaped boulder. A cry from Nuella beside him made it clear that he wasn't the only one to suffer.

Kindan realized that he couldn't see her.

"How can you guys see?" Zenor wondered aloud.

"If you can't see, hold hands," Toldur told the group.

"Grab onto Kisk," Nuella said. "She can see in the dark."

"Second Street," Kindan announced. "Here we are."

"The cave-in is about two meters inside the turn," Toldur said.

"Figures," Kindan muttered, remembering the bad joists he'd encountered.

"We dug out a meter before we stopped," Toldur added.

"So the edge of the cave-in was one meter inside?" Kindan asked. "How low is the ceiling?"

"You'll have to duck," Toldur admitted.

Kindan crouched down and started forward slowly.

"No, you stay behind," Nuella told him, grabbing his shoulder. "I'll go forward."

"Why don't we let Kisk look first?" Kindan suggested.

"What for?" Toldur asked.

"Hot spots," Zenor said. "If Kisk sees heat, a spark would look like a little hot spot, right?"

"Right," Nuella and Kindan agreed in unison.

"You're better at seeing in the dark," Kindan told Nuella. "Why don't you work with Kisk?"

"Thanks," Nuella responded. "Kisk, can you see any little lights? Look for little lights, Kisk."

Nuella concentrated on the image she was looking for. After a moment she got a feeling of comprehension from the green watch-wher and then Kisk diverted her attention to the tunnel ahead. *Ewrrll,* Kisk chirped.

"Stale air," Kindan translated. "Any lights?"

"No," Nuella said. "No lights."

"How about big lights?" Toldur asked. "Like people?"

"No," Nuella responded immediately, in a bleak voice. "No big lights, either."

"You mean no one's alive?" Renna's voice broke the silence. "No one at all?"

"Kisk said there was stale air," Cristov said.

"Kisk can only see heat through about two meters of coal, probably less," Kindan said.

"How do you know?" Toldur asked.

"We tested it," Nuella said simply. She heard Kindan moving beside her. "What are you doing?" she demanded.

"Taking off my boot," Kindan told her.

"Why? Have you got a rock in it?"

"Don't make a spark," Toldur warned as Kindan began to tap the sole of his boot on the hard rails that ran along the floor and into the cave-in.

"How far will that sound travel?" Nuella asked sourly.

"Shh!" Zenor hissed. "It'll travel the length of the rail if you put your ear to it."

Kindan finished tapping out his question and put his ear on the rail. He waited. And waited.

And heard nothing.

"Honestly!" Nuella snarled as Kindan started to rise. "You're making too much noise. Don't you know that you can't hear half as well as I can?"

"Do you hear anything?" Kindan asked hopefully.

"Just you," she snapped. "Shhh!"

Nuella listened. They waited. And waited.

"Eight," Nuella said finally. "I hear eight taps, a long pause, and eight more taps."

"They're alive!" Renna shouted.

"It could just be rocks settling," Toldur suggested soberly.

"Hang on, let me send a different message," Kindan said. "Nuella, lift your head or you'll lose your hearing."

Kindan knelt down again and tapped out a different code. F-A-R.

"Far? You're asking how far they are?" Renna guessed. She had learned her drum codes from Kindan.

"Shh!" Nuella hissed again, her ear on the rail. She waited. And waited.

"Nothing," she reported finally.

"Maybe they weren't listening when you sent that message," Cristov suggested in the dead silence that followed. "Maybe they were still sending their answer. Try again."

Kindan dutifully rapped out the drum code again.

Nuella put her ear on the rail again and waited. After a while she plugged the other ear to shut out Renna's fervent whisper of "please, please, please."

"Nothing—wait! Ten!" Nuella said. "I thought I heard ten." She listened again. "Yes, definitely ten."

"They're alive," Zenor said in profound relief.

"Only eight of them, though," Renna pointed out.

"But they're ten meters down the tunnel," Toldur said. "That means they're eight meters away from us."

"Three days," Cristov muttered sadly. No one needed him to elaborate. It would take crews working around the clock for three days to clear eight meters of rubble, and the trapped miners had less than a day, probably less than half a day, of air left.

"Tell the MasterMiner," Toldur said to Nuella.

"There has to be a way," Cristov said fiercely. "There has to!"

"All that training," Kindan said miserably. "All for nothing. We came this far and we can't save them." He turned to Nuella. "I'm sorry," he said, his voice choked with tears. "Nuella, I'm so sorry."

"I'm not giving up," Nuella said. "And you can't either. You trained Kisk too hard, and we've come too far to give up now."

"What can we do? We can't dig through to them in time. We'd have to go *between* or—"

"Could a dragon get to them?" Renna wondered.

"They're too big," Zenor answered.

"And they have to see where they're going," Nuella added.

"Kisk could do it," Kindan pronounced.

"Watch-whers don't go *between*," Nuella declared.

"Yes, they do, I saw Dask do it," Kindan corrected. He saw that Nuella still looked doubtful and sighed. "Look, watch-whers and dragons were both made from fire lizards, right?"

Nuella nodded dubiously.

"Okay, then," Kindan continued quickly, aware that time was running out for the miners, "if fire lizards can go *between* by themselves to places they know, and dragons can't go *between* to places they *don't* know unless a rider can give them an image—"

"But watch-whers see heat!" Nuella objected.

"Exactly!" Kindan agreed. "That's why you have to ride her. You can give Kisk the right heat images."

"Ride a watch-wher?" Cristov repeated in wonder.

"Danil did it once with Dask," Zenor told him. "I remember."

"She's your watch-wher, Kindan," Nuella protested. "I can't ride her—she's yours."

"I can't ride her: I can't give her the right visual images," Kindan countered. "*You* can."

"Can you?" Renna asked desperately. "Can you save Dalor, Nuella?"

"I'd have to get a good visual image," Nuella complained.

"Take a breath," Kindan said in a low voice close to her ear so that the others couldn't hear. "You can do it, Nuella."

"But she's yours," she protested again.

"I'll loan her to you," Kindan said lightly. "She likes you anyway. You said watch-whers can change bonds, right?"

"Right," Nuella agreed reluctantly. "But how will I know what the image should be?"

"You know your father and how he looks and you know Dalor. Start with them and imagine their heat images in your mind—you can do that, right?"

"I don't know," Nuella admitted nervously.

"You've done it with Dalor, playing hide-and-seek, right?" Reluctantly, Nuella nodded. "And you know the shape of your father, right? And you know what a heat image looks like, so you can imagine his heat image standing next to Dalor."

"Yes, I can."

"Good. Do that," Kindan said. "I'll take care of the rest."

"Do you know how many people Kisk can carry at a time?" Nuella asked him.

"Nine," Kindan answered immediately, lying. "I'm sure the number was nine." To Toldur he said, "Can you take the others back to the main shaft? We need to set up a pattern that Kisk can recognize to go *between* to on this side."

"All right," Toldur said. "She sees in the dark, right?"

"No, she sees heat," Kindan corrected. "What I want is for you to go to the far side of the shaft and form a line across it. Toldur, I want you nearest the shaft, ready to help people out. Renna, you stand beside him. Cristov, next to her. Zenor, you should be touching the west wall. All hold hands until Nuella arrives."

"Nuella, will that work for you?" Kindan asked. "Can you imagine that?"

"I'll tr—" She cut herself off. "Yes, I can," she said firmly. "What if I have to make two trips, though?"

"If you have to make two trips, I'll be there for the second one. I'll stand in front of Renna and Cristov. Will that work?"

"Yes, I can see that," Nuella agreed.

"Okay, Toldur and the others move off now, please," Kindan said. "I've got to tap some instructions to the other side."

"Don't try doing that until they've gone," Nuella cautioned.

"Don't make any sparks!" Toldur reiterated.

"Right," Kindan agreed. "No sparks. Sparks are bad."

◆

Ten minutes later, which seemed like ages to Nuella, Kindan lifted his head up off the rails.

"That could have gone faster if you'd let me listen," Nuella told him sourly.

"You need to stay calm," he reminded her. "And bond to Kisk."

"She's a sweetheart—I've always felt a special bond with her," Nuella assured him.

"That's what I always thought," Kindan admitted cryptically. "Everything's ready now. You need to imagine your father and your brother standing side by side, holding hands. Kisk should arrive with her nose touching Dalor's, and everything will be fine."

"Who's on which side?"

"Dalor's on the right, that's what all my tapping was about,"

Kindan said promptly. "I think you'll want to climb onto Kisk's back, but crouch low on her neck. Let me help you."

Nuella scrambled onto the watch-wher's back and wrapped her arms around the long neck.

"Ready?" Kindan asked.

"Ready."

"Remember, it only lasts as long as it takes to—"

Nuella fixed the image in her mind, two heat-rainbow bodies with a hot spot between them where they held hands, and gave the image to the watch-wher.

The cold of *between* enveloped her. Silence filled her ears.

CHAPTER XIII

Watch-wher, watch-wher, do you know
All the places you can go?

—*C*ough three times.

Ewrrll, the watch-wher chirped. Sound filled Nuella's ears. She took a cautious breath.

"Father," she said, reaching out to where she *knew* he would be, "I came as soon as I could."

"Nuella!" At the sound of her father's voice, tears streamed down Nuella's face.

"Have everyone grab hold of the watch-wher," she said. "If you've got anyone who can't stand, help them onto her back with me."

"She's not big enough," Dalor said doubtfully.

"She'll bear the load," Nuella replied. The watch-wher chirped a bold agreement.

"Hurry, the air's getting too stale," Natalon told the others.

"Let me know when they're ready," Nuella said.

"What are you going to do?" Dalor asked, his voice right beside her ear.

"Don't worry," Nuella said, raising her voice over the others, "we're going to get you out. It's going to be a strange ride but it will only last as long as it takes to—"

"Everyone's ready," Natalon told her.

Nuella brought the image to her mind. Toldur, Renna, Cristov, Zenor. She formed their fiery images and passed them to the watch-wher. "—cough three times," she finished.

———◆———

At Kindan's shout, the miners in the Camp started collecting around them.

"Look, it's Natalon!" someone exclaimed.

"Natalon's been saved!" The shout rang round the Camp.

"Give them room!" Kindan bellowed above the crowd. "And someone send for the Harper and Jenella."

A respectful silence descended as the rescued miners stumbled out of the shaft and collected beside Natalon.

"Who's that with them?" a voice murmured from the back.

Natalon rose to his feet, resting an arm on Nuella's shoulder. She shifted her weight to support him and the watch-wher slithered around to his other side and raised her head under his other hand.

Natalon looked down at the watch-wher and smiled, stroking the ungainly head with affection.

"I have an announcement," he said, pulling himself fully erect. He slipped his arm underneath Nuella's and hugged her tight to his side. "This is my daughter, Nuella. She cannot see, so

I kept her hidden from you all." He paused. "I was afraid that you would hold her lack of sight against her. And me.

"But it is I who have been blind—and foolish," Natalon continued. "Nuella was not blind in our dark mines. She could 'see' where others could not. And so she—with her friends"—Natalon gestured toward Kindan and Zenor—"and the watch-wher rescued us poor, sighted miners."

"You're alive!" Jenella rushed into the crowd, baby Larissa tucked under one arm, and grabbed Natalon with the other. "Oh, you're alive!" She looked around at the crowd of faces. "Who can I thank . . . ?"

Kindan pushed Nuella forward. Jenella looked down at her, eyes brimming with tears.

Nuella tilted her head up to her mother's voice. "Me, mother."

Jenella thrust Larissa into Kindan's arms and grabbed Nuella in a tearful embrace. When she finally recovered enough to stand, she looked around at the crowd and said fiercely, "This is my daughter, Nuella." She looked down at Nuella. "She is my pride and joy."

"She didn't do it alone," Zenor said unexpectedly in the silence. Kindan shot him a look of amazement that Zenor would do anything to risk harming Nuella's acceptance into the Camp. "Her watch-wher helped."

Zenor grinned at Kindan, adding in a voice pitched so that only he could hear, "You knew, didn't you?"

"I was hoping," Kindan answered just as quietly.

Zenor reached over and squeezed his friend on the shoulder, tightly, in thanks and acknowledgment of Kindan's sacrifice.

"Her watch-wher?" Natalon repeated blankly, looking at how

the green sat curled possessively about Nuella without so much as a glance toward Kindan.

"*My* watch-wher?" Nuella repeated, turning toward Kindan.

Kindan nodded. "Ask her her name, Nuella."

Nuella gave him an uncomprehending look, so Kindan explained, "Just like when you *saw*, but with words this time."

Nuella's face took on an abstracted expression that suddenly changed to pure delight. "She says her name is Nuelsk!" She leaped in the air and ran to Kindan. "Her name is Nuelsk! Oh, Kindan," she cried, in bittersweet joy, "you've given me your watch-wher!"

Kindan hugged her tightly and then let her go, smiling. "I think she was always yours, Nuella, and I was just helping you raise her, not the other way around."

Zenor joined them, grabbing Nuella's free hand. Kindan smiled as he watched Nuella squeeze Zenor's hand back, tightly, and then wrap her arm around his shoulder.

"If you kiss him, then everyone will know," Kindan whispered in Nuella's ear.

"Good," Nuella whispered back. She grabbed Zenor's face and kissed him soundly on the lips. The gathered crowd roared with laughter at Zenor's obvious surprise.

"Look after him, please," Kindan begged her when Zenor managed to pull himself away, red-faced with embarrassment and joy.

"Haven't I always?" Nuella replied. Then she frowned. "But Kindan, what about you?"

A figure separated itself from the shadows. "I think I may help." It was Master Zist. "This is an official offer from the MasterHarper of Pern," he said, pressing a parchment into Kindan's hands. Kindan unrolled it and nearly dropped it as he read the words.

"I may be a Harper?" he asked, eyes wide.

"Well, you will certainly have the opportunity to try," Master Zist said with a smile. "No doubt they'll be pumping you for all this lost lore on watch-whers." He leaned in close to Kindan and said in a voice for his ears alone, "You will do fine, lad, just fine."

"So, Kindan," Natalon asked with interest, "what will you do?"

"I think I'll sing," the newest Harper of Pern replied.